Published by
Dreamspinner Press
4760 Preston Road
Suite 244-149
Frisco, TX 75034
http://www.dreamspinnerpress.com/

The Memoirs of Colonel Gérard Vreilhac

Cover Art by Paul Richmond   http://www.paulrichmondstudio.com

ISBN: 978-1-61581-247-9

Printed in the United States of America
First Edition
May, 2010

eBook edition available
eBook ISBN: 978-1-61581-248-6

for D.B. … of the many men in my life,
one I never expected to be *the* man in my life

Preface

HOW STRANGE the workings of memory! I see the men and women of my youth and middle age—friends, lovers, enemies—as clearly as I saw them then, and hear the words we spoke to each other as exactly as if they had just left our lips. When I think of the things that happened and the things I did, it is as though I were living them, doing them. My hands feel what I touched, and the smells that surrounded me fill my nostrils: the dust in the attic where I first made love, the reek of blood at the foot of the guillotine, the fear that permeated Saint-Lazare, the sharp tang of gunpowder, the mingled scents of the Egyptian markets, the bouquet of the wine with which we toasted the Emperor, the night air seeping into the darkness of my bed chamber, the semen. Old joys swell my heart, old sorrows clutch at my throat, my fingers tense with past hatreds, and my muscles feel their lost strength. I remember every face, every name, every street. I could walk through the rooms I lived in with my eyes closed and not trip over anything.

Yet I forget the names of people I met but yesterday, I forget promises I made just this morning, and I could not tell you what I ate for dinner. I am happy we have become a republic once more, though I don't know how long it will last. Phébus tells me they intend to revise the Constitution. I cannot keep track of the shifting politics of the day, and I mix up who is minister of what. The closer an event is in time, the less reliable my memory of it. My memory of the distant past is accurate in every detail; the only difference is that, looking back, I can see what led up to something and where it was headed. I understand now why people did and said what they did, and why I did. The pieces fit together. There is no doubt, no uncertainty.

When I started this memoir, I thought I would have to rack my brain to sort it all out and spend hours researching the battles I participated in. I did not. It was all inside me, every event in the right order, every piece in its right place, but I found that my wartime experiences, though vividly recalled, bored me now, and I rushed through my years in the *Grande Armée*, dwelling only on what was essential to my personal history, for which, I suppose, most readers will fault me. I have passed over the intimate relations I had with women for the same reason. Also, I left things out in my haste and had to go back and add them to my manuscript when I finished it. But that is the forgetfulness of my old age; no sooner do I write something than I forget what I have written. I have now read through these pages, and in reading them I marveled at their accuracy. And their honesty, too. I have no desire to be idolized by posterity; it matters not a whit to me if people find my life scandalous and unnatural.

GÉRARD VREILHAC, COLONEL IN NAPOLEON'S *GRANDE ARMÉE*
SAINT-GERMAIN-EN-LAYE, 20 MARCH 1851

PART I:

My Years of Turmoil

Chapter 1

IN THE spring of 1788, the Jesuits allowed my friend Julien to return to the chateau for two weeks to attend his sister Berthe's wedding—they could hardly refuse a request from the Count d'Airelles—and at the age of fifteen I had sex for the first time.

Berthe had resisted the marriage; she said that she loathed her husband-to-be, the middle-aged and portly Baron de l'Envol, a parvenu who had used his ill-gotten gains to purchase his title the previous year and whose so-called barony was really an abandoned farm in Brittany that had belonged to his grandfather. Knowing he could rise no higher in the nobility on his own, he had immediately asked for Berthe's hand. She had no choice. Her father, the Count, finding it more difficult with every passing year to maintain a household in the grand style, insisted on the marriage, his chaplain delivered lengthy sermons on filial obedience at Sunday Mass, and the King himself had approved it. But Berthe would have objected to any match. From girlhood she had set her heart on becoming a Carmelite nun. Unfortunately, her sister Constance, the Count's second daughter, beat her to it. At sixteen, their mother had found her in bed with her daughters' tutor, and she was packed off to a convent. The tutor had enough sense to flee before the family could deal with him.

Berthe pleaded with her father in vain for permission to join the Carmelites. "I have given one daughter to the Church," the Count said.

"That ought to be enough." Now she was eighteen years old, and like it or not, she was getting married.

Except for Sister Constance of the Holy Innocents, who had not yet pronounced her final vows and would have been granted leave to attend the wedding, but was still in disgrace, the entire family returned to the ancestral domain to celebrate Berthe's marriage. Olivier, the Count's older son and heir, his firstborn, came with his wife, Marie-Catherine, and also the Count's oldest daughter, Jeanne, with her husband and their two children. Preparations for the wedding party had kept us busy for months. Then the guests began to arrive, and we were run ragged.

As the second son and youngest child of the Count d'Airelles, Gaston Dieudonné Alexandre Saint-André Julien de la Motte had more options than his youngest sister. He could choose to enter the Army or the Church. He kept changing his mind and showed no sign of deciding which career to pursue, favoring now one, now the other. Whatever his decision, in a little over a year he would turn sixteen and become either *Monsieur le chevalier* or *Monsieur l'abbé*, and I would have to stop calling him Julien. The Count, who naturally disapproved of Julien's unseemly friendship with his head gardener's son, had expressly forbidden him to seek me out when he came home on holiday. But Julien didn't need to seek me out. He only needed to take a stroll on the grounds and we were certain to run into each other.

Julien and I had been best friends almost from the day of his birth. He was four months and four days younger than me and had been given to my mother to nurse, which made us foster-brothers. His father had accepted, even encouraged our friendship when we were little. Except for some peasants' children from the surrounding farms and in the nearest village, there were no other boys our age to play with. It was only after Julien left to study at the Jesuit college in Paris at the age of ten that the Count felt we were best kept apart. But he had never taken a personal interest in his children, and with no one to enforce them, his wishes went unheeded. When my friend was home, we were virtually inseparable.

It was I who taught Julien to swim, and he gave me my first instruction in fencing, using sticks we found in the forest. Most important, he taught me to read and write. I've been literate since I was five. There are many ways of spelling my name—Vreyac, Veréliac, etc.—and it is written differently on my commission as a foot soldier in the *Grande Armée*, but here I use the spelling Julien taught me, which I assume he invented himself.

I understood the importance of reading and writing—very few of the Count's servants knew how—and I missed Julien's lessons when, at the age of ten, he was sent to study at the Jesuit college in Paris. I looked forward to when he would come back for a month in summer and teach me more, and now he would be able to teach me Latin too. But the first time I made a mistake, he slapped me so hard you could see the red outline of his fingers on my cheek.

"Why did you do that?" I asked, surprised and hurt. As the Count's son he had every right to, but he had never struck me before except by accident when we played at wrestling, and I had done nothing to deserve it.

"So you'll learn. The Fathers always hit us when we get something wrong."

I could not believe that anyone would dare raise his hand to a son of the Count d'Airelles. My father beat me when I made him angry, but I was only a servant.

"They do more than slap us," Julien said. "You'll see when we go for a swim."

I did. His backside was crisscrossed with stripes made by a cane. "They do that to you?" I asked in astonishment.

"How else would I have got them? So there's no reason for you to object to a little slap. I didn't hit you in anger, Gérard."

"How many strokes do they give you?"

"Three, usually. You have to go to the front of the classroom and bend over the desk. Then whomp! whomp! whomp! But if you're punished a third time on the same day you get ten. That hasn't happened to me. The worst part is having to sit on it for the rest of the day."

I didn't need to be told what the rod felt like.

"After supper the boys who were caned are sent to the infirmary," he went on, "and Father Lebreton rubs ointment on our rumps. So it won't leave scars, not to make them feel better, but it does."

"Do you cry when they beat you?"

"I did the first time, because it was so unexpected. I don't anymore. It's unbecoming for a de la Motte."

"Does it really help you learn?"

"I don't know. I know that because of it I do everything I can to get it right, and that I am learning. It doesn't do much good, though. Learning, that is. They don't beat me as often as in the beginning, but I still get caned every week or so and get only bread and water for supper. To tell the truth, I wouldn't go back there if Father didn't make me."

"I don't want to know Latin if it means you're going to hit me," I said.

He seemed to think that getting hit was an integral part of education. "How about this as a compromise? I'll only slap you if you make the same mistake three times in row."

We shook hands on that, because I couldn't imagine being that dense, but he did slap me a few times before he had to return to school.

Father Lebreton's cream proved effective, and at fourteen Julien's ass was unblemished, for now they disciplined him less harshly.

I TRULY believe I was the only one at the chateau Julien looked forward to seeing. He hardly knew his brother and sisters. Olivier was fifteen years his senior, and by the time Julien was three already had a position in the royal retinue at Versailles, and Jeanne was already married and living with her husband on the other side of France, in Lorraine. Constance had no interest in *little* boys, and Berthe, closest to him in age, always had her nose buried in her prayer book. Until the guests arrived, his family more or less ignored him, and he spent nearly all his time with me.

He reveled in not having to act like a grown-up, and we behaved with as much abandon and little dignity as we had when we were young boys, exploring the forest, running across the fields, climbing trees, telling stories and making up silly songs, and we talked about the wedding. I told him how excited about it the servants were.

"It's given them an awful lot of work."

"But none of us are complaining." Julien never used "you" to refer to the servants when he was talking to me. I said "us" to remind him.

"They'll complain enough when they have to clean up afterward."

We also discussed more serious matters, serious for us, that is, such as whether Julien should become a soldier or a priest.

"Why don't you become a gardener like me?" I asked.

"Unfortunately, that isn't one of my choices."

"Then be a soldier. Priests have sour faces and hit people."

"Soldiers kill people."

"But not Frenchmen."

"I've seen them fire on the mob."

"A mob is different."

"I don't think I could do that. Otherwise I would become a soldier. They have a lot more fun."

"If you become an officer, will you make me your aide-de-camp?"

"Don't be silly. You belong to my father. He wouldn't give you to me."

"Why not?"

"Because you're my friend."

Since Julien might be joining the cavalry in couple of years, the Count encouraged him to ride. One day he took his horse and rode off to the woods to wait for me. I chose a feisty mount from the stables when the groom wasn't looking and went to join him. I had not had time to put on a saddle. Julien unsaddled his, and we went for a wild bareback gallop.

When we rode through the village, the peasants doffed their bonnets and bowed. They used to bow to me, too, because I belonged to the Count's household, but only when they came to the chateau.

We slowed our pace so Julien could acknowledge their respects. "Here too," he murmured.

"Here too what?"

"The famine. How thin they are! It's worse in Paris. The people look like sticks."

"The Count has cut back on our bread rations too," I said, "but we'll get to stuff ourselves at your sister's wedding."

When both we and our horses had worked up a sweat, we headed for the river, stripped off our clothes and went for a swim. We wrestled in the water, laughing and ducking each other under the surface. Then we lay on our backs in the grass till the sun had dried us.

Julien ran his eyes over my naked body and placed a hand on my stomach. "Yes," he said, "I can see you've lost weight too. At our age you ought to be filling out."

"I'm still stronger than you," I said. "I have to work, and I have plenty of opportunity to exercise, while you sit all day with your nose in a book except when you get down on your knees to pray."

He left his hand on my stomach for a long time, sometimes rubbing it back and forth and marveling at how thin I had become. In retrospect I think he may have been trying to seduce me, but it didn't occur to me then, and I didn't get hard. We had grown up seeing each other naked, and had always been casual with one another about everything.

We differed as much in physique as we did in rank: I dark-haired and muscular, with the swarthy complexion of the southwest, and half a head taller than Julien; Julien much handsomer, blond, grey-eyed and skin so pale you could see the blue veins of his nobility, so slight of build that he seemed frailer than he in fact was. He would fill out over the next four years, and Julien at eighteen was broad in the shoulder and only a couple of inches shorter than me.

Late in the afternoon we walked slowly back to where we'd left his saddle. I knew the groom wouldn't scold me for taking a horse when we returned because he'd see I'd been with Julien. It was the same with my father. My friendship with the son of the Count d'Airelles flattered him, and he always allowed me to skip work to play with him, though he warned me that when we were grown men our feelings for each other would end.

"Not mine," I protested.

"No, not yours, but the young master's will, and you'll come to accept it."

THE chateau began to fill up, and it became nearly impossible for us to be together. We weren't supposed to be together, and wherever we went someone was bound to see us. There were people wandering all over the grounds. None of them paid Julien any attention except to pat him on the head and tell him what a pretty little curé or brave little dragoon he'd make. Only Berthe spoke to him at any length, and only because she had no one else she dared complain to about her upcoming marriage. He had nothing to do but listen to the musicians rehearse. He was very lonely and very bored.

The day before the wedding Julien came looking for me while I was spreading manure on the flower beds. "Come with me," he said, "I've found a place where we can be alone."

"Where?"

"In the chateau. They've taken about three dozen chairs from the storerooms under the eaves so we'll have enough for the guests to sit on at tomorrow's outdoor reception, and didn't think to lock the door." He pointed to the lawn bordered by the long semi-circular driveway, where the house servants were busy arranging them. We'd had dry weather since the beginning of May, and there was little chance it would rain before morning. People predicted a plentiful wheat crop and said the famine had at last come to an end, but that June more rain fell in Paris than anyone could remember, and it became apparent that the famine would continue at least through next winter and on into the following summer.

"Are you sure they won't come back for more?" I asked.

"They've taken them all, and if they do, what do the servants care if they see us together? I'll wait for you by the small door on the north side; the stairway there goes straight up to the top story. But wash up first."

I told my father that Julien had called for me, rinsed off at the pump, and hurried to meet him.

Inside the north door a wide arched corridor gave access to the front of the chateau. The servants had used it to carry the chairs to the lawn. We turned to a musty stone staircase on the right and followed its zigzags as far as the top story—the stairs, Julien said, continued on to the roof—then through a large wooden door standing open on its hinges into a vast, dusty room lit by narrow windows that appeared to have sat unwashed for generations, the floor, walls and ceiling beams in rough unfinished wood, with chests and furnishings piled high on all sides, and cobwebs everywhere.

I had never been in that part of the building. In fact, I seldom had occasion to go inside the chateau at all. We lived with the other chief outdoor servants—groom, coachman, gamekeeper, etc.—in one of two long, two-story stone outbuildings behind the chateau proper. The other housed the stables, coach room and workroom on the ground floor, and the outside staff slept in a large dormitory above that.

Julien pointed to doors at either end of the room, bolted on the inside. "That's where the minor house servants live," he explained, "men on one side, women and married couples on the other. But most of them are paired up anyway. The bolts on the doors don't keep them apart."

My mother, a cleaning maid, would have lived there had she not married my father. She had never lived there, however. She was a village girl and hadn't worked at the chateau before their marriage. The more important servants, such as the major-domo, the head housekeeper and the cooks, had apartments off the arched corridor on the ground floor. The Count's valet and the Countess's personal maid had small rooms adjoining their bedchambers. It surprised me that the Count and his wife did not share the same apartments.

The door creaked as Julien shut it behind us. He led me to a pile of straw mattresses and torn bedding behind a broken armoire, where we sat.

"Tomorrow's the big day," I said.

"Please, I hear enough about it from everybody. No one talks about anything else, even poor Berthe, who doesn't want it to happen. She pours her heart out to me every chance she gets and makes a scene whenever the family is alone together. She actually threatened to kill herself so she wouldn't have to marry L'Envol."

"What did the Count say to that?"

"Nothing. But my brother Olivier told her point blank that suicide was a greater sin than matrimony. That shut her up."

"I hear that after the wedding night even the most reluctant bride is glad to belong to a man."

It was a daring thing to say about a member of the Count's immediate family; I had never so much as hinted to Julien about his sister Constance's indiscretions, for example. But he didn't seem to notice. "Not all of them," he answered. "It takes time, but eventually you learn to like it, and then you can't get enough of it."

"You sound as if you're talking from experience. You haven't been with a woman, have you, Julien? No, you couldn't have. Not yet."

He answered my question by smiling curiously at me for a long time. Suddenly he said, "That was very uppity of you to make jokes about Berthe's deflowering."

"I wasn't joking."

"I still ought to teach you a lesson."

He threw himself on me. It took a moment for me to realize that he was wrestling in fun and it was all right for me to fight back. In no time I had him pinned beneath me, straddling his hips and holding his wrists above his head in a firm grasp. As I waited for him to admit defeat, I felt his penis hard beneath my scrotum. "Undo my culottes and suck me," he whispered.

It never occurred to me not to obey him, nor did it occur to me that I ought to be shocked. I knew that other boys our age fooled around, so why not us? I opened the buttons and took him in my mouth.

I had no idea how to go about it and did a clumsy job. "I'd better show you how it's done," he said.

He had me stand up, then he knelt in front of me and pulled my britches down to my ankles. "You're soft," he said, surprised. "I'll soon take care of that."

He did. He put the tip of his tongue under my foreskin, swirling it around the head, retracted it. Then he took my penis in his mouth and, pressing it between his tongue and palate, sucked hard, as if he meant to pull all the blood in my body into my shaft. It worked, and I was soon engorged.

He sat back on his knees and said, "You're very big, much bigger than me, and it's very pretty. You should be proud of it." Then he took it back in this mouth and worked me like an expert. It felt more wonderful than anything I had ever experienced. My knees buckled, and even the tight grip of his hands kneading my buttocks wasn't enough to steady me. I fell over backward.

He continued to suck me, stopping only to lick my balls and inside my thighs or take my pubic hair between his teeth and pull back on it before he went back to sucking, his hands caressing my belly or reaching up to pinch my nipples all the while. I came quickly, and he swallowed my ejaculate. Then he got onto his knees and, licking his lips, asked me if I'd liked it.

I could hardly breathe, much less answer. "Where did you ever learn to do that?" I asked.

"Father Lebreton, and I've had a lot of practice with my classmates. He taught me more than that, as you no doubt imagine. Roll onto your stomach, and I'll show you."

He didn't need to tell me what else the priest had taught him. "Won't it hurt?" I asked.

"Less than you think. Roll over." And I did.

He moistened the opening with his spit. He even licked it, a new sensation for me, and in no way unpleasant. Then he inserted a finger and pressed it against the sides of my anus to enlarge it, talking all the time.

"Father Lebreton never bothers with this part," he explained. "He just plows right in. That does hurt until you adjust to having it in you, which doesn't take long. My friends and I figured out that if you get it wet and ready it doesn't hurt, or hardly at all. The first times he took me it hurt from start to finish. It's a good thing he comes quickly. Of course I was smaller then. I shouldn't have any trouble getting it in. After all, you are fifteen."

That didn't sound very reassuring, and I did feel a fair amount of discomfort when he got around to penetrating me, but not what you'd call pain, and the pressure inside me sent waves of pleasure through my body once he started pumping rhythmically. The longer he pumped, the better it felt, and by the time he came I was moaning and pushing back against him to take him as deep as it would go. He collapsed on top of me and kissed my neck, ears and shoulders.

We lay for a long time snuggled close together on the mattress, kissing and exploring parts of our bodies we hadn't touched till that day. "So this is what love is," I thought.

THE COUNT D'AIRELLES had had the absurd notion of marrying his daughter in a "village style" wedding. Instead of holding the ceremony in the chateau chapel, at noon the wedding party, which would consist only of the bride's relations, would walk four miles to the village church, where his chaplain would bless their union. Half his servants would follow behind to fill out the procession, and the other half would remain at the chateau to attend to the needs of the greater part of their noble guests, who would not all fit into the church in any case. Then all but the servants would return to the chateau in carriages for the post-nuptial collation on the lawn followed by dinner and a ball (the last event not at all typical of a peasants' wedding). Only the Count, the Countess and an elderly aunt would go to the village by coach.

It was a scorching hot day, and a thick layer of orange dust covered the road to the village. Except for the soon-to-be-married couple, everyone in the wedding party sweated profusely in their finery and grumbled about what Olivier called a forced march. The reluctant bride shuffled petulantly along in front of the others, not bothering to lift her gown, and when we reached the church the white silk had a terra cotta border that went halfway up her shins. The villagers lined up in front of their homes cheered as we went by. The Count had had the foresight to tell them to shut the pigs in their sties.

Julien wanted to walk back with me, but his father forced him to ride. Tired though we were, we servants trotted all the way to the chateau, eager to eat our fill of the wedding meats that would be laid out for us on a long table by the outbuildings. After that, those of us not called on to wait at table would have a rustic party of our own to celebrate the marriage of our master's daughter.

Julien came to look for me where I was dancing with the village girls. He said he was tired of being patronized by the wedding guests and wanted to spend the remaining time before dinner with me. I was having fun, but I went with him. As I had expected, he led me to the storeroom again. I got hard as soon as I was sure where we were going. He put a hand on my buttocks and worked his fingers between them as we climbed the stairs, kissing my neck as we went. He pressed into me from behind and fondled my cock through my breeches while I shut and bolted the door. Then we hurried to the mattress, undressed, and touched each other intimately.

Julien pleasured me with his mouth as he had the previous afternoon, and then I had a go at him and had my first taste of semen. He complimented me on my cocksucking. I had learned quickly and done a much better job. I asked if he wanted me to fuck him, too, but he wouldn't let me. "You've just come," he said. "Besides, I have to change for dinner now and then put in an appearance at the ball or Father will scold me. Come back here at ten, and we'll play some more and sleep in each other's arms."

A few hours later we met in the storeroom for the third time, and I sucked him again. Then I asked if I could fuck him. He refused.

"Don't you like it?" I asked. "I know I did, both times."

"Oh, I love it, and I'm glad you do too. It's just that… well, with you it just seems wrong, if you know what I mean. Just the… you know. Not the rest. I have no problem sucking you. Now lie on your back and I'll teach you some other positions."

He lifted my legs and played with my hole until it relaxed before he took me. It felt less strange the second time, and I enjoyed it more. He had come just a few minutes before, so he stayed inside me a long time, and the longer it went on, the better it felt. I would have liked to give him the same pleasure and also find out what he was feeling. Later, lying in his arms as he slept peacefully, I remembered what my father had said, that when we grew up, Julien's feelings for me would alter and our friendship would end.

Chapter 2

JULIEN returned to the chateau the second week of August to inform his parents that he had finally decided in favor of soldiering and had arranged to enter the Military Academy in autumn, unaware that they had gone to stay with Jeanne for a month. He immediately took me into the chateau to live with him, which raised some eyebrows, especially the major-domo's. Julien put him in his place. "I'm fifteen now and need my own manservant," he snapped.

He had a small bed moved into his room for me to sleep in. I didn't, of course, but I did lie in it every night long enough to rumple the sheets so the maids would have nothing to gossip about when they came to tidy up in the morning. What they made of the stains on his sheets I couldn't say.

Now that we were lovers, Julien didn't hesitate to fill me in on the details of the personal lives of every member of his family. He seldom saw his brother in Versailles, but he dined once a week with Berthe and her husband in their private hotel in the Marais. While the building itself wasn't particularly grand, he told me, the décor and furnishings were more than luxurious, they were ostentatious, but neither its comforts, nor the Baron's wealth, nor a full sex life (if she had one—de l'Envol had married her for her rank, not her beauty) made Berthe happy. She had, if such a thing were possible, become more pious, and her eyes were always red. Julien felt sorry for her. He considered the Baron a pig, in love with his own insignificant importance.

Julien used his father's money to have me outfitted with the family livery, and declared that I looked very fine in it indeed. Moreover, he said that if I was to be his manservant, he would have to teach me how to behave like a gentleman. My father disapproved of the project, but he didn't dare protest. He feared nothing would come of it except to give me impossible ideas of rising above my station. My mother, on the other hand, envisioned a bright future for me. If she, a peasant's daughter, could work at the chateau, why shouldn't I also be able to move up in the world? "No, *Monsieur le chevalier* has found a new game, that's all," my father told us. That he had!—Julien taught me much, much more in the privacy of our bedchamber. So I suspected he had other reasons than preparing me to become a house servant. Surely he meant for us to go on like this forever. Why else would his instruction have including riding and swordsmanship?

Thus, while Berthe may not have enjoyed a full sex life, Julien and I did. He would not let me penetrate him, but he gave me a great deal of pleasure, in front as well as behind, and always saw to it I was fully satisfied. I'm afraid I often exhausted him in the process. I had become a very proficient cocksucker. As for taking the man's role, I was determined to have my way with one of the village girls after he left, and I did. In the meantime, I had no cause to complain. He allowed me a free hand in everything else, even to insert a finger in his ass while I sucked him, and it drove him wild. Much as I would have liked to feel my cock inside Julien and do myself proud by making him beg for more, I would enjoy my affair with him to the hilt while it lasted if it should prove no more than an idyllic interlude, and if it turned into something permanent, I did not doubt that sooner or later I would enjoy him to the hilt as well.

For the moment, just being with him gave me more enjoyment than I had ever had, and I don't only mean in bed. I saw more of him than I had since infancy. During those two weeks we were together twenty-four hours a day, every day, I ate like a king, and I didn't have to work. Working in the garden would have been unbearable in that heat, and I went swimming every day. My only responsibilities were to help him out of his clothes at night, a task which I performed quite differently from other *valets de chambre*, and to pour his bath and stand by holding a towel while he bathed. I poured his bath, but what I did once he had got in it one would hardly call "standing by". And how many menservants are undressed by their masters?

My first stint as a house servant came to an abrupt end upon the return of the Count and Countess. *Monsieur le comte* told Julien in no uncertain terms that, except for princes of the blood, schoolboys did not have personal servants and he could damn well wait until he received his first commission. He also took away my livery and sent me back to the gardens. I was afraid he'd have me whipped, but he was so pleased with Julien's choice of career that his discipline went no further. I had not expected it to last after Julien left for the Military Academy anyway.

THE COUNT took his son to Paris to outfit him for the Academy two days later. I was disappointed that he was not allowed to say goodbye to me. As things turned out, however, our separation was a brief one.

Julien lived in the barracks, but from ten o'clock Saturday morning until Monday he stayed at the Hotel L'Envol. He had to leave at six in the morning to get to the Academy in time for roll call. At the end of November, Berthe wrote her mother a long letter complaining of loneliness and asked that two of her former maids, whom she believed to be very devout, come to Paris to serve her. (According to Julien, both slept with their lovers in their rooms on the top floor of the chateau.) Berthe also wrote that not a single soul who had grown up in a city like Paris knew the first thing about gardening, and might she have "that charming little boy who used to be friends with Julien" to tend her flower beds? The Countess, who felt guilty for having forced her into a marriage she herself would have refused, was anxious to oblige her daughter, but the Count was adamant. The maids, Lucie and Henriette, left for Paris without me. Only after Berthe came to spend Christmas away from her husband and the Count found himself beset on two sides did he give in to his daughter's tears and the Countess's pleading and accede to their wishes. When Berthe returned to Paris the day after Epiphany, it had been decided that I would join her there toward the end of the month.

Before then I made good on the promise I had made myself to have sex with a woman. All the girls in the village knew me for a friend of the Count's younger son, and I had no difficulty turning their heads. The following spring I learned from Julien that I was a father, though he couldn't say for sure which of my many conquests was the child's mother. I promptly forgot about them, having left that life behind me.

I ARRIVED at the Hotel L'Envol to assume my new duties on Candlemas. I discovered that Berthe's entire garden consisted of two potted trees in the courtyard on either side of the main entrance and not a single flower. It was, of course, Julien who had engineered my transfer to Paris. He had become his sister's only tie to her former life, and her affection for him bordered on worship. She went out of her way to humor him, and he wanted his own manservant for the two days a week he spent at the hotel.

I found my livery ready and waiting for me to try on. I saw at once what Julien had meant by the Baron's ostentation. Compared with what the servants wore at the Chateau d'Airelles, I could have passed for a duke.

They put my bed in a small, windowless space, not much more than a closet, connected by an inner door to the room reserved for Julien's visits. In fact, I had to pass through his room to get to it. It was my responsibility to keep it tidy and dusted in his absence and to help the other male servants in their duties, such as waiting at table when the Baron entertained. With only two weeks' experience as a household servant, my manners were far from adequate, but neither were the Baron's, and my blunders in etiquette passed by him unnoticed.

I learned much waiting at table, for the unrest in Paris was on everyone's lips. I pressed Julien for more information. He shrugged off the notion that the Estates-General would actually meet, though the King had agreed to summon them two months earlier and my fellow servants were certain it would happen. On whether they would accomplish anything their opinion was divided.

The most accurate information I picked up in the streets. Being the youngest servant by several years, I was often sent out on errands. During my tenure in the de l'Envols' employ Berthe must have had me go to every church in Paris to light a taper for one reason or another, and after a few weeks of regularly losing my way, I came to know the city quite well. I had never been in any city before, much less one as vast and crowded as Paris. Our village had only three streets, one with two rows of houses facing each other, and behind them kitchen gardens, each with two or three chickens, then another row of houses on either side facing across the fields where the peasants grazed a small herd of communal cattle and planted grain, nine-tenths of which went to the Count, the King's bailiffs or the Bishop of Angoulême. The parish church where Berthe was married stood at one end of the central street, and at the other, at the bottom of an incline, the smithy and the village barn and granary. The peasants thought the Count owned their village, the Count thought he owned the peasants, and the pigs who lazed in the street thought they owned everything and knew as much about politics as the villagers. Life there, in short, was worlds removed from life in the capital.

It soon became clear to me that I should not give credence to Julien's views on how the situation would work itself out, although I continued to question him about it. He took little interest in political matters and simply repeated what he had last heard from one or another equally ignorant fellow student at the Academy. He didn't even know about *Qu'est-ce que le tiers état*, the pamphlet circulated by the Abbé Sieyès calling for all members to the Estates-General to vote as a body instead of in three separate groups, which a servant had smuggled into the Hotel and we all devoured. All that was to change three months later after the Tennis Court Oath, when everyone at his school had to move to Versailles. I didn't know that until his next visit, a week or two after the fall of the Bastille, and by then the National Constituent Assembly was well on its way to drafting a constitution and the King was already wearing the tricolor cockade.

In the meantime I had witnessed the rioting in Paris that preceded the march on the Bastille and the French Guard supporting the insurgents. I was curious to see with whom Julien would side. My sympathies, of course, lay with the commoners.

The violence angered Julien, but he was not entirely unsympathetic to the mob's demands. In reaction to the Declaration of the Rights of Man, he voiced the opinion that however admirable the principles it expressed, he didn't see why we needed a constitution to implement them. His point of view, though naïve, was more honest than that of the Baron, who, himself a commoner until quite recently, waxed indignant at the suggestion that all men were created equal. Why should any person's right be considered inalienable when he had had to pay for his? This led to fights at the dinner table whenever Julien was present. Berthe inevitably sided with her brother, although she understood not a word of what either of them said, and both Julien and the Baron told her so. It goes without saying that we servants kept our mouths shut.

In bed with Julien I could say anything I wanted, with one exception: that I considered my right to fuck him to be among those covered in the Declaration. In his eyes our disagreements were as trivial as I knew them to be profound. I recognized the National Assembly as legitimate; he did not. But in those days people finally (or should I say still?) felt free to speak their minds, and I took our differences of opinion as proof that we had entered a new age. Of course I was not so radical as to demand the abdication of His Majesty. I don't believe the thought had yet entered anyone's head.

AT THE beginning of October, the women of Paris marched on Versailles, and it became clear that Louis XVI was a weakling who would grant the people almost anything they asked for. The royal family took up residence in the Louvre, and Olivier and his wife followed them to Paris. There were nowhere near as many apartments available in the Louvre as in Versailles, so they came to live at the Hotel L'Envol, to the extreme mortification of Olivier, who thought Berthe an insipid ninny and held an even lower opinion of the Baron than Julien. From then on the dinner table arguments became more heated. It was close to impossible to say exactly where Olivier stood on anything, because although he believed with all his heart in an absolute monarchy, he couldn't bring himself to agree openly with the Baron on anything. Berthe, having no opinions of her own, was at a loss to express any, which did not prevent her from speaking up and making a fool of herself by contradicting what she had just said every time she opened her mouth, until they passed the Civil Constitution of the Clergy and at last everything fell into place for her, or seemed to. When the King signed it at the end of the year, she was crushed.

By then Julien was no longer in Paris. He had received his commission and been sent to put down some of the counter-revolutionary uprisings that had broken out in the provinces without the personal servant the Count had promised him. In early February, almost two years to the day since I had first donned the de l'Envol livery, the Count and Countess d'Airelles arrived in Paris to seek safety in numbers. The spirit of the Revolution had taken hold of the peasants, and not a single aristocrat remained within forty leagues of the chateau. They brought with them half a dozen servants and five times the belongings they needed. The Baron gave them the second story of the Hotel. More people were living in the Hotel L'Envol than there was room for, and I knew myself to be unwelcome to everyone there but Berthe, who loathed only her husband and was indifferent to everyone and everything else except her God, so I left and ceased being a servant forever.

I WAS on my own. At nineteen years old, I owned nothing but the clothes on my back which no longer fit me, I knew no one in Paris, and I had no place to go. I wandered aimlessly around the city, feeling hungrier by the hour, until a stout man in his mid-forties wearing the red Jacobin bonnet spotted me staring in the window of the café where he was eating supper. He waved to me to join him, shook my hand enthusiastically, introduced himself as Jacques Gombert, *citoyen*, and inquired about my circumstances.

Citizen Gombert heartily approved of my decision to leave the service of a family he called an enemy of the people. I should work for the Revolution, he said. The Revolution took care of its own, and no Frenchman would ever be destitute again. He paid for my supper, taught me the "Carmagnole", and invited me to stay with him until I found work and could set up on my own. I went home with him to his garret, furnished only with a table, two chairs, and a straw mattress on an unswept floor. I collapsed onto the mattress and immediately fell asleep. In the middle of the night, he raped me.

Although he had raped me, in other ways Citizen Gombert was true to his word. The next day he introduced me to the Jacobin Club, and when I told them I could read and write, they offered me a position as clerk. Gombert promised to find me affordable lodgings, but I did not think he would look very hard since he enjoyed the nighttime companionship I provided, while I took no pleasure in his at any time of day. Unless I myself found a place to live I would have little choice but to put up with my host's unwelcome lust. Until then only Julien had possessed me. Though I had had my fun with Henriette more than once during Julien's absences while I lived at the Hotel L'Envol, I had yet to discover what it was like to penetrate another man, and I had no desire for Gombert to be that man, nor would he have agreed to it.

It took me a week of walking around with ravaged innards before I could secure suitable lodgings, for I worked all day and was only free to look in the evening. I don't know how long I might have had to endure Gombert's below-the-waist abuse if one of my co-workers, Citizen Rivaillon, had not mentioned that an elderly invalid who rented a room in a boardinghouse run by some friends of his had died that morning. I asked if he would take me there before someone else snapped up the room, and we talked the head clerk into giving us an hour off work to see it. Rivaillon's friends lived in that tangle of narrow, twisting, trash-littered streets near the central market off the rue Saint-Denis at the foot of the rue Montmartre. Outside the house appeared run down, but once we had passed through the entrance into the open courtyard I saw that inside it was clean and in good repair. What's more, I would have use of the furniture the deceased had left behind. I had received my first week's pay the day before and could give a fortnight's rent in advance. I ran to Gombert's after work, grabbed the satchel that contained everything I owned, and moved in immediately. I would sooner sleep in a bed in which a man unknown to me had died of unknown causes the night before than spend one more night on the floor under Citizen Gombert.

My new landlady, Madame Leforgeron, took an immediate liking to me and took me under her wing, because she, too, came from the southwest and recognized a fellow countryman in the name Vreilhac. She told me to call her Artémis. Her protection was invaluable, because she was the most rabid and bloodthirsty Jacobin I ever met and nothing escaped her notice. She called me her curé, which disconcerted me until I realized she meant it in jest, because I didn't have a mistress and for the time being led a celibate life. Lying beneath Jacques Gombert's malodorous body and enduring his inconsiderate thrusting had well-nigh destroyed my interest in sex. Had I wanted a woman to share my bed, I had but to say the word. Sandrine, a plump and perky little blonde from Normandy, about twenty-five years old, who had a room across the landing from mine, did not hide that she fancied me. She had wide hips and earned a meager living sewing flowers out of crepe, taffeta and other fabrics. But I sensed that an intimate involvement of any kind with anyone was becoming more perilous by the day, and attractive women were held in particular suspicion.

On the other hand, Artémis despised my in-name-only benefactor as much as she liked me, and I subtly encouraged her low opinion of him. Citizen Gombert was far too sure of himself to realize that nobody she counted as her enemy could be safe for long. I admit that I was perhaps as ignorant as he, but I had the advantage of being less self-assured. I grasped the uncertainty of the times but did not yet see the full extent of it.

Artémis Leforgeron was a tall, big-boned woman with a beaked nose and an unruly shock of long, dark brown hair. I never saw her without her linen apron and her yellow woolen shawl draped over her broad, manlike shoulders. Her knitting hardly ever left her bony hands, and when she gesticulated wildly, as she did whenever she spoke about politics, you had to step back so as not to be poked with one of her needles.

She spoke about little else, but in troubled times everything becomes political, from the shortage of bread to your neighbors' morals. I kept my ears open and my mouth shut lest I say something to compromise me, but I heard only one side of the story and believed everything I heard. I owe my political education to Artémis and her lodgers, whereas my upbringing at the chateau and in a country village had formed my sense of right and wrong, and I judged people according to what they did, not what they thought. Thus I was often appalled by the Jacobins' methods, but I shared their principles and kept my thoughts to myself. My reactions to the major events of the day were identical to theirs: indignation at the King's attempt to flee the country, elation when we became a republic, distrust of the Austrians and the belief that we should go on the offensive and attack them before they attacked us. At the same time, I could tell that the crowd I frequented was ten times more volatile than the political situation.

I had fallen in with the Jacobins entirely by chance. Though I had listened eagerly to the servants' gossip at the Hotel L'Envol, except for royalist and republican I could not tell one faction from the other. I was unaware that the Jacobins were the most radical of the lot, and, quite frankly, I didn't care. Not until I witnessed the hysteria that accompanied the King's execution did I realize that the world had been stood on its head. The animals had become the zookeepers, they had begun to prey on each other, and before long the most savage of them would be in charge.

Since Artémis never mentioned their names when she ran through her litany of enemies of the State, I blithely assumed that the people I had once known were safe. It occurred to me that she might have lumped them together with the *émigrés*, whom she hated most of all, but that, too, would have meant they were safe. I only learned of what became of my former masters, or rather, what led each of them to their respective fates, when Julien sought me out two years later, hoping that I could help him. After the King's abortive flight to Varennes, only the Baron de l'Envol, stupid though he was, had enough sense to foresee the inevitable and left for Holland, taking his wife and her maid, Lucie, with him. He had, in any case, long grown weary of his in-laws' undisguised scorn. So in the end, the marriage Berthe loathed saved her life. Olivier waited until the King was sentenced to the guillotine before fleeing to England, leaving Marie-Catherine behind. She had just learned she was pregnant after years of trying to conceive, and Olivier thought the journey too great a risk. He felt certain that the Revolutionaries would not harm a woman who was carrying a baby. But the *gendarmes* came soon after the Legislative Assembly declared the Republic and arrested all of them for carrying on seditious correspondence with *émigrés*, as they undoubtedly were. Berthe had been living in Holland for a year and a half, Jeanne's family had fled to Austria shortly before we declared war on them, and now Olivier was in London. Only Julien, an officer in the Republican Army, was in no immediate danger. But the situation was unstable, and the time would come when the Terror cast its eye on him as well.

Chapter 3

AT WORK my name was Citizen Vreilhac. I was one of five clerks. Our job consisted of turning rough drafts into clean copy. It might be anything the leaders took it into their heads to write—memos, letters, orders, notices, inventories, pamphlets, accusations, even an occasional poem. People were always talking and there were always disagreements, and from my first day on the job, as if warned by instinct, I refrained from saying anything until I had assessed in what direction the majority opinion was headed before seconding anyone's point of view. If someone asked why I didn't speak up more often, I'd say, "I'm listening; I want to know the facts. Of course I have opinions, but what is my opinion worth next to that of the Friend of People?" The Friend of the People was Jean-Paul Marat, and when a document arrived written in his hand, we fought for the honor of copying it.

One would think that as I grew more familiar with my new circle of acquaintances I would venture to express an opinion, but the longer I stayed with them, the warier I became. These people changed opinions from day to day without realizing they were contradicting themselves, but their memories were long when it came to what another person had said or done. Very seldom did I forget to hide my true feelings, but when the royal family was arrested they must have seen the shock on my face, because Citizen Rivaillon, the most outspoken of them all, turned to me and said, "What's the matter, Citizen? Don't you think Capet is a traitor?"

"There's no doubt we're safer with him in prison," I answered, covering up as best I could. "It's just that I never thought the Girondists would have the courage to do what's right."

This sparked an argument over what faction ought to be credited with the King's arrest. To suggest that it was the Girondists was a serious blunder. I had dug myself into a hole, and it was imperative that I extricate myself quickly.

"It was we who convinced them to vote as they should," I said, "and it wasn't easy."

That mollified Rivaillon. "You're right, Citizen," he said. "The Girondists are unreliable. They can't be counted on to take strong measures when they're needed. Don't they understand we're at war? You'd think they had water in their veins."

A few months later the Girondists would no longer be unreliable; they would be devious, and after that, traitors. And when they went to the guillotine we saw that their blood flowed as red as anybody's.

I CAME to realize that the surest way of taking the Jacobin pulse was to listen to Artémis. We lodgers gathered in her kitchen every evening to drink a glass of wine and talk about recent events and what they meant for the future of the nation. Unlike at work, we called each other by our first names, except for a mild-mannered humanist and intellectual who liked to sprinkle his conversation with quotes from the classics, whom we addressed as Citizen Brotteaux, following Artémis's lead. In addition to our landlady and her husband, a taciturn man who sat in the corner puffing away at his pipe despite a hacking cough, Brotteaux and Sandrine, my fellow lodgers included an elderly, obese blind woman, Madelon, cared for by her twelve-year-old grandson, a frail lad who could have passed for ten; twin brothers, Philippe and Thomas, who avoided telling us their profession (Artémis informed me they were gravediggers); and a fellow named Clément, a carter whose bawdy sense of humor irritated Artémis. Thierry, a burly, balding, pockmarked porter at les Halles who left for work at three in the morning, seldom joined us.

Artémis often chided me for my silence, so I hit on the idea of reading popular novels aloud to my companions, a chapter a night. I had not yet read any of them myself and chose them by reputation. Citizen Brotteaux knew them well but said I was a good reader and that he enjoyed listening to me. The others had heard of the books, but none of them were readers. I began with Rousseau's *La nouvelle Héloïse*. Jean-Jacques Rousseau was the idol of all good patriots, but when I first opened the book and read the title page, where he calls himself "Citizen of Geneva", Artémis corrected me: "He was a citizen of the world."

"That is very true, Madame Leforgeron," Brotteaux agreed, "but our revered Jean-Jacques was very proud of the city of his birth, though his fellow citizens may not have deserved it."

"Love of one's fatherland is a noble sentiment," Madelon said, and her blind eyes filled with tears. Her two sons and eldest grandson had joined the army to fight the Prussians, and she had not heard from them in weeks.

"Rousseau had unshakable faith in the goodness of man," Brotteaux continued (Artémis smiled and nodded), "although one would think experience would have taught him otherwise. He loved humanity as a whole, yet he maintained that everyone persecuted him."

"People are born with good hearts," Artémis replied. "It's the conditions of our daily lives that corrupt so many of us. When we all live in freedom and our basic needs are met, the Age of Goodness will begin. The Revolution will see to that—'Liberty, Equality, Fraternity'. But let's listen to Gérard. The Friend of the People speaks highly of this book, and I'm sure Gérard is a wonderful reader."

I began the story of Julie and Saint-Preux. Reading the book kept us occupied for months. We were all moved by the main characters' trials and tribulations, especially the women. Their innocence and devotion stirred even Artémis, so uncompromising and severe and practical in every other way. She often interrupted my reading to express sympathy for them or ask me to read an especially romantic passage a second time.

The story also gave Sandrine an opening to hint to me about her feelings. She asked if I had ever been in love.

"Love is a luxury in these unsettled times," I told her. "Our enemies attack us on all sides and the nation is ripped apart by internal divisions. We never know from one day to the next how we'll keep ourselves alive—where we'll spend the night, how we'll clothe ourselves, or where our next meal will come from. A man has to think about these things."

"Isn't that a reason for two people to seek consolation in love and support each other? It only makes life harder when you have no one to turn to."

I shook my head sadly. "What man doesn't want a wife and children, and what man doesn't have a right to them? But no, not yet. For now we can only live for the future."

Influenced perhaps by Sandrine's unrequited love—my landlady saw everything—Artémis inquired about what she called my shyness with women. "A man has needs," she said, no doubt thinking of Thomas and Philippe, who often brought a woman to their room, never the same one, and probably shared her. Artémis pretended not to know they were all prostitutes.

Reading *La nouvelle Héloïse* had revealed the tender spot in her hard heart, and I made up a story about an unhappy love affair and a son I had never seen, alive somewhere in the Charentais and whose whereabouts remained a mystery, however desperately I looked for him. (I couldn't remember if Julien had told me whether the child was a boy or a girl.) Artémis embraced me and thanked me for my honesty. I made her promise not to tell Sandrine.

Of all Artémis's lodgers I was most drawn to Brotteaux, but I kept my distance from him, though he repeatedly tried to engage me in conversation. He was a talkative gentleman and did not hold back his opinions, which were eclectic and often cynical, which meant they were at odds with the prevailing idealism. I never contradicted him lest he seize the opportunity to draw me out, because, to tell the truth, I found his ideas more astute and convincing than the empty clichés everyone else seemed to spout. I thought it inevitable that he would end his days under the guillotine.

NOT all my work as a clerk consisted of producing clean copies of rough drafts hastily penned and full of words scratched out or written over. We were also called on to take dictation, most often of public notices and manifestos, which would then be taken to the print shop to be typeset, run off, and posted around Paris. My ability to take dictation quickly brought me to the notice of Citizen Andrieux, the man in charge of our workroom. I had a clear hand, excellent spelling, and I wrote quickly and was able to remember word for word what had been dictated to me, though I had heard those words while I was writing what he said two sentences earlier. It always fell to me to take dictation from the most important Jacobins, except Marat, who wrote everything in his own hand. One day Robespierre, whom we would later call "The Incorruptible", dictated what almost amounted to a pamphlet off the top of his head, speaking so quickly it seemed as if he never stopped to take a breath. I seldom had to ask him to repeat himself and only asked him to stop twice so I could sharpen my quill. The finished product I gave him was so accurate and legible that he complimented me and asked for my name. My fellow workers were envious. They said that Robespierre never forgot anyone who made a good impression on him, and he was certain to use his influence to advance my career, but for a long time nothing came of it.

TWO celebrations from those days stand out in mind. The first occurred on the twenty-first of September 1792. The day before, we had ceased being a constitutional monarchy and become a republic.

It was a crisp autumn day. The crowds began arriving early at the Champs de Mars to honor the infant Republic. People came dressed in their best clothes and carrying picnic baskets. They played games, partied, toasted the Republic, and congratulated one another on the nation's achievements. Nobody gave thought to the armies massed at our borders. The festivities went on all day, and there was a display of fireworks in the evening.

It seemed as if the entire population of Paris had turned out to celebrate, though of course they could not all have fit even into so large an area. I am told almost as many people gathered at Vincennes and a smaller crowd in the Tuileries Gardens. I went with Artémis, Monsieur Leforgeron, Sandrine, Clément, and Thierry, with Brotteaux tagging along behind. Philippe and Thomas went on their own, I assume so they would have a free hand to flirt with the ladies and perhaps find a couple they could screw on the banks of the Seine after dark. Old Madelon and her grandson stayed home, afraid she would be jostled by the crowd and lose her way among them.

We wandered about the grounds in search of old friends, smiling and laughing. Brotteaux stopped to chat with everyone we passed, and we soon lost sight of him. Everybody seemed to know and like him. That didn't surprise me. I have seldom met a man more friendly.

Citizen Brotteaux had nothing but praise for the Republic, which he compared to Ancient Rome, and for the new constitution that would now be written, and was unwisely generous in his suggestions as to the system of governance he hoped it would establish. On the other hand, he had nothing but ridicule for the proposed Republican Calendar, which he called pompous and foolish. "How disappointing they should waste their time on such trivialities when so much needs to be done!"

he said. "What will people in the deserts of Arabia think of a month with the name Pluviôse, or of Thermidor on the frozen tundra, when we bring the Revolution to the rest of the world? And it is our aim to share its blessings with all mankind, is it not?"

I could not have agreed with him more, but I nonetheless praised their "sublime logic" and words like July or April never passed my lips for as long as the calendar was in force. For some bizarre reason I even remember some of the things they used to replace the saints in order to banish religion from it. Under the new calendar my name day became the ox, Julien's knotgrass, and it flattered Artémis's vanity to learn that hers was the amaryllis. (I believe Citizen Brotteaux's was the grape.) Ironically, the calendar proved the most long-lasting of their accomplishments, though even most Jacobins paid no attention to the idiocy of a ten-day week.

The second was not so much a celebration as a spontaneous outburst of wild joy that seized hold of the mob when the guillotine severed Louis XVI's head from his body on the Place de la Révolution.

I did not attend executions often, but my absence at so important an event would be noticed. Not to go would be taken as a sign that I did not support the majority's decision. I was right; I could see that everyone who recognized me made a mental note of my presence. The size of the crowd was unprecedented, and I thought that many people had come there for the same reason I had. I realized my error when I saw their reaction.

People had shaken their fists, yelled insults, even hurled mud at him when the procession rolled by them in the streets, and the crowd gathered around the scaffold was abuzz with holiday expectation. But when he stepped from the tumbrel a hush fell over the Place de la Révolution. It seemed as if everyone had stopped breathing at once, as if in awe, or perhaps all were afraid of missing the tiniest detail, as we sometimes see in the theater. The wheeze of the descending blade sounded like a consumptive struggling to inhale, and the noise of it hitting the wood as it fell into its slot and of the head when it rolled into the basket sounded like a suspended heartbeat.

The throng surged forward en masse, carrying me with them. People reached into the basket to grab the head, and the lucky woman who was first to sink her fingers into his thinning hair held it high in the air and let the blood pour down over her. Others pushed in close to her to share in the gory shower. Still others seized the bucket of collected blood and thrust their arms into it, then pulled them out and smeared their faces with it or licked their fingers clean. Some gathered up the blood in their cupped hands to spray on the people who pressed in on all sides but were unable to reach their goal. They howled with joy and turned to wipe their hands on the shirts of those standing closest to them. They hugged each other and laughed. They danced in the streets and sang "Ça ira" and the "Carmagnole". Those who had brought their children held them up so they could see better. This uncouth and primitive behavior subsided in an hour or two, but the excitement lasted for days.

A GENERAL panic set in with the uprising in the Vendée. Almost overnight people began to see spies and traitors at every turn. The arrests multiplied, and trials were held almost round the clock. My fellow clerks had been right in saying that Robespierre had an iron memory. On his recommendation I was given a position as court recorder for the Revolutionary Tribunal. The jurors' bench was perpendicular to the judges' table, a few yards to their left. I sat at a small table to the right of the judges, where it was my responsibility to write down every word spoken at a trial or hearing. Artémis called it a high honor.

Recording the proceedings was less difficult than it sounds. People seldom had a chance to speak in their own defense, and since we had so many cases to get through, the prosecutor soon stopped giving speeches denouncing the sedition and wickedness of those accused. He simply read through the act of accusation, a copy of which had been given me in advance, the judges pronounced sentence, and that was that.

The inordinate number of accused soon made it impossible to grant everyone a preliminary hearing, and once the Terror was in full swing they often dispensed with a trial as well. I was none too happy with my new job, in spite of a significant increase in salary and the chance to associate with the heroes of the Revolution, which made my situation less precarious at a time when it seemed no one was above suspicion.

My first day on the job reassured me somewhat. By chance, about a quarter of the crimes we had to judge were not political. (I say "we" because just being present at a trial made me feel implicated in every execution they ordered, though I had no say in the matter.) Among the first to face the Tribunal was Jacques Gombert, accused of raping a ten-year-old boy. I immediately thought, not of what he done to me, but of Julien's sexual initiation by the Jesuits. The child's mother testified, and the details she gave were horrific. The doctor who treated him confirmed what she said. The people in the stands wept openly.

There was no doubt what the verdict would be; all Revolutionaries considered the protection of children a sacred trust. The presiding judge even delivered a speech on the heinousness of his crime. They sent Gombert to the guillotine, and he wept when he heard his sentence. I felt an enormous satisfaction in having participated in bringing a criminal—especially that criminal—to justice, and I told Artémis about it. She spat and called him a vile man. We went together to see him guillotined.

I don't believe I ever again volunteered information on a trial, although Artémis was ever curious and pressed me for details, in which case I had to speak about it. On the other hand, she often came to observe the proceedings and sat in the first row with a dozen or so women and their knitting, who glared at the accused and invariably clamored for their death. That evening in the kitchen she would tell everyone what happened, turning to me to confirm what she said.

However, Citizen Gombert was an exception. Nearly every person brought before the Tribunal was charged with a political crime, and not all the executions were just—far from it. The jeers and loud cries for condemnation from the crowds that came to witness the proceedings reminded me of the insanity I had witnessed below the former King's scaffold, and the small role I played weighed heavily on my conscience. This hysteria could not go on forever, and I feared that I would be punished when it came to an end, along with the judges who every day condemned so many to death with impunity. I felt trapped, and it would eventually give me nightmares. After my second nightmare I stopped attending executions. However, Artémis literally dragged me by the arm to Charlotte Corday's and I felt obliged to be present at one other.

I REMEMBER the events of one other day as vividly as the festivities that accompanied the inauguration of the Republic and the savage glee that followed the King's execution. Here, too, the death of a prominent figure was the occasion for an outpouring of emotion, but it was the exact opposite of a celebration.

It was a beautiful early summer day. I had been excused from work for a week to nurse an injured right wrist. The Leforgerons and I were sitting by the street door. I had moved out three chairs so we could enjoy the sunshine. I remember we were not discussing politics. We talked about my nightmares, which had begun a few days earlier. Sandrine had heard me call out in my sleep and rushed into my room to find me bathed in sweat and staring straight ahead with open eyes, though I was still asleep.

We were interrupted by a hubbub of running feet. From where we were sitting we could see to the corner and people running in the larger street, women tearing their hair, grown men weeping. Some stopped for a moment to talk to each other, gesticulating wildly.

Artémis and I sat there stunned, unable to grasp what the commotion was about. I hurried to the corner to ask. People were yelling questions to one another amid the sobs and cries: "Is it true?" "How did it happen?" "In his bath, did you say?" "Who would do such a thing?" "What will become of us?" A man called out to me, "They've murdered Marat!"

Artémis screamed and staggered to her feet when I told her. "Your dreams were an omen!" she wailed, and ran to join the ever-growing crowd. I followed her, leaving her husband to watch the house.

Nowadays everyone knows the name Charlotte Corday, but few remember what she looked like. I know I don't. But who among us cannot picture David's famous portrait of Marat in his bath, deathly pale and slumped to his right, his dangling arm still holding a quill, and the livid red gash in his chest? Yet when I think of Marat, what comes to mind is not David's portrait, but the inconsolable grief of a populace that clamored unremittingly for the blood of all and sundry, and their lamentations.

Corday's brave but senseless act sealed the Girondists' fate. Less than a month later the Incorruptible established the Committee of Public Safety, and from then on one event followed another with dizzying rapidity. On days when Clément had no loads to deliver—and there were many of them, for few people had money to pay to move their belongings—his cart was used to carry people to the guillotine. The bodies piled up in Paris as on a battlefield, while life went on as always and people pretended that everything was normal.

Not long afterwards, the former Count and Countess d'Airelles and their very pregnant daughter-in-law, Marie-Catherine, and even Berthe's former maid Henriette, came up for trial. I hadn't known they'd been arrested. I wondered why Berthe and the others were not with them. I learned that Olivier was an *émigré* in London when they read the accusation. I thought him despicable for having left his wife behind. But more than anything, I felt relief that Julien was not there and that his name was nowhere mentioned in the accusation. Surely he was safely out of the country. An officer at the front could easily desert and escape across the border.

They were condemned to death; everyone always was. They deferred Marie-Catherine's sentence and sent her back to the

Conciergerie because she was with child. With luck they would forget about her; it had happened before.

I kept my eyes glued to the page in front of me, but I felt the Count's piercing gaze forcing me to look up. He was glaring at me. Had he been permitted to speak, I'm sure he would have unleashed all his hatred on me.

When we had finished for the day, one of the judges came to me and said, "He recognized you, didn't he, Citizen?"

"Who?"

"That ex-Count Something-or-other. You knew him, too. Your hands were shaking."

"D'Airelles," I said. "My father used to be his gardener."

"Then I'm sure his execution is one you won't want to miss."

I didn't, though I kept well back in the crowd and observed in silence. I didn't want the Count to think I had come there to gloat. As he mounted the scaffold, I caught sight of Julien a short distance away from me. We had not seen each other in nearly three years. He was not in uniform. I was certain he recognized me. I moved toward him; he seemed to back away, but it might have been the press forcing him deeper into the crowd. Then came that terrible whishhh! and heart-stopping thump!, and a roar rose from the crowd. Samson was holding up the Count's head for all to see. When I turned around to look for Julien, he had disappeared.

Chapter 4

MY MOST difficult moment at the Tribunal came when they condemned Citizen Brotteaux to death on the most ridiculous charges imaginable, for conspiring with a well-to-do society lady, an innocuous, simple-minded priest, and a good-hearted girl they called a notorious prostitute. The list of accusations was such a jumble of contradictions that they made an exception and called on him to answer them. They were particularly curious about the little book he had in his pocket, which they had seen him reading while they called the others on trial to stand before them and summarily sentenced one after the other. When he told them it was a copy of Lucretius they asked if he was a revolutionary. "Yes," Brotteaux replied, "in his own way, he was."

Brotteaux accepted his fate stoically and smiled at me kindly when they pronounced his sentence. "Here," I thought, "is a man who will die with a clear conscience and does not blame me for the atrocities of the Terror."

Artémis was unmoved. In fact, she had been present at his arrest and had not spoken up to defend him. And I had thought she was fond of him!

"He amused me," she said.

I no longer read aloud when we got together in the evening. We had put our last novel aside unfinished shortly after Marat's assassination. We hardly spoke anymore about the war or the problems of daily life. The bread shortage was attributed to hoarding, our army's reversals to the generals' sedition. We spoke only of guilt and punishment, of tracking down the culprits and chopping off their heads with all possible speed.

"When all the enemies of the Revolution have been destroyed, then we can have peace and justice," Artémis repeated nightly, like a litany.

"Yes," I thought, "but who will be left to enjoy the new order when everyone who doesn't agree with you on every insignificant detail is an enemy of the Revolution?"

I lived in fear that sooner or later I would let something slip and open my thoughts to the most rabid Jacobins, the *enragés*, who were now in control. I saw myself mounting the steps of the guillotine. I was doomed.

One night, when Sandrine and I had walked up to our rooms together, she turned to me on the landing and whispered, "Madame Leforgeron terrifies me."

I immediately suspected a trap. Had someone asked her to draw me out. "Artémis?" I asked, feigning innocence. "Life terrifies me. Living in Paris terrifies me." I stopped short, realizing how my words would probably be taken. "Paris is surrounded by enemies, inside and out," I explained, "and we're all of us at their mercy. Why single out Artémis?"

WHEN I left the Conciergerie late one cold, wet evening near the beginning of Brumaire and headed for the Pont au Change, a man wrapped in a greatcoat stepped out of the shadows of the building and followed me across the bridge. The streets were nearly empty because of the weather, but my path along the Quai de la Mégisserie was well traveled and it did not surprise me to hear his footsteps on the paving stones behind me. Something, however, aroused my suspicions, and I tested him to see if he was following me. I was not mistaken. He stopped when I stopped, waiting for me to move on, and kept four or five houses behind me. Had the Terror sent its spies to watch my comings and goings? Had I inadvertently said something to compromise myself? Perhaps one of my former fellow clerks, jealous of my transfer to the Tribunal, had dredged up some idle comment I had made in the past, a bit of Jacobin dogma that had since become anathema, and turned it against me?

As soon as I turned into the small side streets and alleyways surrounding Artémis's house, I ducked around a corner and waited for him to catch up. His footsteps sped up as soon as he lost sight of me, and, when he turned the corner, he ran straight into me.

"*Monsieur le chevalier*!" I exclaimed. It was Julien.

"Don't call me that," he said. "I don't want anyone to know me as a *ci-devant*." He paused and added, "I need your help."

"Are they after you?" I asked, relieved that he had sought me out. It meant he didn't think I was one of them.

"No, I don't think so. Marie-Catherine had her baby. A boy. She named him Phébus."

"And?"

"They took him away from her and said they would give him to a wet nurse."

"How do you know all this?"

"Through a neighbor whose uncle was in prison with her. For forgery."

"And?"

"They guillotined her this afternoon."

"I'm sorry. I didn't know."

"You wouldn't. There was no need to send her before the Tribunal a second time."

"Then you know where I work."

"I saw you at my parents' trial."

"You were there? I didn't see you."

"No, you kept your nose buried in your papers."

"I saw you at their execution. You avoided me, as if you thought their blood was on my hands."

"Nobody's hands are clean anymore, Gérard. I don't blame you. What could you have done? People have to put themselves first to survive. Will you help me?"

"What do you want?"

"I want you to find the infant, my brother's son."

"To make sure he's safe?"

"To bring him to me."

"Julien, are you mad? A man on the run? Because if you aren't now, you will be soon."

"I want to take him to London and give him to his father."

"Does he deserve to have him, abandoning his mother like that?"

"She was pregnant, and he had to leave France in secret. You know—going on foot, wading across rivers, sleeping under bridges. He was afraid she'd lose the baby."

"And the others? Berthe…"

"Some other time. Do you think you can help me get out of the country?"

"I'll do my best. You know I'd risk anything to save your life, don't you, Julien? But first I have to find the baby. Do have any clues who this nurse is?"

"None whatsoever. I thought you might ask. You have contacts."

"It will take some time. Asking questions makes people suspicious. How can I get in touch with you?"

"You can't. I don't stay in one place for long. Who knows where I'll be when you find my nephew? I'll contact you."

"Well, goodbye then."

"Goodbye. And thank you."

We shook hands, and he disappeared into the fog.

It took me only two days to locate Marie-Catherine's baby, but what would I do with him until I found Julien again? I told the woman that I knew a barren couple who were looking for a child. They would pay handsomely.

"How much?"

I named a price, more than I could afford. Once she accepted, she'd take less if we couldn't honor our promise. Perhaps Julien had something he could sell. His cavalry sword?

"And what will I tell the police if they come looking for it?"

"Tell them he sickened and died. As I said, they're willing to pay, but it may take a while before they can raise the money."

"I can wait. This brat isn't going anywhere."

I waited for Julien to contact me. Time passed, and I grew anxious. I told the child's nurse that the woman who was to be the child's mother had fallen ill and did not want to take it into her home until she had recovered. She complained that her milk was drying up because of an inadequate diet, and I gave her money. I was relieved to learn that nobody had inquired about the child since he was first given to her.

JULIEN came looking for me during the last days of Nivôse. As before, he waited outside the Tribunal and followed me home. As soon as we had turned off from the main thoroughfare, he ran to catch up with me and grabbed me by the arm. His first words were not about the baby.

"The Committee of Public Safety is on my trail," he said breathlessly.

"How long have you known?"

"Three weeks. I've been on the move ever since, staying with friends when I can, or else sitting up all night in cafés, sometimes sleeping under archways or wagons in les Halles. I heard this afternoon that they arrested a man who put me up for a day or two after I left my lodgings."

"They must be closing in on you."

"They are. I'm sure they'd never find me once I was out of the city but there are guards posted at all the gates."

"Wandering the countryside alone at this time of year? Where would you go? How would you keep warm? What would you eat?"

"Oh, I'd be all right. My time in the cavalry taught me how to survive in the wild. Gérard, do you know of anywhere I can hide until I find a way out of Paris?"

I answered without hesitating. "In my room."

"Didn't you hear me? They arrest people who let me stay with them."

"My room is the last place they'll look. The house I live in is a nest of the some of the most fanatic *sans culottes* in Paris. Their devotion to the Revolution is beyond question. Our only problem is getting you past my landlady, who's a Jacobin Cerberus, and once you're in my room you won't be able to leave and will have to be as quiet as mouse."

"Then how will we get past her?"

"I'll think of a way. Here's the address. Wait for me somewhere where you can see the doorway without being seen yourself. I'll leave the house a little after midnight. But disguise yourself somehow. Do something to change your appearance. Shave that mustache and take the ribbon out of your hair so it will hang free. Dye it if you can. Most important, find yourself a red Jacobin cap."

Sneaking him into Artémis's would not be easy. To reach the stairs to my room you had to cross an inner courtyard, and the Leforgerons' ground floor windows looked directly into it, and Artémis often stayed up all night. Her husband's cough, which had all but disappeared over the summer, had returned with a vengeance when the cold weather set in, and he hadn't left his bed in over a month, hacking incessantly and spitting blood.

I kept a small bottle of brandy in my room and also a few packets of herbs I used to make infusions to warm me on cold nights. I would bring a cup down to the kitchen for Artémis to fill with boiling water. That night I made a mixture of the strongest smelling herbs, broke off the end of a stick of licorice, and put them into a vial with a measure of brandy and a little oil, had Artémis fill my cup, and set the vial to stand in the hot water so the ingredients would blend. Toward midnight, I slipped the vial into my coat pocket and left the house, aware that Artémis had seen me go.

I joined Julien and waited with him in the shadows. He had altered his appearance in the way I had instructed. After half an hour, I handed him the vial and whispered, "Follow my lead and play your part well. Now come."

We entered the courtyard and knocked on the Leforgerons' door. "You husband's coughing woke me three flights up," I told Artémis, hoping that Citizen Leforgeron was not having a quiet night. "I went to get my friend here, Citizen Mautal. He's an apothecary."

Julien made a show of examining Leforgeron's sputum before handing the vial to Artémis, telling her to empty its contents into a glass of hot wine and have her husband drink it slowly. She thanked us and reached into her purse for a few coins, but Julien refused, saying that free Frenchmen should not have to pay for a doctor's care. We climbed the stairs to my room while she was busy administering the medicine.

When I closed the door behind us, Julien whispered, "I can't stay here forever. How will I get back out?"

"Now that she thinks you're my friend we can simply walk out together in broad daylight. She doesn't stay home all day, you know. She'll assume you stopped by while she was at the market. My next task is finding a way for you to leave the city. I located your nephew, by the way."

"You have? Unfortunately, I don't see how I can take him with me now. No infant could survive living outdoors in the winter."

We stood staring at each other. I had only one small bed, and my room was freezing.

"It's late," I said. "Get undressed and come to bed. We'll be warm under the quilt."

He smiled and said, "Like old times," and let me kiss him.

He was trembling, however, and not with cold. Then he relaxed and returned my kisses. I pushed his greatcoat off his shoulders, and it slid to the floor. Then I untied the rope belt on his britches and undid the buttons. He stepped out of them, and I took him by the hand and led him to the bed, both of us in just our shirts.

I had not had sex since Gombert had generously let me share his bed—with ulterior motives. That night I took the man's role for the first time except with women, and I remained the man for as long as he stayed with me. In bed he would lie on his side with his back turned toward me, I would drape my arm across him, and he would press back against me in open invitation. I would reach for the oil I had used to concoct Leforgeron's elixir, moisten the orifice nestled between his buttocks and slide into him. Then, when the sweet sensations of sex seized hold of him, he would roll onto his stomach, and I would rut on top of him while he buried his face in the bolster to stifle his sighs.

We took it for granted it was my prerogative to fuck him. He depended on me. I did not consciously acknowledge this as the reason then, and he may not have either. I simply wanted him and now he was letting me have him. We made love every night, and not once did he ask to enter me. I made love to him as gently and carefully as he had taken me when we were boys, and I could see I gave him pleasure.

Still, there were differences. Julien had become more muscular, more manly. He had hair on his chest, and his scent was more pronounced. Our boyish sex had been playful; now it was more purposeful, more intense. But his body was as familiar to me as ever, and my desire for him greater, and when we reached climax together, our satisfaction more profound.

MY JOB at the Revolutionary Tribunal gave me access to the seals of every member of the Committee of Public Safety. I found an old letter of accusation signed by Saint-Just and practiced duplicating his handwriting in order to prepare false identity papers for Julien, leaving a space to fill in the alias we had not yet chosen.

A few days after I had succeeded in hiding Julien in my room, Artémis stopped me in the courtyard when I came home from work. "I knew it wouldn't last," she said, smiling. "I'm glad for you."

I looked at her, puzzled. She pinched my cheek. "Don't you go playing the innocent with me! You know what I mean."

I climbed the stairs to my room, unable to guess her meaning. It worried me. Artémis knew something, and I didn't know what it was.

Sandrine was waiting for me on the landing. "Artémis heard someone in your room last night and asked me if I had seen anyone. I told her it was me and that we were lovers. I know you're hiding a friend there." Then, blushing, she asked, "Is it a woman?" I nodded. "Is she your mistress?" I shook my head. "Is she in trouble?" I nodded again. "Then you can count on my help," she said.

"You have already," I answered, "immensely."

Sandrine's lie to Artémis and her questions to me gave me an idea. I explained it to Julien, and he approved. In addition to the false papers I would write out a passport and safe conduct for Julie Verlan. That way he could travel by coach to Valenciennes and cross into Belgium with Olivier's infant son, pretending he was the child's mother. I took his measurements that night so I could procure women's clothes for him. Though I didn't tell him yet, I had already made up my mind to accompany them as far as the border.

I made up a story about some business I had to attend to in Valenciennes and requested a week's leave to see to it. The Incorruptible told me to write myself a safe conduct for him to sign, thus making himself a party to my excusable corruption.

I had just about given up finding a pair of women's shoes to fit him—no one would go out in slippers in the middle of winter—but in the end the clothes I found for Julien fit him perfectly. We improvised a curling iron. His hair was long enough to wear in the latest feminine fashion. He made a lovely woman.

I reserved two places on the post coach and told the wet nurse that we would come to pick up the child in the morning two days later, because I wanted to take Julien out before we left to see if his disguise would pass muster. She asked for five pounds, far more than either of us could spare. I bargained her down to forty *sous*.

We went for a stroll among the arcades of the Palais-Royal, where to my distress we saw Artémis. She saw us too. She did not recognize "Citizen Mautal" in his new disguise, but she glared at us, angered by my supposed infidelity to Sandrine. I braved her ire, and later that afternoon I brazenly walked across her courtyard and up to my room with Julie Verlan hanging lovingly on my arm.

Artémis had already told Sandrine everything, and, true to her word, Sandrine deceived her with fake tears and locked herself in her room. We heard Artémis bring her some leftover stew that evening and try to encourage her to eat. I opened my door and told Artémis that I was leaving for Valenciennes in the morning and would be absent for a few days. She answered me coldly; her attention was fixed on Sandrine, who pretended she could not be comforted, but I knew I was in for a stern lecture when I returned.

To spite Artémis, Julien and I made love unrestrainedly that night. I'm sure the entire house heard us. We may not have shaken the rafters and rattled the window panes, but his cries were loud enough to keep everyone awake. We reveled in our coupling, thinking only of ourselves and how little time was left us. I realized how cruel I had been to Sandrine when I saw her puffy eyes the next morning. She might easily have taken revenge on me, but her soul was too honest to denounce a woman whose life was in danger and had sought my protection.

WE LEFT early, each of us carrying a small suitcase. We would make the journey in stages, stopping for the night at Senlis, Noyon, Péronne and Cambrai, with a final night in Valenciennes, since Julie Verlan was not the type of mother who could nurse her child in public. So that she would not have to share a room with other female travelers at the inns, I had forged our marriage certificate and dated it a week earlier, too late for her to have her name changed on her travel documents, which made Phébus my son born out of wedlock. The return journey would take me two days.

So now Julien was playing the woman's role by day as well as at night. Every time we slept together, we made love. I could have let him penetrate me, and there were three good reasons why I should have. For one, he might think that I was taking advantage of the circumstances to compel him to submit to me, even making him dress as a woman, to get even for the years he would not let me do it because I was his servant; second, because I had not forgotten what a wonderful lover he was and longed to feel his hardness between my thighs. I missed feeling his weight pressing down on me, his arms holding me, the sound and the warmth of his heavy breathing in my ear, and I missed the sensation of his throbbing inside me when he came. But I never suggested we switch places, and he never took the initiative, not by so much as a gesture.

The third reason was that there was a grain of truth to the first. Not that it was a revenge, no more than Julien had fucked me to show his superiority when I had been in his family's service. He was an aristocrat and I a free Frenchman, and I instinctively adjusted our relationship in keeping with our altered status. It did not occur to me that it proved that the noble sentiments of the Declaration of the Rights of Man were far from becoming a reality. The Revolution had not made all men equal.

In Valenciennes, our last night together, he lay on his back, his legs locked behind mine. We clung desperately to each other, joined at the mouth and below the waist. He dug his fingers into my buttocks and pulled me into him. His body stiffened, and his mouth fell open with a sudden inhaled whimper. "Wait—" he said. I felt three brief spasms trill against my glans, and with each trill he spurted onto his stomach. I pushed deeper into him, and my orgasm was unleashed.

I remained inside him until my penis softened and slipped out on its own; then I wriggled my body lower in the bed to lap up the sticky pool that had poured onto his belly, opening and closing my mouth around his skin like a fish sucking water through its gills. "Will you come to London with me?" he whispered.

I waited until I had licked him clean before answering. "No, my place for the time being is in France. I hate what's happening here, but I could not stand by and watch battalions march forth to attack my country."

"Then I'll come back after I've given my brother the baby."

"Are you mad? A hunted man, and then to return as an *émigré*!"

"Don't you want me with you?"

"I want you alive."

"I could come back as Julie."

I shook my head. I didn't love Julie; I loved Julien. But I didn't say it.

"We may not see each other again," he went on.

"I lived three years without seeing you."

"But this time it will probably be forever."

"I know. It's not me; it's the times we live in."

"If it weren't for the Revolution, I would have made you my aide-de-camp."

"If it weren't for the Revolution, your commanding officer would have forbidden it. A commoner, a man with no breeding. But we have the Revolution, and someday, if we're ever reunited, we can come together as equals."

"You still support the Revolution, don't you, in spite of everything. You were always a dreamer."

The next morning I rode with Julien as far as the border. We stepped out of the coach and walked slowly to the barrier. I carried the baby; I had left my suitcase at the inn. I stood beside him in the queue of people waiting to show their papers. "I'll write you when I get to London," he said when the man ahead of him stepped up to the makeshift counter.

"Don't. A letter from an *émigré* can be a death sentence."

"Then I suppose this is goodbye."

We faced each other, sorrowful but calm. I handed him the baby, and he held him up for me to kiss, the last action but one of our charade.

"Goodbye," I said. My lips brushed over his in a brief and gentle kiss, a man and his wife taking leave of each other for a short time.

"Next," the guard barked, and I turned and walked down the road to Valenciennes without looking back.

Chapter 5

On my return to Artémis's, I apologized to Sandrine for our audible display of the week before. "Why apologize?" she asked. "It was no concern of mine."

"I could see that it affected you."

Her eyes flashed in anger at the implication that she'd wished she had been the woman in my bed. "I was miffed because you lied to me," she said coldly. "You told me she wasn't your mistress. I realized after that I had been foolish to think a man could share his bedroom with a pretty woman night after night and not give in to Nature. What passed between you was to be expected. I have nothing to forgive."

Sandrine was hurt but not resentful. However, from then on she kept her distance from me, and we exchanged no more than a few polite words when we chanced to meet. Artémis took it differently. Without saying anything, she made it known that her feelings for me had cooled. I could no longer count on her support. Unwisely, I stopped attending the evening gatherings in her kitchen.

A week or so after my return she did climb the stairs once to knock on my door, to ask for more medicine for her husband from my apothecary friend. I lied and said he had enlisted and left Paris. Citizen Leforgeron died the following night. Thomas and Philippe refused to accept money for digging his grave.

I had to work, so I could not attend his burial. The Tribunal was in session almost every day from dawn to dusk, yet we could barely keep up with the number of prisoners who came before us for judgment. The guillotine was far more efficient and disposed of them quickly. I put in a brief appearance in the kitchen that evening to offer my condolences. The deceased, who since I had come to live there had sat in the corner without anyone addressing so much as a word to him, monopolized the conversation in his absence. They spoke of his devotion to the Revolution, the numerous sacrifices he had made, and how the nation would regret his loss, though I had never seen him lift a finger except to take a sip from his wine glass, bring his pipe to his lips, or scratch his neck. Madelon said she would present her grandson to Robespierre as all she had left to give to France in her hour of need. No doubt we lost countless soldiers on the battlefield every day, but Citizen Leforgeron had not been one of them.

I BECAME a loner, which, too, was suspect. I sat at my table at work, disconnected from my surroundings, and wrote down the words I heard. I could not pretend that the accused were not human beings, nor could I adhere to the fiction that all were guilty. Instead I tried to think of my workplace as an island of unreality from which the men and women emerged into a sane world after playing out their little nightmarish drama, but time and again the actors themselves would shatter my fantasy. They seemed unaware that they had come before us to die, and when the judge read their sentence they turned pale, screamed or dissolved into tears. Many had to be dragged back to their prison, or carried there if they fainted, as some women did.

When I left the Tribunal, I would go eat a light supper at a nearby brasserie before I returned to Artémis's, crossed the courtyard and went directly to my room without saying good evening to the lodgers who had come to sit in her kitchen to enjoy each other's company. They were often singing revolutionary songs. The "Carmagnole" with its exaggerated mockery of the aristocracy, and "Ça ira" with its gleeful chorus at the prospect of stringing them up on the lamppost, sickened me, but the noble strains of the "Hymn of the Battalion of the Rhine" never lost its power to stir my soul.

I had read the handwriting on the wall months before, the day they executed Citizen Égalité, but did I not begin to fear for my own safety until the middle of the month of Germinal, when they accused Danton, the head of the Committee of Public Safety himself, of being too lenient and sent him to the guillotine. Dantonists, Hébertists and an ever larger number of Girondists followed him there. On the first day of the third ten-day week, or decade, of Prairial, I arrived at work to see an armed escort waiting for me and another clerk sitting in my place. The bailiff told me I had been arrested. I asked on what charges. He did not know, nor would the judges until I came to trial. I was led downstairs to where the prisoners were kept. The jailer entered my name into his register and read me the accusation.

My crime was not political; I was under suspicion of engaging in the illegal commerce of buying and selling children. An emissary of the Republic had gone to the wet nurse's lodgings the day before to see if Phébus was thriving and ready to be weaned. When she told him the child had died, he berated her for not informing the authorities and demanded she show him the death certificate. She broke down and confessed that she had entrusted the child to me on the understanding I would give him to a childless couple to raise. If I could prove that I had not accepted payment, he said, they would probably release me.

Three days passed before I was called on to provide the proof they wanted. In the meantime the other prisoners shunned me as the only one there not under sentence of death. A magistrate came to the prison to take my statement. I told him that not only had I not profited from the transaction, but it was the wet nurse who sold him for forty *sous*. The price astounded him, and he made a note of it saying that the nurse would be severely punished if it were true.

He then asked why I had agreed to act as middleman and why the couple had been willing to pay so handsomely. I answered that the child had not, in fact, been given to a barren couple, but to his father.

My interrogator removed his spectacles and looked at me severely. "To the child's father?" he asked incredulously. "To the ex-aristocrat Roger Christian Olivier de la Motte, formerly the Count d'Airelles? An *émigré*! An enemy of the State, tried and condemned to death *in absentia* for conspiring against the Republic! This affair is more serious than I imagined."

I quickly made up a story I hoped they would not be able to disprove, fabricating details as I went along. "No, his father's name is Jacques Verlan, a tailor from Valenciennes, whom I knew as an acquaintance when he spent a few months in Paris two years ago."

"Are you saying that de la Motte's wife was a whore? How can you be sure this Verlan was the father?"

"He told me so himself. I knew of Marie-Catherine's infidelities when I was in the family's service, as did all the domestics. Monsieur Olivier neglected her."

"I must ask you for his address."

"Jacques Verlan's?"

"Of course Citizen Verlan's," he snapped. "Did you think I was asking for de la Motte's address in London?"

"I couldn't give you the address of any *émigré*; I have not been in communication with any of them. As for Citizen Verlan, I only know that Jacques lives in Valenciennes."

"But he wrote to you concerning the child. Have you kept his letter?"

"He didn't write. His sister Julie came to Paris and asked me to help her find him."

"I see. We shall look into verifying your story." He had me sign my statement and stuffed it into a folder. Then he summoned the jailer to escort me back to the exercise yard.

A fellow prisoner hailed me sarcastically. "Hey, kidnapper! How does the Republic punish people who traffic in human flesh?"

I silenced him with a scornful stare. "They claim I amassed a fortune returning the children of ex-aristocrats to their families in exile," I answered.

"Then it was foolish of you not to reunite young Capet with his Austrian grandparents," said another. "You'd be rich enough to buy off the Incorruptible Maximilien."

I had become one of them.

The justice meted out by the Committee of Public Safety was as swift as it was merciless, so I expected to be hauled before the Tribunal in a day or two, but I heard no more for over a month. Either they had forgotten about me or they were preparing an iron-clad case against me, which seemed unlikely since they felt themselves free to condemn at whim. Knowing this, I did not spend untold hours preparing a defense, a pointless activity a number of my fellow prisoners engaged in. Until the morning I stood before the men I used to work for and who would now judge me, I had not expected to be given the opportunity to defend myself, and, in fact, I was not, but they asked me questions as if it were a real trial. I hoped I could remember the lies I had told the examining magistrate.

Accusations were read and sentences handed down. I was the only one they interrogated. My crime: abducting an infant and smuggling him out of the country so he could be given to his father, Roger Christian Olivier de la Motte, an *émigré* and ex-aristocrat, in return for which I had received an undisclosed amount of money.

I answered that the child in question was not de la Motte's, but the natural son of my friend Jacques Verlan, on whose behalf I had acted in taking the child, and that I had taken no money from him.

"But surely he offered to compensate you for efforts."

"He did, and I refused it." I had seen the nurse in the women's courtyard at Saint-Lazare, so I knew she had confessed to the forty *sous*. They could have no evidence that any other sum had changed hands.

"Do you deny that your accomplice repaid you with sexual favors?"

So they had questioned Artémis on my activities. "The woman you are referring to is Julie Verlan, the child's aunt. Someone must have seen us together and taken her for my mistress."

"Yet you accompanied her and the child to Valenciennes and slept in the same room with them, pretending you were husband and wife."

"Yes, to see to it that she and the child arrived in Valenciennes safely. We did not engage in intimate relations at any time."

"I find that hard to believe. Furthermore, you made the journey using a safe conduct you had secured from this Tribunal on the pretext of a matter of personal business in Valenciennes."

"That is true. My business was to deliver the child to his father."

"And you handed him to your friend in person?"

I sensed a trap. "No. Julie took the child and left me as soon as we arrived at the post relay. I spent a night at the inn and returned to Paris in the morning."

"There is no one of the name of Jacques Verlan living in Valenciennes."

"I knew a Jacques Verlan in Paris. He told me he was from Valenciennes."

"A woman going by the name of Julie Verlan crossed the border into Belgium with an infant on 15 Pluviôse, using what we believe was a forged passport."

"I did not know that."

"A man accompanied her to the Custom House but remained in France."

"Again, I know nothing of it. I was not that man."

"Four days afterward, the younger de la Motte disembarked in England. He had a child with him."

I gestured to indicate my ignorance of that fact.

"The Committee of Public Safety has in its possession reliable evidence that you and he were close."

"As boys. We were the same age, and my mother was his wet nurse."

"You were a domestic servant of the ex-Baron de l'Envol and his wife, sister of de la Motte, *émigrés* currently residing in Holland."

"I did not know they were in Holland. I have not seen them since I left their service."

"Before that you worked as a gardener for his father, a traitor condemned by this Tribunal and guillotined for his crimes last summer."

"I know. I was present at his trial."

"You were also present when, at the same trial, we condemned the child's mother, Marie-Catherine de la Motte, and deferred her sentence until after the birth."

I acknowledged it was true.

"At which time you wrote the father of her unborn child in London, promising you would arrange to have it brought to him if he paid you two thousand *livres*, and have remained in contact with him ever since."

It was untrue, and I denied it, but the Committee of Public Safety did not concern itself with truth and falsehood, and I was sentenced to die by the guillotine.

Most of the condemned—and only rarely was anybody acquitted—went directly from the Revolutionary Tribunal back to cells in the Conciergerie and from there immediately, or the next morning at the latest, to the Place de la République, but for some reason I and a handful of other prisoners were marched under guard to the prison at

Saint-Lazare by a squadron of musketeers. People hooted and jeered at us in the streets.

I expected the next morning to be my last, but my name was not called. Sandrine came to visit me that afternoon with sausage, cheese and pastries. That I had risked my life to save an innocent child—for she firmly believed that the Revolution would eventually turn against them because of the blood that flowed in their veins—made me a hero in her eyes. I refused to answer her questions, saying that to have any knowledge that I had withheld from the judges would make her an accomplice. I forbade her to visit me again. She would probably not find me there anyway.

They didn't come for me the next day either, nor the day after, nor the day after that. The people who had been tried the same day had all gone to their deaths. Only I was left, apparently forgotten.

I BELONGED to a select group of condemned men stuck somewhere in the Terror's inexorable murder machine before it could spit us out. Or perhaps the machine had overflowed—over thirteen hundred people lost their lives in the final six weeks of the Terror—and the men responsible for its upkeep were too busy feeding victims into one end and watching their heads roll out the other to sweep up around it. One or two had been in Saint-Lazare for more than a year. These forgotten men and others awaiting trial, who got stuck in the machine more often than those who made it as far as the Tribunal, were my constant cohorts. When the Tribunal called for them, we would wish them luck instead of bidding each other farewell. The few we saw again would return to the prison for a day or two at most, listless and taciturn, and would keep to themselves.

Among the prisoners who were with us a few days, left for their trials, and never returned, was one Barnabas Lebreton, an ex-Jesuit. I questioned him and concluded it was indeed he who had sodomized Julien between the ages of ten and fifteen, and I rejoiced that he had not escaped the Jacobins' clutches. On the other hand, if he had controlled his lechery and not forced himself on his luckless charges, Julien might never have introduced me to the practice. When he left for his trial, I bluntly told him what to expect. He blanched and said, "But I thought—"

"Not men of the cloth. They always lose their heads."

He did not catch my double meaning. The other prisoners thought me cruel until I told them about Julien. What he'd done made them so irate I believe they would have torn him limb from limb if he had been returned to Saint-Lazare to await execution after his trial.

We were a mixed bag of aristocrats, clerics, professional men, tradesmen, unskilled laborers and peasants, royalists, republicans and radicals from every corner of France. Some of them I met again during my years in the *Grande Armée*, others after the Bourbons returned to power. Most had been condemned for hoarding, overcharging customers, counterfeiting, passing *assignats*, desertion and the like, all of which counted as political crimes. I believe I was the only one there who openly admitted having done what I'd been accused of, though I denied I had done it for gain. All protested their innocence, but I thought it more than likely they were guilty. (Almost everyone who could hoarded, including Artémis). Those accused of conspiring against the nation I generally presumed were innocent, though with ex-noblemen, former monks and priests, and financiers who had invested money abroad before the Revolution, one could never tell. As for those accused of lack of revolutionary zeal, harboring seditious thoughts and—would you believe?—atheism, their guilt or innocence was to me a matter of total indifference.

Though but a lowly clerk, I fit in best with the small group of professionals—two doctors, a lawyer, two notaries, a banker, a disgraced magistrate and an architect—for I had first learned manners at the Hotel L'Envol and afterward by observing such highly educated men as Danton and Robespierre, whose behavior was reserved and invariably correct when they weren't giving inflammatory speeches, and above all Citizen Brotteaux, whose natural kindness and unaffected elegance I had greatly admired. However, my closest friends were a printer named Thibaud and Laurent Pavot, a waiter whom I believed innocent, because he lived in an attic room above the restaurant where he worked and had been arrested on the presumption he had aided his employer, a notorious hoarder. It turned out that Thibaud, who had been in Saint-Lazare for almost two years, had printed many of the handbills and manifestos I had been given to copy before I went to work for the Revolutionary Tribunal and had even been arrested for one of them. He was a few years older than me. Laurent was a lovely, slim youth with delicate features, the only one among us who never boasted of his amorous exploits. We didn't find it unusual that a seventeen-year-old would have none to boast of, but his large brown eyes often came to rest on me in a way that led me to wonder if under more fortunate circumstances I would have found him a willing bedfellow. The strong and unmistakable attraction I felt toward him caught me off guard, since my nasty experience with Citizen Gombert had convinced me that, except for Julien, whom I loved, having sex with men did not interest me. However, I had no choice but to ignore the urge. We had no privacy in Saint-Lazare, and our companions' reaction to Father Lebreton made it clear they would not have approved of that kind of intimacy.

I played so many games of cards during the two months of my incarceration, one before my trial and one after it, that I did not play again for my entire military career and only took it up again when the fashionable English games the *émigrés* brought back with them had become all the rage in the wealthier bourgeois salons of Paris.

Occasionally someone I knew would arrive. Our reunion was always brief, but I gave him what little hope and comfort I could. I made some new friends, only to lose them a few days later. I remember none of them.

AT THE beginning of Thermidor I saw the last d'Airelles remaining in France in the women's exercise yard on the other side of the grille. I called to out her and asked if she remembered me. She did not, but ex-Sister Constance of the Holy Innocents was not the kind of nun who passes up an opportunity to talk with a well-built and not unhandsome man in his early twenties.

The convent had been closed and the ex-Carmelite nuns forbidden to associate with one another since the Republic had expropriated the property of the Catholic Church after passing the Civil Constitution of the Clergy. Sister Constance of the Holy Innocents had made the most of her newfound liberty. She had not lacked a roof over her head or a bed to sleep in and managed to keep her stomach full, from above and from below, although she would have been able to live more comfortably if the new government hadn't also taken possession of her family's ancestral estates.

"I should have stayed on with Camille," she sighed. "He was a pretty man, and more virile than I would have thought, to judge by his demeanor. He used to be our chaplain at the convent and heard our confessions, so he knew what to expect when I came knocking on his door, though for me it was a pleasant surprise. Unfortunately, he was afraid the Committee of Public Safety would misinterpret our relationship if it found us together, and he sent me away."

Except for her sister Berthe, whose marriage she envied and gloated over in turn, Constance showed little interest in the fate of her parents, brothers and sisters, for whom she had ceased to exist the moment the convent door slammed behind her. She gave a little laugh when I told her that my crime was having sent Olivier's son to his father in England.

She forgave the Revolution's stupidity for having rounded her up along with her sisters in religion and charging them all with conspiring with Rome to overthrow the Republic. She said that, given the choice between the veil and the guillotine, she would prefer the latter, but it galled her that she would mount its steps in the company of "those horrible, dried up, bead-counting women who waste their time praying for the return of the Monarchy" and would be considered a martyr when her real martyrdom was having lived seven years with them.

I only spoke to her once, for the jailer read the Carmelite nuns their sentence that evening. The Tribunal had condemned them without a trial. Had their execution been scheduled for two days later, they would have survived.

THE end came so quickly it was over before we knew it had started. On 9 Thermidor the National Convention turned on Robespierre, who had by then succeeded in ridding himself of nearly all his most powerful allies. He foolishly appealed to the right for support, who hated him more than the left, though they were less prone to let their hatred carry them away. He, the rest of the Revolutionary Tribunal, and most of the members of the Committee of Public Safety were put under arrest. The Commune sent troops to free them, but the Convention's soldiers defeated them in short order. The next day Robespierre, Saint-Just and others received the justice they had meted out, perhaps to as many as forty thousand others.

Upon our release, we prisoners embraced and congratulated one another on the end of our long ordeal. We paid no heed to the philosopher among us who observed that the fall of a bad regime does not necessarily herald the birth of a good one, an opinion Citizen Brotteaux would no doubt have shared. In fact, the surviving Girondists immediately launched a little Terror of their own and sent the entire Committee of Public Safety, everyone who had been associated with the Revolutionary Tribunal, and a large number of other Jacobins to their deaths. They spared me because of my insignificance and because my name was on the Tribunal's list of those condemned. Neither of those circumstances alone would have saved me. In short, I owe my life to my death sentence, and ultimately to Phébus.

PART II:

My Years of War

Chapter 1

I WAS alive and I was free, and I would be hard put to say which of the two gave me more satisfaction. Thibaud, Laurent and I resolved to stick together until we could ascertain what, if anything, remained of our former lives for us to go back to. We had little hope of recuperating the belongings we had left behind, we had little doubt that other people had taken over our lodgings, we could not count on returning to our former employment (I certainly couldn't), and we had no way of knowing if the friends we could rely on were alive and, if so, where they lived now.

Since I had only been arrested two months earlier, Thibaud proposed we begin by going to the house I had lived in, but I explained that Artémis's had been a center of Jacobin activity and that if the Girondists raided it and found us there we would end up right back where we started. Laurent's restaurant was located outside the city walls on the road to Vincennes, so we went to see if Thibaud's old print shop was still in operation. He had worked out of his home on the Île Saint-Louis, so if it was we would probably find his wife, Adrienne, there.

"I don't expect her to be a Penelope after two years of separation," he said. "I don't think she knows I survived. The last time I saw her she was in the gallery of the Tribunal, clamoring for my death."

"Then I seriously doubt she'll welcome you with open arms," I said.

"Oh, she didn't mean it. She had to pretend. If she had said a word in my support or even kept silent, they would have hauled her up there alongside me."

Thibaud lived in a narrow three-story house tucked away in a tiny dead-end side street, not much more than an alley. The large front room on the ground floor was taken up by the print shop, with a bench in front of the window, a long counter across from it, and behind it the press. There were two rooms in back, a small office and the kitchen, which also served as a dining room, and a stair to the upper stories between them. A door from the kitchen opened onto a small back courtyard with an outhouse and two large sheds for storing the equipment needed for the printing press. I hadn't known any of the houses on the island had a courtyard.

We found the print shop up and running with Adrienne in charge. She couldn't believe her eyes when she saw us. She rushed forward to embrace her husband but came to a stop two feet away and exclaimed in disgust, "Lice!"

Adrienne marched us into the courtyard, ordered us to strip, and brought a bucket of powdered lye. She stood there, hands on hips, watching us throw handfuls of the powder at each other until we were coated from head to toe in white. The shop assistants, youths she had hired since Thibaud's arrest, gathered at the back door to have a peek at us, and they giggled at the sight of their mistress lording it over three strangers.

We waited fifteen minutes before she let us dust ourselves off and comb through the matted hair on our heads and the tangles above our groins. That still was not enough for her. We had to douse ourselves with turpentine and rub the thick, foul-smelling liquid into every patch of hair on our bodies. Finally she had the shop boys bring out a large iron tub and fill it with hot water, and she gave us a bar of lye soap to scrub ourselves with. By the time we finished we felt cleaner than we had in months. It was a good feeling, but we could not get rid of the odor.

Adrienne made lunch for us, and Thibaud gave us some money, and Laurent and I set out for La Poule Qui Caquette, Laurent's restaurant, feeling optimistic that it had been so easy for Thibaud to pick up his life where he had left off.

The restaurant, now called Le Bresson, was under new management. The proprietor, a jolly, heavyset man named Claude with grey hair and very pink cheeks, told us in a thick Lyon accent that he had all the help he needed. He had never been up to the attic. It was locked and no one could tell him where to find the key. He thought it too much of a bother to break down the door. He was surprised to learn that someone had once lived in it. He gave us permission to see if Laurent's belongings were still there, and said we were welcome to stay there at no cost for as long as we wished but that we would have to pay for our meals if we ate at the restaurant. This gave us a roof over our heads until we could find work, but the jobs were in Paris, and Le Bresson was an hour's walk from the city gates.

We climbed the stairs to the attic, and Laurent took the key from its hiding place. Laurent found his room just as he had left it but covered in a thick layer of dust and cobwebs. Even the little box where he kept the money he put aside was untouched. There was plenty of room for two, and I thought we would be quite comfortable there once we had cleaned up.

We opened the window and tossed the rug and bedding into the garden so we wouldn't have to carry it through the dining room. Then I went downstairs to beat the dust out of it while Laurent stayed in the room to sweep the floor and wash the furniture. Getting the attic back in shape took us all afternoon and evening. Claude sold us a loaf of bread, some cheese, two apples and bottle of wine for a fraction more than he had paid for them. We brought our supper up to the attic and ate it at Laurent's little table before going to bed.

We lay in bed side by side. Laurent moved closer to me. When he saw I didn't pull away from him, he touched me—oh, so hesitantly!—unsure how I would react. I reassured him. "It's all right, Laurent," I said.

"You can take me if you want."

I expect he thought I would fuck him quickly and be done with it. To his surprise, I leaned over him and blew on his belly, running a finger gently around his nipple; then I opened my mouth, closed my lips over a patch of skin, and began to lick him.

I pulled back almost immediately. "You don't have to do this if you don't want to," he said.

"Turpentine!" I gave him the back of my hand to taste.

We had become used to the smell but would never find the taste palatable. Laurent pulled a medium-sized bathtub to the center of the room, took a bar of scented soap out of a drawer and handed me a bucket. I made five trips to the pump outside to fill the tub. The last bucketful we put on the stove and poured it in with the rest when it came to a boil. We tested the temperature of the water; then we soaped each other all over, rinsed each other off, soaped and rinsed again, and dried each other with the same towel. Then we sampled each other in various places, and when we found burying our tongues in each other's pubic bush left no unpleasant aftertaste, we returned to bed, I thoroughly acquainted with his body and he with mine.

Under the circumstances, it seemed natural to concentrate on oral pleasures. We lay down head to crotch and pleasured one another simultaneously. Laurent had been with far more men than I had, most often on his knees in front of them, but I was the more experienced. He was used to getting a man off quickly and taking care of his own needs manually. Reciprocation was as much a novelty for him as making the pleasure last as long as possible. Though he had taken many cocks in his mouth, he had never done anything but suck on the shaft. From me he learned how many other sensitive places a man has on his body, more sensitive, in fact—the knob on top, the underside of the foreskin, the testicles, the base of the belly, the crease between the legs and the scrotum, the ridge of skin leading from the scrotum to the base of the buttocks, and the inside of the thighs. I also showed him how inserting a finger into a man's anus while you suck him from the other side increases his pleasure tenfold. The more we teased and toyed with each other below the waist, the more passionate he became. "Where have you been all my life?" he asked.

I came first, which was a good thing, because two minutes later his orgasm so overpowered him that he would not have been able to go on sucking. His whole body lurched into spasm and continued trembling after I had sucked out his last drop of ejaculate. I cradled him in my arms and kissed him tenderly.

"How long has it been for you?" he asked when his overwrought nerves had grown calm again.

I thought back and said, "14 Pluviôse."

"Me too, more or less, but it wasn't anything like this." He had been arrested at about the same time I was helping Julien escape.

Julien and Laurent looked as different as two beautiful men could. Had I wanted to, I could not have pretended that one was the other, not even in the dark. Laurent's lanky body and almost hairless, translucent skin in no way resembled the solid build and broad shoulders of Julien the man. Still, Laurent's boyish figure reminded me of the fun we used to have at the chateau and the Hotel L'Envol, and that added to his attraction. On top of that, he had a very pretty cock, a bit on the thin side, but with loose foreskin, not so long that it extended like a nozzle, with a bright pink head beneath it. I found sex with him enormously pleasurable, and his enthusiasm was undeniable. If I had to make a list of my favorite male lovers, I would put him among the top three.

We spent most of the next day in bed. There were many things we hadn't tried, and he was eager to try them all. When I said I wanted to mount him, he hurriedly got onto his knees and spread his cheeks with his hands. It startled him when I placed my tongue between them instead of my cock. It startled him more when I entered him slowly. He had taken as many cocks in his ass as he had in his mouth, but in his experience the ineffable pleasure had always been preceded by stabbing pain. It delighted him when I didn't finish in under five minutes, and when I flipped him onto his back and raised his hips till he was balanced on his shoulder blades so I could thrust straight down into him, the depth of my penetration awed him. Most of all, he was grateful that I did not stop after my orgasm but spent a long time servicing him with my mouth so as not to leave him unsatisfied.

Laurent was the third man I had sex with and the only one besides Julien with whom I had wanted to. I had thought that, except for Julien, I preferred women. I now modified my opinion to "except Julien and Laurent". I don't think I was lying to myself. I had had sex with three men and about half a dozen women, and if I ranked them in order of my desire for them and how much pleasure they gave me, my list would have read: Julien, Laurent, the women, and last of all Jacques Gombert. As far as I could tell, I was no different from other men, and if other men not only preferred women but claimed to be attracted only to women, I assumed they hadn't met their Julien or Laurent, though I readily believed a woman might be at the top of their list. Of course I knew what people had to say about men who loved men and how they persecuted them sometimes, and if the Terror had taught me anything, it was not to disagree openly with public prejudice. The prevailing view made no sense to me—why make such a fuss over something as trivial as who had sex with whom? I was not ashamed of what I had done with Julien and was doing with Laurent, and I had no intention of giving it up, but I didn't argue the point and kept those activities secret.

Over the next few years I would have affairs or one-time rolls in the hay with other women, who would take their place on my list with the others, right after Laurent. Another four years would pass before I decided I definitely preferred men, with the exception of Gombert.

WE WALKED back to Paris to look for work the second day after we moved into Laurent's attic. We made a detour so I could show Laurent where I used to live. While I was telling him about Artémis and the people who rented rooms from her, standing in the very spot Julien had waited for me, Sandrine stepped out the front door. She screamed, ran across the street, and threw her arms around me. "You're alive!" she gasped.

I didn't want to attract attention, so I hurried her back into the courtyard with Laurent behind us. Sandrine's greeting had convinced him she'd been my mistress, and he didn't want to let us out of his sight.

Artémis had gone into hiding. A man who imagined himself a poet and supported himself repairing shoes was living in my old room. Thierry still worked at les Halles. The Terror had kept Thomas and Philippe very busy digging graves, and they hoped they wouldn't have to work so hard now that it was over. Madelon's grandson had become a soldier and was defending our eastern border. The old woman was pining for him and seldom left her room. Four militiamen had come and taken away Clément's cart, the one that had borne so many to the guillotine. It was still being used for the same purpose, but on its first trip Clément ridden in it as a passenger instead of as the driver. The loft over the stable where he used to live was empty. My friend and I could move in there.

I asked if the police came by to look for people. "Only once so far," she answered.

"Then I wouldn't be safe here, but I'll come back next week if I've found work and see how things stand."

"Are they looking for you?"

"You forget I used to work for the Tribunal."

Our matter-of-fact conversation had reassured Laurent, but as we turned to leave Sandrine asked if I'd heard from Julie. When I told her I hadn't she said, "And you two were so close to each other! You must be disappointed. Such a pretty woman, too!"

Laurent now thought I had had two mistresses, and he was consumed with jealousy. In just two days the poor boy had fallen head over heels in love with me. As soon as we were back in the street, he started berating me. I explained that Julie was really Julien disguised as a woman so we could travel as man and wife in order get his nephew safely across the Belgian border. Laurent knew about the baby, but not the details of how I'd gone about it. It didn't take him long to put two and two together: Sandrine thought Julie was my mistress, Julie was a man, I had spent four nights with him on our way to Valenciennes, the last time I'd had sex before we made love in Laurent's attic was on 14 Pluviôse... His jealousy flared up again, and he began to cry.

"You're in love with him," he said, choking back his tears. "He'll come back, and you'll leave me."

"No, he won't. Just look at his situation, Laurent. We're at war with England. He's an *émigré*, a wanted man. The Revolution has confiscated everything his family ever owned. I'll probably never see him again."

"Am I as good a lover as he is?"

"You're starting to sound like a woman."

"I want to know. Am I as good as he is?"

"Was. And you will be. You've just begun to learn how two men can please each other, and you're learning quickly."

"Have you had sex with women too?"

"Yes."

"That's what you really want, isn't it?—a woman. I'm just a temporary substitute."

I held him by the shoulders and turned him to face me. "Believe me, Laurent. I'd rather be with you."

Instead of looking for work, we spent the afternoon buying me clothes. Everything I'd left at Artémis's had disappeared, and I had only two outfits to my name. We would have to dip into Laurent's savings to pay for them, so we asked the tailor to put them aside for us until tomorrow.

We left Paris as soon as the shops started closing, because they shut the gates at sunset. We returned to Le Bresson tired and dusty, purchased a small supper from Claude, filled the tub and had fun bathing each other, something Julien and I had never done, and then went to bed and did things Julien and I had done together countless times.

That became our routine for the rest of the week. As I had predicted, Laurent was already as good a bed partner as Julien, but as a companion he had begun to annoy me. His insecurity knew no bounds. He kept asking about Julien, and every little detail he wormed out of me made him more jealous. Julien had never cared who else I had sex with; Sandrine had cried all night when she heard our sex noises in the room next to hers, and she wasn't even my mistress. Laurent *was* my lover, and he was a hundred times more possessive than Sandrine.

Not only was he behaving like a woman, he saw himself as one. According to him, I was the man. We argued about it. I pointed out that he was a man too. If I wanted to have sex with a woman, I'd find one and have sex with her. Not that I wanted him to fuck me—I didn't—but I wished *he* would want to. A man should think of himself as a man, whatever role he took when we made love. That made no sense to Laurent. He said he had always been somebody's bitch, and now he had someone who treated him like a queen. Didn't that mean he was the woman? We left it at that.

WE HAD had no luck finding work, and we agreed that our chances would be better if we looked separately. When we met up at the end of the day, Laurent told me he had found a job peeling vegetables and cutting up meat at the post inn, but he had to start work at six in the morning and work for twelve hours with an hour off for lunch. He would have to get up at four to arrive in time if we stayed at Le Bresson, and in winter the city gates would be shut when he left work and not yet open when he arrived. We went to see if it was safe to move into the loft Clément had occupied.

The militiamen had not come by the house since they had come for Clément, and Artémis had returned from hiding. She acted as if everything had been forgotten and she was glad to see me. We could have the loft, but we'd have to pay a week's rent in advance. Laurent's savings more than covered it, but they were back in the attic. We told her we'd take it and would return after work the next day with the money. In the meantime, could we please see the loft?

It was big enough for the two of us, but the police had stripped it bare. There wasn't a stick of furniture in it. We would have to arrange for a cart on Laurent's day off to move as much of what he had in his attic as would fit. Until then we'd sleep on the floor. Would she lend us a couple of blankets? She answered that when she saw her money, we'd see our blankets, but we could only keep them one week and would have to launder them before we gave them back.

That settled, we headed back to Le Bresson so we would get to bed early and wake up in time for Laurent to get to work, but knowing we would have to sleep on a hard floor for the next ten days, we stayed up late making love and only got four hours' sleep.

I was desperate to find work. While I did not see myself as the man in our relationship, I didn't want Laurent to support me either. A couple of days after he started his job, I was hired as a stable hand at the same post relay where he worked in the kitchen. Laurent was delighted, I suspect because he would be able to keep an eye on me— his jealousy had not abated. I wished I had been able to find something less dirty than mucking out the stables. I rinsed off at the pump with the other stable hands at the end of the day, but I had no way of taking a real bath, and by the time we got around to moving some of Laurent's furniture from the attic into Clément's loft (we still didn't think of it as ours), I stank. The first thing we did after unloading the cart was to fill the tub halfway with water from the pump and borrow Artémis's soup cauldron and put it up to boil on her stove, but it was clear that we would no longer enjoy the luxury of a nightly bath. Artémis informed us that every fifth day was bath day. If I wanted to bathe more often I could pay to use the public baths. Laurent and I went there occasionally, but we couldn't play.

Once we had moved in, we had less space to move about in than we had in the attic, but we enjoyed living one on top of the other. (In bed it was always me on top of him.) We bought our meals from a caterer and ate in our loft instead of with Artémis and her lodgers, and we didn't socialize with them in her kitchen in the evening. Instead we would go out, sometimes to visit Thibaud and Adrienne, who made for better company. Until the weather turned cold, they would leave their assistants to tend the shop when Laurent and I had a day off, and we'd all go on an outing in the country.

Artémis called us "the Inseparables". I replied that, like Thomas and Philippe, we worked in the same place, and, unlike them, we had Saint-Lazare in common. She hadn't known we'd been prisoners together.

One evening Thomas had a headache, and Philippe went out on the town without him. He returned with two tramps, one for each of them, but by then Thomas was feeling much worse, so Philippe offered me one of them to share with Laurent. Sooner than arouse his suspicions about us, I picked Rosalie.

Laurent was appalled. "You've brought a woman into our room!" he exclaimed.

"What did you expect him to bring, a monkey?" Rosalie asked. She touched him through his clothes but couldn't get him hard. I said he was embarrassed in front of me. She laughed and called him a prude. "If he watches us, maybe he'll get over it," she said. "I hope he does. He's such a pretty boy!"

Laurent watched, and he suffered horribly the whole time. When she left, he burst into tears and made me promise never to do it again. I said that Rosalie would tell the brothers how our little orgy had turned out, and it was unlikely they would repeat the offer.

That didn't satisfy him, and we had another argument, as we sometimes did about Julien. I told him I hadn't wanted to fuck Rosalie, I *had* to. He said I liked it, that having sex with him wasn't enough for me, that all I wanted was someone to suck my cock until I found a full-time mistress. I told him he was out of his mind.

That night Laurent stayed on his side of the bed, as close to the edge as he could without falling off, and he pushed me away if I tried to come near him. When we got off work the next day, he dragged me to the public baths.

Chapter 2

THE political situation during the year that followed the Terror was no more idyllic than my affair with Laurent, but people hoped that the new Constitution would mean an end to the wars and usher in a period of enduring stability, just as I hoped that the stability of our relationship would eventually cure Laurent's paranoia.

While anything would have been an improvement after the Terror, the Directory did not bring the promised stability. Almost everyone who did not own property objected to the idea of limited suffrage, and violence broke out in Paris. Napoleon Bonaparte, the young Corsican who had been made a general and become a national hero for lifting the blockade of Toulon, stepped in and restored peace by shelling the insurgents as mercilessly as he had shelled the English fleet. I had had enough. I told Laurent that I was thinking of enlisting in the army. Naturally, he opposed the idea and put forth every argument he could think of to dissuade me.

"That doesn't make any sense," he said, "joining the army because you can't take any more violence."

"An army is disciplined and well ordered," I answered naïvely. "What we have in Paris is chaos."

"What you really want is to get away from me."

It had not occurred to me before he said it, but I realized he was not entirely wrong. To avoid another argument I suggested he enlist with me, knowing full well he wouldn't. Instead of enlisting, Laurent enlisted Thibaud and Adrienne to talk me out of it, but my mind was made up.

Laurent would not go on living at Artémis's without me. He had no friends there, and he hated Thomas and Philippe because of Rosalie, and Sandrine because he believed we had had an affair. Thibaud invited him to live with them. Newspapers had once again started proliferating in Paris, and he had decided to start one of his own. He needed more helpers and would teach him to operate a printing press.

Artémis praised my decision to fight in defense of the nation, but it was obvious she was glad to be rid of us. She considered Laurent a nonentity. Heartbroken though he was, Laurent proved his devotion by selling his furniture, which he wouldn't need at Thibaud's, and using a large part of what he got for it to outfit me as a soldier. We had to pay for our uniforms and were expected to provide our own weapons.

I stayed with Laurent for the rest of the month in the room below the attic Thibaud had given him, until my military training began and I moved into the barracks at the École Militaire, Julien's old school, which now accepted enlistees from all classes of society. In the other two, smaller bedrooms on that level they kept large cans of ink, thousands of packages of different sizes of paper, and trays of extra letters in a variety of typefaces, which they might someday need but never used except to replace those that broke. Thibaud and Adrienne lived on the first floor, where, in addition to their bedroom, was a second bedroom reserved for the children they planned to have and the parlor where the four of used to chat together after the shop assistants had left for the day. It was a cozy parlor, simply furnished with wooden chairs each with its own little cushion, two oil lamps on two small round tables for our wine glasses and plates of *amuse-bouche*, a massive hutch for those plates and glasses and also bottles of sweet dessert wines and brandy, and a fireplace.

Our friends didn't raise an eyebrow at us sleeping together in the same tiny bed right above their heads. They had figured out that we were lovers and knew what we would be doing in it. On the other hand, the men who worked there found a source of amusement in Laurent's displays of affection. I think some of them would have roughed him up if he hadn't been a friend of their employer.

IT HADN'T occurred to me that foot soldiers had to go through training as well as officers. I imagined they would stick a gun in my hands and send me straight into battle. Of course they would have to teach me to use a firearm, but how hard could that be? And didn't everybody know how to march?

When he learned I had worked as a domestic servant and a clerk, the officer in charge of our training concluded that I was a hopeless case who didn't know his right from his left, and singled me out as a prime candidate for bullying. It didn't take him long to realize his mistake. I mastered the basic commands more quickly than the other recruits and didn't have to think in order to execute them properly. I tired less easily. I was a better wrestler than any of them. Thanks to my experience as a domestic in an aristocratic household, my uniform was always perfect at inspection. He only had to show me once how to take apart and reassemble a bayonet, and I seldom missed the target. When he saw I knew how to handle a sword, his eyes almost popped out of his head. Moreover, I spent my afternoon leaves with Thibaud, Adrienne and Laurent instead of getting drunk and paying for prostitutes. When we finished training six weeks later, he recommended me for another program that prepared men to serve in the artillery. Everyone else was sent north to attack Holland.

The program would start in two weeks. Until then I was free to live as a civilian. I went back to Thibaud's and sleeping with Laurent, who was as happy to learn I wouldn't be leaving Paris as he was to have sex with me again. Except for missing me, he was much happier than when he'd lived at Artémis's, and although it was hard physical labor, he preferred the printing press to the tedium of peeling vegetables. He looked as boyish as ever, but when we got to bed I discovered that he had developed some muscle, which made it more exciting to touch him.

He was insatiable and couldn't get enough of my cock. "We have two weeks," I told him. "Don't wear us both out." He replied that except for his time in prison, he had never gone this long without sex.

"You didn't have to deprive yourself," I said. "There are plenty of men in Paris who'd pay you for a blowjob."

"I'm not a whore. I've never taken money."

"I didn't mean it that way. I only meant you would have had no trouble finding someone to have sex with."

"Those days are over. I've found the man of my dreams, and when they send him to front, I'll wait for him to come back, even if I have to wait forever."

That night he didn't have to wait.

He was all devotion and appreciation now, too afraid of losing me to accuse me of infidelity, perhaps too afraid to care. I would not have minded coming back to Laurent. When I enlisted, I'd had the idea of following the Army to the ends of the earth, although of course I had no idea how far in that direction Bonaparte would lead it. Now I could imagine returning to Paris when my tour of duty was over and settling down with Laurent into a life of domestic bliss.

When Adrienne saw us in the morning, she said, "Laurent! You look radiant!" then turning to me, "And you look wrung out." It was the first time she had openly acknowledged that we were sexually involved. Thibaud grinned, and winked at us. After that, when we stayed up late talking with them after the workers had gone home, I would sit on the floor with Laurent's head in my lap and stroke his hair and give him a kiss if he asked for one. Artémis had called us "the inseparables"; Adrienne called us "the lovebirds". Laurent was in heaven.

A day or two before I left to become an artillery man, Adrienne learned she was pregnant. Laurent said that now I'd have to come back to see the baby.

"Don't be silly," Adrienne said. "He'll come back to see you."

I did well in training, and they promoted me to corporal even though I had never seen action. That meant yet another training program—this time a short one—to learn how to give orders and maintain discipline. Then, instead of sending me to fight, they told me I was to remain in Paris for the time being. They had decided that my first assignment would be in Italy, but it was uncertain when I would leave. Bonaparte was waiting for the Directory to approve his plans to take it from the Austrians. They gave me a list of the equipment I would need, purchased at my own expense, of course. I was sure it would weigh a ton. I was collecting a salary now. They paid me in worthless chits, but their suppliers were obliged to accept them.

WE SET out on 16 Ventôse. Those of us who lived nearby spent the night before with our families. Laurent made me fuck him so many times that my balls ached, and I marched out of Paris dragging my feet. My fellow soldiers thought it very funny. You can always tell by how a man walks if he has sore testicles. Of course they took it for granted I had been with a woman.

We reached Nice fifteen days later. I wrote Laurent a letter saying that Southern France was so beautiful, only an idiot would choose to live in Paris.

I didn't have time to enjoy Nice. The fighting started before we'd had time to stretch our limbs, with Bonaparte taking the offensive, although the enemy outnumbered us almost two to one. His strategy was brilliant. He divided his forces and launched a two-pronged attack. I followed General Masséna up the Roya to Saorge and through the mountain passes into the Piedmont, while Bonaparte swept along the coast as far as Savona, the vanguard reaching the outskirts of Genoa.

From Savona he swung north and routed the Austrians at the Battle of Montenotte. Two days later the two halves came together and crushed them at Dego. It took only three weeks to occupy the entire Piedmont and most of Liguria. They had lost more than three times as many men as we had. A month later Nice and Savoy became part of France.

From there we went on to conquer the northern half of Italy. We marched into Lombardy. Reinforcements arrived, doubling our numbers. We besieged the Austrian garrison in Mantua but were unable to take the city, so we left a blockade around it and turned south. We overran Tuscany and the Papal States. Meanwhile the Austrians, who considered Mantua their most crucial stronghold, sent troops to lift the blockade. We left a division behind to occupy the region so as not to lose the foothold we had gained and returned north to confront the Austrians. We forced them to retreat up the Adige River to the Alps, but they returned three more times, keeping us on the move throughout the area to the east of Lake Garda for nearly four months.

During the three weeks to a month between each relief effort, I got to know the local population and discovered that they looked on the Austrians as an army of occupation and us as their liberators. Many had espoused republican principles, though few understood them. They certainly could make neither heads nor tails of the republican calendar. I lost track of it myself, and until I returned to France I kept track of the date in the traditional way.

Had I remained in Tuscany with the occupying force and not been sent back to Mantua, during those four months I would have lived in relative peace in a warm and gentle countryside with people who knew how to set some time aside every day to enjoy life. No doubt I would have spent them in the company of a Tuscan mistress, but my Tuscan mistress would not have been Luciana.

I MET Luciana in the village of Albaredo on the left bank of the Adige two or three days after the Austrian Field Marshal Würmser and his troops found themselves trapped inside Mantua with the garrison they had been sent to relieve. In ten days we had gone in a big circle around the entire region in pursuit of the enemy and come back to our starting point. First we marched north along the Adige to Rovereto, where we put Field Marshal Davidovich's division to flight, then we turned east to engage Würmser. We met up with him near Bassano and trounced him thoroughly. He fled toward Mantua with us close on his heels, took refuge inside its walls, and there he stayed until the Austrians surrendered the city four months later.

When first I saw Luciana she was leaving the market with a heavy basket of eggplants, tomatoes, zucchini and other vegetables. I helped her carry it home and gave her the sausage I had bought to share with some friends that night. She thanked me for my kindness and told me that all French soldiers were heroes. Had I taken part in the fighting at Cerea? She could hear the explosions all the way from Albaredo and was terrified. (I had. We had lost that one, though she evidently assumed we'd won.) And all the time she was talking, her eyes said she thought me handsome.

Six months of living with soldiers and listening to them tell about their sexual conquests (I made up quite a few stories myself) had renewed my interest in women. Luciana's heavy mane of dark hair and olive complexion made her stand out from the other village girls, but what I noticed first were her ample bosom and wide hips.

Our paths crossed again the next morning, and she waved to me. Bonaparte's orders against looting were very strict and we were expected to treat the Italian people with respect. Ironically, that made the village girls all the more willing to sleep with us, and a number of my comrades had three, four or even five mistresses in different towns around western Venetia. That evening she met me outside a hut where the villagers moored their boats, and I gave her a different kind of sausage. She knew what she was doing and that I would never marry her.

After we had made love, she asked if she would ever see me again. I asked if it would be possible for her to get to Verona, expecting her to say no. She told me she had cousins there. From then on I sent word to her whenever we were stationed in the area, and we'd arrange to meet. Neither of us expected our affair to last; Mantua would fall, and the French Army would move on to other conquests. I did not expect I would still be there five months later.

I learned from Luciana not to make generalizations about women. She did not agonize over our inevitable separation and made as few demands on me as Julien. Her only fear was that she might get pregnant. If it had been at all possible, Laurent would have done everything in his power to become pregnant in order to tie me to him. But as hot-blooded and passionate as Luciana was, she didn't really know how to please a man. She only knew how to let him take his pleasure with her.

I SAW Luciana almost every week for a month and a half. Then the Austrians appointed a new commander to push our armies back from Mantua, this time attacking from the west, and I returned to Bassano with General Masséna. We fared less well this time and were forced to retreat to Verona, but we were redeployed north along the Adige before I could send word to Luciana. The Austrians continued to get the better of us on every front. We owe our victory to the sluggishness of their eastern flank. Believing that Masséna was still in the neighborhood of Bassano, they stayed so long in the area that the other divisions of their Army came together too late to occupy a superior position. In the meantime, Masséna circled around them to the south while Bonaparte moved his divisions down from the north, meeting up near Arcole, to the east of the Austrians' main force, whereas they had expected to encounter us on the west. We faced each other on either bank of the Arpole River just north of where it flows into the Adige, a few kilometers from Luciana's village.

Bonaparte's strategy was to prevent the Austrians from crossing to our side of the river. We would attack them across the narrow bridge and hold them bunched up between the marshes and the river, where they could not spread out to take advantage of their superior numbers. Another division would build a pontoon across the Adige to the south and move north to cut their lines of communication.

The fighting went on for three days. We succeeded in crossing the bridge on the first day, but they drove us back. We spent the rest of the battle fighting to hold it, which was difficult, because even to reach it we had to expose ourselves to enemy fire, but the Austrians knew they were in a disadvantageous position and concentrated on pulling back their artillery so we wouldn't capture it if we took the bridge, which we had to do before their eastern flank arrived.

Bonaparte distinguished himself by staying in full view of the enemy, and many soldiers in his entourage were killed. Our casualties were nearly equal to theirs. At last we forced them to withdraw, we held the land between them and Mantua, and their divisions had been separated. It was by no means a stunning victory, but it had achieved its purpose, and Bonaparte made many battlefield promotions to mark its importance. I had been made a lieutenant after our victory at Dego, and now I was promoted to captain, a commissioned officer in charge of my own battery. Many of us enlisted men received promotions after Arcole to replace the officers who had fallen.

Bonaparte then turned to encounter their advancing eastern flank and drove them back. Their third attempt to lift the siege ended in failure. Würmser, thinking the enemy had got the better of us, led his troops out of Mantua only to find himself facing the French lines and had to retreat once again into the city, where they continued to suffer from hunger and disease. By the time Mantua surrendered, thousands of them had died. More than half of those remaining were too weak to leave the city on their own.

By now only a handful of the men who had marched with me to Nice were still alive. I had come through it all unscathed, with no injuries worth mentioning, certainly nothing that qualified as a wound: my temple grazed by a bullet, a concussion when a rock thrown up by a cannonball exploding some fifty yards away knocked me to the ground, grapeshot embedded below the skin on my left shoulder blade, cuts and scratches from flying debris, while all around me men lay dead and dying. I had seen more blood shed than during the Terror, but those who died had died defending themselves, not led like sheep to the slaughter, and I was fighting their killers. All in all, I preferred the violence of war to the cold-blooded murders of the Terror, and I felt safer under enemy fire than I had standing before the Revolutionary Tribunal.

The men in my battery speculated on whether we had seen the last of the fighting or if Austria would again send troops to lift the siege. Bonaparte knew they would: he said we would not control Italy until Mantua surrendered. As always, he was right.

After the Austrians had withdrawn from Arcole, I walked the short distance to Albaredo to show Luciana my new rank, but the people who lived there had fled, leaving the village just about empty. I figured her family had taken refuge in Verona. As it turned out, they would stay there for as long as I remained in Italy.

DURING the six weeks until the Austrians returned at the beginning of January, I spent most of my time in Verona, where Luciana finally introduced me to her family. I took her to restaurants and walked openly in the streets with her on my arm. I had no trouble arranging for some place where we could be alone. Her parents thought I was courting her. They may have suspected we were doing more, but flattered by the attentions their daughter was receiving from a French officer—times were hard, and whenever I came to visit I brought some luxury food item as a gift—they did not protest. At least they didn't to me. I can only guess what they may have said to Luciana when I wasn't there.

THE Austrians began massing troops in the mountains east of Lake Garda at the beginning of January and sent diversionary forces from Padua and Vicenza to advance on Verona. Not until General Joubert, who held the Adige Valley, sent word to us did we realize that the main attack would come from the north. By then it was almost too late. We set out immediately, leaving three smaller divisions behind to prevent the troops threatening us from the east from breaking through to Mantua. By forced march we arrived at the town of Rivoli and took our position on the Trambasore Heights overlooking the Rivoli Plain, a combined force of about twenty-three thousand men.

From our vantage point on the heights we had a view of the enemy such as a general needs to have in his mind's eye in order to develop his strategy. We who worked the heavy guns always had the enemy in our sights, of course, but most often we saw only his front ranks. My fellow soldiers were thrilled at being able to take in the entire field and follow the progress of the battle beyond the exhilaration they always felt when we engaged the enemy. Most men joke and swear in the heat of battle to show bravura and encourage one another. It serves both to release tension and as an expression of team spirit; they think and feel, not as individuals, but as a unit. I reacted that way in my first engagements at Montenotte and Dego, the result, I think, of apprehension, of my not knowing what to expect or how I would conduct myself. Since then I had not allowed myself to think or feel, except at Arcole, where every one of us was downright terrified. Here and in our other battles I went about my business, adjusting the angle of the cannon when a ball fell short or overshot the enemy and nodding silent approval when it landed in their ranks, but not cheering with the others. A single cannonball, I'd tell them dryly, does not win the day. After it was over, of course, I felt the same pride in our victory and relief at being alive we all did, and celebrated boisterously with the others unless we were all too exhausted to move a muscle.

Although the artillery was the least glamorous branch of the military, and we had to do more physical labor—loading and unloading the heavy guns from the wagons, moving them from place to place, positioning them, hauling cannonballs and crates of shells, building defenses (everyone pitched in there, but we did most of the work)—I was, all in all, glad to be there. For one, we played the decisive role in nearly all Bonaparte's successes. But more than that, I appreciated the greater distance that separated us from the enemy, not because I was afraid, but because having seen so many of my comrades fall and die next to me I was uncertain I could kill a man face to face. I know that makes no sense. A man you've killed is no less dead however far away he is.

With the entire field of battle stretched out below us, I was fascinated by how both sides deployed their troops, as if observing a giant chess game whose stakes were life and death. Despite Bonaparte's brilliance as a strategist, the outcome of any given maneuver was anything but assured. Although we faced the enemy on three sides, we held the advantageous position. But their dragoons cut through the Rivoli Gorge along the river to the left of us and overran the plain to the south, putting the entire Austrian Army between us and Mantua. Foolishly, the Austrian commander ordered them to attack us. We blasted them with artillery while our cavalry and infantry swooped down on them, forcing them back into the gorge, and their retreat caused the troops advancing through it behind them to take to their heels. The next day Joubert chased the Austrians' broken columns up the Adige, and we turned south with Masséna to deal with the troops outside Verona.

It was a decisive victory. Their losses were four times greater than ours, not to mention the four thousand men we took prisoner. On 2 February Würmser surrendered the city. Two and a half weeks later, the Papal States sued for peace. We were in possession of most of northern Italy, and Bonaparte was free to turn his attention to the invasion of Austria.

Chapter 3

BONAPARTE had moved east and was threatening the Tyrol, Masséna was visiting his wife and children in Antibes, and we were left behind to hold on to our Italian territories. The units that had fought in the Italian campaign were granted two weeks' leave on a rotating basis. Ours would not come until April. My regiment was stationed in Verona, so I was able to pursue my affair with Luciana.

I had fallen in love—with Italy, not with Luciana—and I thought seriously about resigning my commission and settling there. I didn't tell Luciana. She took it for granted that I would return to France when the war in Germany and Austria came to an end, and if I let her think I might be staying on, I was afraid she would also start thinking about marriage. I could imagine myself married to Luciana, but I was not ready to make a commitment.

When my leave came, I said goodbye to Luciana, telling her I would return in two weeks. I planned to spend the time in Nice, which was now part of France. But when I reached Genoa, I learned that the Austrian Emperor had asked to negotiate a peace, and I changed my plans. I proceeded to Antibes, where I presented myself to Masséna and requested permission to return to Paris pending further orders, given that it seemed the war was over and my presence was not required in Italy. He granted my request, and I wrote to tell Luciana that I had been sent to Paris. I took my time on the journey and arrived early in May, or, as I now called it, the middle of Floréal.

I found Thibaud's print shop still in operation but much less busy. The Directory had shut down his newspaper along with most of the others, and he and Laurent had joined the Army and were fighting in General Mortier's brigade in Germany. Adrienne oversaw the shop while taking care of her seven-month-old daughter, Lisette.

When I walked into the shop her reaction was the same as Sandrine's after my release from prison: "You're alive!" They had not had a letter from me since I'd written to tell them of my promotion after the Battle of Dego a year ago. I excused myself by telling her I had seen almost constant action during our blockade of Mantua.

News had arrived that both sides had reached a preliminary peace accord and the hostilities were over. We expected Thibaud and Laurent to return any day. But it seemed that Bonaparte had no intention of withdrawing his armies until a permanent treaty was finalized and signed. We thought it would happen soon, but it took close to six months. In the meantime, we received a letter from Thibaud saying they were both well, and Adrienne wrote them I was back in Paris.

My affair with Luciana had convinced me that except for Laurent (and Julien, if I ever saw him again) I was only interested in sex with women. I was not on active duty—in fact, I was a civilian in all but name—but I always wore my officer's uniform, which assured me I would not lack for an admiring woman to sleep with whenever I felt like it. I slept with many, but when I look back on those days, I wonder if I didn't enjoy the admiration more than the sex.

France and Austria signed the Treaty of Campo-Formio on 26 Vendémaire of the sixth year of the Republic. Our eastern border now extended to the Rhine, and Belgium, Lombardy, the Piedmont and Savoy were ours along with half of Venetia. The First Coalition was dissolved, and only England remained at war with us. I resigned my commission.

MORE than a month later, my friends still had not returned. We finally heard from Thibaud. They had come as far as Bavaria when Laurent came down with a bad cough. As winter had set in and they were traveling on foot, they thought it wise to interrupt their journey lest the cough turn into pneumonia. Laurent urged Thibaud to go ahead without him, but he would not leave his friend and was staying on to take care of him. We could expect them in spring, if not sooner.

I did not stay in Paris long enough to see them. The Directory approved Bonaparte's plan to conquer Egypt, which he had been pressing for half a year. He argued we could use it as a base to establish relations with the Moslems in India and become their allies in their struggle against the British, the only nation in Europe that had not made peace with us. My time in Italy had given me a taste for foreign countries, and I could imagine none more exotic than Egypt. I volunteered for the expedition without hesitation and left to wait in Marseille until we were ready to sail.

We took control of Malta, landed in Alexandria on the first of Messidor, and encountered the Mamelukes and utterly destroyed their cavalry outside Cairo in the Battle of the Pyramids—they lost twenty times as many men as we did—only to lose our entire fleet to Lord Nelson a week later in the Battle of the Nile. But on land we held Egypt firmly in our grasp. We had units stationed in Alexandria and the Sinai Peninsula, but most of our troops were billeted in Cairo in houses Bonaparte requisitioned for us, and I saw little action except for an occasional skirmish.

We were, on the whole, unwelcome guests. The Egyptians were fiercely protective of their women, but their men were fair game, and it didn't take me long to realize that many French soldiers were sleeping with the adolescent boys they had taken on as servants. Long-neglected desires stirred inside me, but remembering Father Lebreton and what he had done to Julien, I did not follow their example. All that changed four months later. I met Akmoud, whom at eighteen I did not consider still a boy.

It was Akmoud who approached me in the side streets of the bazaar, where I had come to look for a rug with a fellow-officer, the captain of another unit, and his twelve-year-old personal (very personal) servant, Jabir. We thought he wanted to sell us something and perhaps pick our pockets in the process, so we pushed on by him, but he followed us, and we were obliged to turn and hear him out. He knew only a few words of French, and between my friend and me we had only a smattering of Arabic, so we had to rely on Jabir to interpret.

Jabir told us he was seeking employment as a houseboy for a French officer, and as he had seen the two of us with only one servant, he thought that one of us might be willing to hire him. This aroused my suspicions, and I proceeded to question him. It was more than likely that the soldier he worked for had thrown him out for thievery. No, he had not worked as a servant for another Frenchman. Why had he not looked for a position sooner? He hadn't thought we would remain in Cairo so long. How had he supported himself till now? As a porter.

Since I was asking the questions, Akmoud knew that it was I he would work for if I decided to take him on, and he turned all his attention on me. He had incredibly large, oval brown eyes, a sandy-brown complexion, and—unusual for a lower-class Egyptian—perfect teeth. He was thin but solidly built, and he had strong hands. When he saw that I was studying him, his mouth broadened into a winning smile that was an open invitation for sex. "Do you think I can trust him?" I asked Jabir.

"Oh, yes. He's very honest. My family knows his family."

I agreed to hire him on a trial basis. He said he would be back in ten minutes with his belongings and ran off, pushing his way through the crowd.

Akmoud's belongings consisted of a djellaba, a pair of loose-fitting shin-length britches, a *chèche*, a woolen shawl, a pair of sandals, a little book which I assumed was the Koran, a prayer mat, a sleeping mat, a stringed instrument I did not recognize, a small brass tea kettle, a hookah, and a pouch of tobacco. I led him to my house and pointed to the spot outside my bedroom door where he should put his sleeping mat. He did not sleep on it.

After piling his other belongings the corner, he asked me in gestures to show him my stove and then put his kettle to boil and made tea. He noticed my metal bathtub behind the stove, pointed at me, and imitated taking a bath. I shook my head no and made signs to indicate that I bathed before bed. He nodded vigorously and smiled, then indicated he wanted to see the rest of the house. Finally, he asked my name. I said Vreilhac. He stumbled hopelessly over the *vr* and *lh*, so I told him to call me *capitaine*. By the next morning he was calling me Gérard, but only when we were alone together.

Next he turned my kitchen upside down to see what provisions I had, shaking his head over the lack of what he considered essential. I showed him a shoulder of goat meat, and his eyes lit up; then he shook his head sadly when he saw my meager collection of spices. He signaled me he'd be right back and returned with a loaf of Arab bread he had begged from the neighbors, and again managed to convey by signs that tomorrow he would go to the market and stock my pantry properly. Then he stretched out his prayer mat and went through his routine of evening prayers. I was beginning to have fun communicating with him without words.

The supper he cooked for me using what little I had convinced me I had found a pearl. He had evidently heard from somewhere that we French eat our meals in three courses. Our first course consisted of three slices of cheese sprinkled with pepper and olive oil, our main course of eggs deliciously scrambled with herbs, tomato and onions, and dates for dessert. I gestured for him to eat with me. He hesitated, smiled, and sat down at the table across from me, jumping up to run to the kitchen, bring the next course, and serve me. I poured myself a glass of wine and offered him some, but he would not touch it and drank water instead. He ate with his hands.

After supper he washed and put away the dishes; then, as if following a time-honored and immutable routine, he locked the front door, brought the lantern into my bedroom, turned down the covers and lowered the mosquito netting around my bed, carried the bathtub into the middle of my bedroom (though I kept gesturing that I bathed in the kitchen) and poured my bath. Then he stood by waiting for me to undress. I knew by now that it would do no good if he had made up his mind to stay and watch me. He waited until I had lowered myself in the tub and then left, only to return with the bar of soap and a towel I had not thought to bring from the kitchen. I thanked him and waited for him to hand me the soap, but instead he knelt beside the tub and began bathing me. After he dried me, he led me to the bed, had me lie on my stomach, and massaged my neck, back and shoulders for half an hour. Then he went back to the tub and washed his upper half thoroughly, turned his back from me and washed his crotch. Finally, he looked up at me questioningly.

I patted the mattress to invite him to join me. He grinned, stood up and faced me, already fully erect. His penis was massive. I wondered if all Egyptian men sported equally generous endowments. If so, I understood why so many of my comrades did not complain that they had to forgo women.

He proceeded to pleasure me manually. My foreskin fascinated him. I showed him how to pull it back and expose the glans. He knew intuitively that the head of an uncircumcised penis would be extremely sensitive and handled it gently. I indicated my desire to touch him there too. My request surprised him, but he welcomed my fondling. I was curious to know if I could fit so large a thing into my mouth, but I remembered our difference in status and what I had hired him for, and did not act on it—this time. Instead I signaled him to suck me, and he performed like an expert, watching me carefully to judge how I enjoyed his variety of maneuvers. In an instant, any misconception I had entertained about preferring women was dispelled. When it came to sucking cock, Akmoud, then Julien and Laurent topped my list of favorite lovers, and a chasm separated them from the women below them. Before the night was over I would conclude that the same held true for fucking.

After giving me fifteen minutes of the most exquisite pleasure I could remember, he patted his rear and cocked his head. I nodded. He got onto his knees with his backside high in the air, moistened the opening with spit—my cock was dripping with his saliva—and pressed his head against the mattress, his body tensed as if he anticipated pain. When I slid slowly and carefully into him, he emitted a long-drawn sigh, and his body relaxed. He turned his head to me and smiled to let me know I had done well. Soon I was bucking like a jackass kicking backward and grinding away inside him, my balls slapping against his buttocks. He pushed back into my thrusts, rotated his hips, clawed at the mattress, and gave a short, low-pitched grunt every time I slammed into him.

He made a move to get out of bed after I came, but I signed that he should finish himself off. That, too, surprised him. He left a copious white puddle on his stomach; then he went for the towel and cleaned us both off. Then he went into the main room. I saw through the door that he had unrolled his prayer mat. He bowed countless times to the east, mumbling all the time. Then he rolled up the prayer mat and leaned over to stretch out the other mat to sleep on. I called out to him and patted the mattress next to me. He grinned, came back to bed, and curled up beside me for the night.

I WOKE up in the morning lying behind him on my side, rock hard, my erection pressing into his buttocks. A movement from him showed me that it was he who was pressing his buttocks into my erection. He moistened us with his saliva, positioned my cock against his hole, and wriggled back until I was deep inside him. I grabbed his cock and pumped it furiously while I fucked him. We both came in a few minutes. Then he got out of bed to say his morning prayers.

After we dressed, he had me tell him the name of everything in the house. Then he picked up my shopping basket to show he was going to the market. He rubbed his thumb rapidly back and forth across his fingertips to signal that I should give him money. I gave him some, but he wanted more. I added to the sum, but he still wanted more. The third time he asked for more I gestured that I would come with him.

He had not asked for too much. He filled the basket to overflowing with vegetables, fruit, dried beans, spices, oil, flour, milk, yoghurt, pastries, and cooking utensils I didn't own. I taught him the French word for every item he purchased. Before he was done shopping I had to buy him another basket. He haggled over everything, and it cost him a quarter of what I would have paid. My mouth watered thinking about the lunch he would cook for us.

When Akmoud gave me my bath in the evening I signed for him to take off his clothes and examined his balls and circumcised cock (as much a novelty for me as mine was for him) in minute detail. I ran my finger over the head and traced the ridge around it and the spot below the slit where the two sides meet. I watched his shaft engorge as he stiffened in my hand. I longed to take him in my mouth... but I restrained myself.

In bed that night he was lavish with his attentions, and I reciprocated by caressing his body. He kissed me tentatively, and I responded passionately. When it came time to fuck him, he held his cheeks apart and was impatient for me to enter him. Afterward we lay in bed and I taught him the French word for every part of his body. In a few days he could communicate simple things to me in very rudimentary French. When he knew enough to answer more detailed questions I asked if he had been circumcised because his religion required it, like the Hebrews. (The difference between our two penises was an endless source of fascination for us, perhaps because it offered an excuse to indulge our fascination with any penis.) He didn't know; it was just something one had to do for a boy to become a man. I pointed out that I had become a man without it. "Europeans must be different," he said.

At the end of the first week I sucked him off, but it was another month before I could take the full length of that monster in my mouth without choking. Even if I only went down on him half way, I thought its thickness would dislocate my jaw.

I fucked him in other places than the bedroom, like with him leaning over the table in the main room or lying on it on his back. I put a finger (of the left hand, of course) in his asshole and massaged him inside while I masturbated him. I sucked his balls. And he always looked for new ways to pleasure me.

ONE day Akmoud dropped a wine glass in the kitchen. He swept up the shards and showed them to me; then he handed me a stick. He expected me to beat him. "Akmoud," I said, "it's only glass, and you didn't break it on purpose."

"I was clumsy," he said. "I deserve to be punished."

I told him use his own money to buy me another. He didn't think me severe enough. "Then tonight you sleep on your mat," I said.

He shook his head. "For a week."

After two nights I decided I had punished myself enough and ordered him into my bed. He was all smiles and eagerness to join me, and we played together as if nothing had happened. But after I fucked him he got up and returned to his mat.

Akmoud wanted only to please me. He struggled to master the French language. He taught himself to cook French dishes but would not make wine sauces, although I tried to explain that the alcohol evaporated when you heated it. He dressed me in a djellaba and showed me parts of Cairo where no Frenchman would ever venture. He shaved his beard and let his hair grow over his ears. He learned to piss standing up. He readily acquiesced to my zaniest whim. He did his chores in the nude. He danced for me naked. He twisted and contorted his body into awkward positions so I could fuck him from a new angle. He let me tie him up. He consented to do things no devout Moslem would. He smeared me with couscous and licked it from my body. He probed my asshole with his tongue. (Of course I never asked him to drink wine or taste pork.) And he made no demands on me whatsoever.

I CONVINCED Akmoud to redecorate my main room to resemble the tent of an important sheik, filled with carpets and cushions and brass trays. I had him move the table into the kitchen, and we used it only when he prepared a French meal. Otherwise we sat on the floor and ate with our hands, Egyptian style. At night we sat cross-legged on a pile of carpets and shared his hookah, but what he put in it wasn't tobacco. It made us silly and we made love on the floor. I bought a large tent made of animal skins and we rented camels for a weeklong excursion to the pyramids. I dressed as an Egyptian. The peasants we encountered recognized me as French, but they greeted me in a friendly manner. We pitched our tent in the shadow of the pyramids, leaving the flaps open, and made love with the cool desert breezes blowing over our naked skin. But Akmoud made me cut our trip short after three nights because he was afraid thieves would break into my house.

My comrades despised Egypt, but thanks to Akmoud I fell in love with it. He explained the local customs and told me all the things he loved about his native land. He spoke rapturously about its history. He opened my eyes to the beauty of the desert. He helped me understand why his countrymen hated the French. He showed me what behavior would get them to accept me. I began to feel at home in this alien landscape and foreign culture, as different from that of Europe as night is from day.

ABOUT half a year after we took up residence in Cairo, Bonaparte learned that the Turkish Sultan had gathered a force of forty thousand men to drive us from Egypt. Bonaparte realized the only way to defeat them was to engage them in Syria before the allies they had enlisted in the Balkans could join them and double their number. We prepared to move into the Levant.

Then my luck turned; I can't say whether for better or worse. Until then I had received no serious wounds. I felt so comfortable in Cairo and was so used to moving freely in its crowds that I had grown careless and forgotten how unpopular we were with the populace as a whole. I went out walking alone, and a man came up behind me and stabbed me three times in a street less than a quarter-mile from my house. A woman who had often seen me pass by with Akmoud ran to tell him, though it would not surprise me if she would just as soon have let me die. Had she not gone for him, I surely would have bled to death. On the other hand, I might well have died of plague in Jaffa if I hadn't been stabbed.

I was too weak to leave my bed for ten days, and it was another two months before my wounds completely healed. Akmoud gave me a Koran. "I don't read Arabic," I said, and he answered, "To protect you." I could not have asked for a more loving and attentive nurse than Akmoud during my long convalescence. He dressed my wounds, applied poultices, set bowls of boiling water with herbs floating in it by my bedside, and massaged my feet. The army surgeon came every day for a week; then he told Akmoud that he was caring for me better than any physician and from now on he would only come every other week. He explained how to send for him if I needed him. Akmoud asked when I could get up, and the surgeon answered, "When you think he's ready, and feed him what you think he can eat."

When I was able to stand on my own, he carried me to the roof and had me pace its length in the sunshine. The next day we walked in the street in front of my house. That night he slept beside me in bed. Then he started taking me for walks, a little farther every day. When I could walk three miles without tiring, he announced that I was well enough to make love again. I felt I had been more than ready for that for a while, and jokingly asked if he had asked the surgeon's opinion. "Do you want him to know?" he replied.

The first time we had sex again, he was very careful in bed. We lay on our sides when I took him. He would not get on all fours and let me mount him the way animals do, saying that I'd overexert myself.

One night I had him lie on his back so I could look at him while I caressed his body. I told him he was very beautiful. I sat with one knee bent and my foot on the other side of him. Before going to bed, I had smeared cooking oil between my buttocks without his knowing it. When he was fully erect I raised my hips and lowered myself onto him. His eyes widened in astonishment; then his face relaxed into a smile. Then my eyes widened. He was very large, and I hadn't done this in six years. It seemed my hole had to stretch until it gaped. But by slow determination I succeeded in fitting all of him into me. I rocked back and forth on him, and the sweet, familiar feeling returned. Instead of grunting as he did when I fucked him, he hummed while I rode him until he exploded inside me. He actually hummed!

We had crossed a threshold. After that he fucked me about once a week, but he would not get on top of me; I had to ride him. He put his finger in my ass when he beat me off. It didn't faze him when I did things Egyptians thought demeaning for a man of higher status, such as bathing him or tonguing his asshole.

BONAPARTE returned toward the end of spring, at the same time the Nile flooded. Many of the French had died of plague, we had not conquered the Levant, much less moved on to India, but it seemed the Turks no longer threatened us and that Egypt was secure. They made a last attempt, and I was called to fight at Abukir, where we trounced them yet again. Then Bonaparte sailed for France, somehow managing to sneak through the British line of blockade, leaving the Army behind under General Kléber. The troops looked on his action as a desertion. It had been agreed we would follow him. Instead the British naval commander sent the Mamelukes to attack us again, but we drove them off.

We remained in Egypt for two more years. I can say without exaggeration that I was the only soldier in the Army who was content to stay. Even a bout of dysentery, two of malaria, and the hostility of the people did not disturb my idyll with Akmoud. His French became fluent, and we lived together as near equals, but he never forgot he was my servant. I had fallen in love with him, more deeply in love than I had been with Julien. As I had considered staying in Italy and marrying Luciana, I thought about converting to Islam and staying in Egypt with him forever, but I knew I was fooling myself. It was not the ordeal of circumcision that dissuaded me, but honesty. I could not imagine myself kneeling on my prayer mat next to Akmoud and banging my head on the ground five times a day. I no more believed in the teachings of the prophet than in those of the Church. And however much I loved Akmoud, I was a Frenchman to the core.

We were constantly harassed by the populace and had to face the Turks and the British repeatedly. Disease likewise took its toll on our numbers—especially disease. Kléber was killed by an assassin, and General Menou took over. The men were dying; they were homesick and discouraged; they resented being in Egypt and fought half-heartedly to defend it. Menou capitulated. The British agreed to bring us back to France.

The day we were to leave for the harbor at Alexandria, I packed my personal belongings along with a few souvenirs of my time in Egypt—an ancient statuette, two intricately woven rugs, the Koran Akmoud had given me. Akmoud pleaded with me to take him with me. He wept. He knelt in front of me and embraced my ankles. But it was impossible. "They won't allow it," I said. "They won't let you on the ship." I gave him my watch as a keepsake. "To remember me by," I said. I extended my right arm and swung it slowly out to the side. "This whole house is yours, and everything in it." I gave him half my money and embraced him. Then I walked briskly out of the house. I left him in the center of the main room with tears streaming down his cheeks.

Chapter 4

I GOT back to Paris at the beginning of autumn. The Directory was a thing of the past, and no one seemed to regret its demise. Bonaparte had staged a coup two years before and established the Consulate. The Executive consisted of three Consuls, whose power far exceeded that of the parliamentary assemblies, and Bonaparte, ever popular, had been elected First Consul. One could no longer call us a republic.

Thibaud and Adrienne still ran their print shop, Laurent still lived with them, and Lisette idolized him. She had grown into a pretty little three-year-old who chattered incessantly and whose boundless energy ran her mother ragged. Adrienne was chasing her down the street when I turned the corner. I grabbed the child and tucked her under my arm. Adrienne was upset to see a stranger toting her daughter like a package. Then she realized who I was and exclaimed once again, "You're alive!" Everyone had heard about the sickly Egyptian climate and plague in Jaffa.

So I was finally reunited with my old friends from Saint-Lazare after five and a half years. Thibaud shook my hand heartily; Laurent hung back, unsure how to greet me, until I opened my arms for a hug. Then he clung to me and would not let go until I kissed him on the forehead, firmly removed the arms that enfolded me, and took a step back to look at him. Ever boyish, he had hardly changed at all.

We sat up talking late into the night. I shared my enthusiasm for Egypt with my friends and fascinated them with my stories about the exotic lands in the mysterious East. Thibaud, Laurent and I compared notes on the experiences we had had as soldiers. From the way he spoke of them, it seemed that Laurent had found his calling in the military. I have no explanation for why it was I who was promoted to colonel and he never advanced in the ranks. I was a proficient artilleryman but totally unsuitable for hand-to-hand combat. Laurent loved it. The noise and confusion of the battlefield exhilarated him, as did the thought that he might at any moment be struck by a bullet or an artillery shell would blow him to bits, as though he at once defied death and sought it out. It astonished me to hear him speak passionately of the exaltation of subduing an enemy, of the feeling of power that galvanized him when he thrust his bayonet deep into his enemy's chest—Laurent, who could not bring himself to thrust his penis into my ass even when I wanted him to! Thibaud agreed that everyone admired his courage, but in his opinion, Laurent took unnecessary risks. Yet despite his rashness, not once was he wounded in battle.

They had had a second tour of duty in Germany while I was in Egypt. Our old enemies had reunited to form a Second Coalition in Bonaparte's absence, this time joined by the Russians. Austria and Bavaria hoped to regain the territories they had ceded to us under the Treaty of Campo-Formio and were largely successful, most notably in Italy and the Rhineland, until Bonaparte returned to France. Then the tide turned against them. By the time I left Egypt we had regained control and made peace with the Austrians. It now seemed that Great Britain would follow suit, and we would have a lasting peace. We signed the Treaty of Amiens five months later.

At length Adrienne said, "Well, it's about time we all went to bed. I'm sure you two want to get reacquainted." Laurent had been unable to tear his eyes from me all evening. It was obvious he was itching to make love.

"First I'm going to have a bath," I said. "I'm still dirty from my trip." Laurent was ready to bathe with me, but I told him I'd be upstairs in half an hour.

He was waiting impatiently for me, naked under the quilt. He watched me undress, his eyes wide with longing and expectation. I slipped into bed next to him.

"I've missed you terribly," he whispered, nuzzling up against me. He didn't tell me he'd been faithful, so I assumed he hadn't been, which was fine with me. Who he had sex with was his business, not mine.

I stroked his arm; he put his hand on my chest, caressing my skin as his fingers passed over my body, and slowly lowered it to my genitals. He cupped his hand under my balls and ran his thumb over my penis, as if to reassure himself that it was still as he remembered it. I touched him there, too. His average size erection seemed almost insignificant after Akmoud's. He was dripping copiously. I brought my fingers to my mouth and tasted it, then kissed him on a nipple. He raised my head and pulled it to his lips and kissed me passionately, clutching me against him. Then he went down on me.

Good as it felt to have a mouth around my cock again, I couldn't help comparing him to Akmoud. He didn't keep at it for long. "Take me," he said, and rolled onto his stomach. I entered him in one swift thrust, something I had never done before. He gasped. Then he said, "I can't tell how long I've dreamed of feeling you inside me again."

It felt good having an ass to plow again, too, and it felt good to give a man the most intense pleasure a man can feel and to hear his moans and sighs as his bottom wriggled back to meet my cock, asking for more, more! With Akmoud I learned how to delay my orgasm indefinitely, and I fucked Laurent for over an hour without stopping, till his head fell to the side, his eyes rolled up in their sockets, his thighs twitched furiously, and his toes curled down so tightly I thought his feet would snap in two. The floor squeaked with my pumping, and his cries of pleasure echoed through the house. I could only imagine what Adrienne would have to say in the morning. She said nothing; she was occupied with Lisette when we came downstairs. But Thibaud made it clear he had heard everything. He winked at me and gave Laurent a friendly slap on the butt.

When I came, Laurent's back arched in a spasm so violent it almost threw me to the floor. I was afraid his heart would burst, so long did he lie panting, his eyes glazed, unable to move, the waves of orgasm still crashing in his body like an angry surf. The sheet was drenched where he'd been lying on it, and not with sweat. He had probably ejaculated several times.

"Did you have enough?" I asked.

He was still too overcome to answer. At last he caught his breath and said, "Where did you learn to do that?"

It would have been cruel to tell him the truth. "It comes from having gone so long without you," I said, and kissed him gently on the ear.

In this way we resumed our habit of nightly sex, but I did not repeat my performance of the first night. I did introduce him to a few things I had discovered with Akmoud, pretending I was making them up on the spur of the moment, like massaging him inside with a finger while I licked his balls and swirled the other hand up his shaft, over the head, and back down to the base, and taking him in my mouth when I felt he was about to spurt, which he loved almost as much as getting fucked. And I tried other new things I hadn't done in Egypt. If I had learned anything from Akmoud (and he taught me a lot), it was to be inventive.

SOME *émigrés* began returning to France after the Treaty of Amiens: not too many, and of course not from England. Though they had made peace with us, our relations with that nation were fragile indeed. Berthe and her Baron were among the first to return. I didn't learn they were living in Paris for a few weeks, but it was only to be expected, since we controlled the Netherlands, where they had taken refuge.

I no longer collected a salary, though I always wore my uniform, and had yet to find work, but the money I had brought back from Egypt was more than adequate since I didn't have to pay for lodgings and Thibaud would not accept money for my board. He said I was family. I helped Adrienne by taking care of Lisette, doing the marketing, and I sometimes made dinner for them. I introduced them to the spicy exotic dishes Akmoud had cooked for me. To Laurent's distress, I spent many an evening at a café with my comrades from Egypt.

I learned of Berthe's return when I ran into Lucie at the butcher shop. She was now the Envols' only female servant. The Baron could easily have afforded more, but he no longer owned his hotel and lacked the space to house them. He was pressuring the government to let him take possession of his former property but had not met with much success. I asked if her mistress was yet a mother. "She would make a good one," I said.

"I fear the Baroness will never have a child."

"Indeed?"

"They have separate bedchambers," she whispered, "and they never sleep together."

"Are you sure?"

"My room connects to hers."

I asked if they would welcome me if I paid them a call and called her attention to my uniform. She assured me they would, and told me where they lived and on what days they received.

"Will they look on me as a servant?"

She hesitated for a second and answered, "Not the Baroness."

It was Berthe I wanted to see, and only to have news of Julien. I had not heard from him or of him since we parted at the Belgian border eight years ago. Were it not for that, I would not have gone to see them.

The Baron was surprised to see me and greeted me awkwardly. On the one hand, I was a former servant; on the other, my uniform impressed him. I had worn my sword. Berthe did not disguise her pleasure. I had been close to her favorite brother, and my military rank allowed her to speak to me, if not as an equal, as a not-too-close friend. Had I been one grade higher—say, a commandant—she could have invited me to a dinner party.

I inquired about her family. Her eyes teared up.

"They guillotined Father and *Maman*," she said, "and Marie-Catherine, too."

"I know, Baroness, I was present at their executions. Out of respect, you understand. I hope they didn't misinterpret my being there if they saw me in the crowd. But I didn't hear about your sister-in-law till afterward."

"Olivier has remarried," she said off-handedly. "An Englishwoman. I haven't met her and don't know her rank."

"She's the Countess d'Airelles."

"Is there such a thing?" She clearly took no interest in her Olivier's bride and immediately went on, "And poor Constance!"

"I met her in Saint-Lazare, you know. I was also in prison. She was very brave."

"Constance died a martyr for her faith. I envy her that." I was tempted to tell her that her sister the martyr thought having her head cut off less cruel than having to spend her life in the convent. It annoyed me that it made no impression on her that I had almost been a victim of the Terror.

Berthe sighed. "But I suppose we all have our martyrdoms. And poor Henriette! So many people died at the hands of the Terror! But they went after the aristocracy with a vengeance."

She couldn't have been more wrong. Peasants and laborers accounted for three-quarters of its victims.

"And your other sister? Is she doing well?" I asked, seeing that she had no interest in my experiences under the Terror.

"I've written several times to urge Jeanne to come back to France, but she dislikes Napoleon and doesn't trust him at all. She says she can feel in her bones there'll be another war. She has also developed a great loyalty to Austria. I hope that doesn't offend you. Her children have grown up there and hardly remember France at all. That gives her another reason not to leave Vienna."

"And her husband?"

"Killed in Italy trying to relieve the fortress in Mantua. He fell at the Battle of Rivoli your Napoleon is so proud of."

I did not say I had fought in it. "And Monsieur Julien?" I finally asked. He was the one member of the family I could refer to by first name.

"Married, to an Englishwoman of no rank to speak of. Olivier is quite disgusted with the match."

"Do you hear from him?"

"Very rarely. He keeps his distance from the family. He maintains there's no future for the nobility in France, and ultimately not anywhere."

"Has he turned republican, then?"

"I really couldn't say. Julien was always the realist of the family. He may like the idea of an aristocracy and only think their—our—days are numbered. I do hope he isn't right."

"I think it will just become more frequent that commoners like me advance themselves in society, Baroness," I said, continuing to play the hypocrite.

"Oh, I should not mind that at all, provided they earn their titles for heroism or service to their King. I mean, the Nation."

The Baron had bought his.

We had exhausted the subject of her family. The conversation now turned to politics, a subject on which she was woefully ignorant. Nothing really interested her there except the Concordat with Pope Pius VII, which had to a limited extent relegitimized the status of the Catholic Church in France, the one thing Bonaparte had done of which she approved, though with reservations. That Catholicism was recognized as the religion of "the majority of the French" did not mean much to her if people were free to believe or disbelieve in anything they wanted. Why, they could believe in nothing at all if they so chose! I pointed out that he had reintroduced the seven-day week with Sunday reserved for rest and worship. That also made her happy. Personally, I thought that if the first day of the week didn't coincide with the first day of the Republican months, the simplicity the new calendar had aimed to achieve had been thrown into chaos, and what he had was a mongrel calendar that confused everyone.

Having exhausted politics as well, we chatted a while longer, until she stopped disguising the fact that my company bored her, and I took my leave. The Baron had not said a word during my entire visit.

EVERY so often Lucie and I would chance to cross paths. As the Baron had received me in his salon, she thought herself far below me, but I was friendly to her, and when we met I more often asked her about herself than the Envols. She commented on how good it was of me, a war hero, to take an interest in a mere lady's maid.

"My life isn't really all that different from yours," I told her. "My closest friends run a print shop. I'll introduce you to them on your next day off, and you'll see."

True to form, Laurent jumped to the conclusion she was my latest mistress. When I came to bed that night, he berated me for what he called my "need to have sex with women." Didn't he satisfy me? Could I ask for a more devoted lover?

"I promise you, Laurent, I have no interest in women whatsoever. I haven't been with a woman since Italy. They used to attract me, but now I'm like you. I love men."

"So you've had other men besides me."

"One. An Egyptian lad. He was my servant. A lot of soldiers had sex with their Egyptian servants. We had no other outlet."

"Did you love him?"

"I told you. He was a servant. *My* servant."

"What about the other soldiers?"

"*What* about the other soldiers?"

"Did you have sex with them?"

"Lord, no. We wouldn't have dreamt of having sex with each other. We all pretended we were sleeping with our servants because there were no women available. For most of them, that was the truth."

"But not for you."

"No, not for me. But I only had sex with Akmoud. I didn't dare let on. You ought to know. You served in the Army.

"And you don't want a woman? They don't even tempt you?"

"No."

"Then just how do you know this Lucie?"

When I told him, he immediately suspected I was in contact with Julien, and his jealousy knew no bounds.

"I lost track of Julien when he fled from France. I haven't seen him, haven't heard from him. I hear he's married."

"So you've asked about him."

"Lucie told me when we met at the butcher's. That's when I found out she was back in France. She told me about all the de la Mottes. That's all we have in common. Quite honestly, I don't think Julien even remembers me."

"But you remember him."

"Is it a crime to remember people you knew long ago?"

"Do you love me, Gérard? Do you *really* love me?"

"The only thing I don't love about you is your insane refusal to believe that I've chosen *you* as my man. You pry into corners of my past that no longer matter and where there's nothing worth knowing about."

"If you really loved me, you'd want to know everything about me, too."

"I'm sure you would tell me if there was anything I ought to know about. I don't question the sincerity of *your* love, Laurent."

Akmoud had been no less devoted to me, but he let me live my own life. He was ten times more beautiful than Laurent, and his body was more manly. He gave better blowjobs, too, and was a better fuck. And he fucked me. How I longed to feel a dick in my ass again! Any dick would do, but would I find one as huge as his on any man in France? What was I thinking when I obeyed the call of duty and left Egypt!

I had to argue for a long time before Laurent was finally appeased, but I didn't think he believed me about Julien. He didn't suspect I had been in love with Akmoud. By the time we dropped the subject, I was too overwrought and exhausted to make love. I lay back and let him service me and fell asleep before he had finished, only to wake with a start when I came.

KNOWING I would have to find employment sooner or later, I turned to the military and was given an office position in their bureaucracy. My principal assets were good spelling, a rudimentary knowledge of Italian, and familiarity with Bonaparte's campaigns in Europe. I hoped I might distinguish myself and earn a promotion, but the work was routine and we who did it seemed to go unnoticed. In retrospect, however, I may have my job in the War Ministry to thank for my subsequent rapid rise in the ranks. When you hear a name often enough, even if you aren't paying attention, you tend to remember it, and although you may not remember what was said about the person, so long as he has not been criticized, you assume that people have spoken well of him. Thus when the Emperor promoted me as a reward for wounds I would not have received had I been a more competent soldier, the name Gérard Vreilhac may have been lurking at the back of his mind.

To those Frenchmen who had no real access to the inner workings of the Consulate, it seemed that we had achieved a lasting peace. It was common knowledge that England had taken umbrage over what they called our "interference" in Haiti, but the Antilles seemed so very far away and unimportant. Only Europe concerned us.

I saw that this was not the case when I began working for the military. There was no love lost between our two nations. The majority of people in England had opposed the Treaty of Amiens from the beginning. Haiti was little more than an excuse for them to renew hostilities. The British demanded ever more concessions, and Bonaparte steadfastly refused to make them. They recalled their ambassador, and five days later their Parliament began to debate whether they ought to declare war on us. On 2 Prairial Bonaparte ordered the arrest of every British citizen on French soil. War with Great Britain was not only inevitable, it had to all intents and purposes begun.

Laurent, who needed no excuse for war other than his enthusiasm for soldiering, said it was all for the better. The English had been our enemies throughout history; we had always been at war. They had chopped off their King's head, then changed their mind and put his successor back on the throne. They had opposed our King in everything he did when we had a king, and now that we had got rid of him, they wanted to restore the Monarchy. Their uncontested control of the seas put a stranglehold on shipping and threatened not only our shores but those of every territory in the Empire. Laurent came up with an astonishing number of reasons and argued them heatedly. I had no trouble seeing through his rantings. Another motive why he favored waging war with England was that Julien was there.

As it appeared more than likely that most of the fighting would take place at sea, Thibaud, Laurent and I were not mobilized. I suspected, however, that Bonaparte's true motives were that he expected the war in Europe to resume before long. No country in

Europe trusted him, and since he had seized power and established the Consulate they could only wonder how far his ambition would lead him. Their governments feared the republican elements in their midst, for the ideas of the Revolution had spread with his conquests. I told my friends what I thought; they called me a pessimist; and for a long time it seemed they were right. Two more years were to go by before we faced the Third Coalition.

If the peace in Europe was fragile, the situation in France was no more stable. Royalists and Jacobins alike schemed against the First Consul. When a plot to assassinate him was uncovered the next year, he used it as an excuse to send dragoons across the border in secret and kidnap the Duke d'Enghien, a Prince of the Blood who had fought against us since the earliest days of the Revolution but was not even remotely involved in the plot. Although we were not at war with Germany, where he now resided, the Consulate put him on trial as an enemy of the Republic (which of course we were not) and executed him. Our enemies raised the cry of martyrdom, and I was certain Germany would declare war for our illegal incursion into their sovereign territory, but nothing came of this blatant provocation.

A very different motive lay behind Bonaparte's action. It made it seem that the attempt on his life had been part of an international conspiracy. Patriotism and devotion to the First Consul reached fever pitch, and in less than two months the Senate had voted to dissolve the Consulate and acclaim him Emperor. In Notre-Dame Cathedral on 3 Nivôse, at a ceremony so sumptuous that no monarch since Louis XIV could have matched its magnificence, he crowned himself Emperor of the French.

His Empire already more or less covered that of Charlemagne. Would he stop there?

Chapter 5

WALKING along the Seine toward the Châtelet with Lucie one day not long after Napoleon's coronation, I heard a woman's footsteps running after me, and a voice called out, "Monsieur Gérard! Monsieur Gérard!" We were on our way to join a couple of my Army companions at a café. Jacques and Armand had said they would be bringing their mistresses, and as the Baroness had given Lucie the afternoon off, I had asked her to accompany me for the sake of appearance. I didn't know about Armand, but back in Egypt Jacques had not been above having sex with his Khalil. But we weren't in Egypt. In Paris such things were considered disgraceful.

I turned to see who had called me. It was Artémis.

How she recognized me from behind in a three-cornered hat and heavy cape I shall never know. When I turned to face her, she exclaimed, "My, don't you look dashing in your *captain's* uniform!"

"A battlefield promotion," I told her. "In Italy."

"Were you at Marengo?" Her eyes gleamed in admiration.

"No, I was in Egypt then. I was promoted after the siege of Mantua."

"In Egypt? Under the Emperor himself? Were you serving under him at Mantua, too?"

"Under General Masséna."

"One of our greatest heroes." He was back in the Emperor's favor again and would soon be named a Marshal of France. Artémis the Jacobin had become a dyed-in-the-wool Bonapartist. As she had taken it for granted I was a loyal Jacobin, she now took it granted that I was one of the Emperor's most fervent supporters.

Lucie had been patiently waiting for me to introduce her. I toyed with my former landlady's enthusiastic ignorance by introducing her as "Mademoiselle Lucie Labonne, of the household of the Baron de l'Envol."

Lucie blushed, thinking I was making fun of her (Labonne was not her family name), but she soon realized that she was not the butt of my sarcasm. Artémis had completely forgotten the name and mistook the Baron for one of Napoleon's generals. "Ah, yes, the Baron," she said in a tone that suggested she held the very name in awe. "All Paris is singing praises of his valor."

"The Baroness's *personal*... maid," I added.

"Oh," she answered, deflated.

One could not take the wind out of Artémis's sails for long. I asked her for news. She drew herself up, puffed out her bosom in simulated dignity, and announced, "I'm Madame Tournant now." She had married Thierry.

I congratulated her. "And you, are you still living with your friend?" she asked.

"When we're both in Paris at the same time. He was in the Army too, in Germany. We stay with Thibaud, the printer. All three of us were in Saint-Lazare together."

"What terrible times those were," she said mournfully, "but now we've come to the dawn of a new and glorious age. Don't you agree, Monsieur Gérard?" My brain reeled at the depth of her hypocrisy. Or was it shortness of memory?

She filled me in on the people who had been my co-lodgers when I lived with her. Madelon had died years ago, but her grandson had returned from the front and grown up to become a fine young man, though with only one arm. Thomas and Philippe had died in a military hospital in Germany. (Of the pox, I thought.) Then she cut herself short and said, "But I really must be running. How fortunate that we ran into each other! Good evening, Mademoiselle."

She walked away a few steps, turned, and added in a significant tone of voice, "I won't forget to tell Mademoiselle Sandrine you send your respects."

"Who is Mademoiselle Sandrine?" Lucie wanted to know.

"A young woman who covered for me when I hid Monsieur Julien in my room before I helped him escape from France."

"You helped him escape? I didn't know that. Madame Tournant made it sound as if she was your mistress."

"Artémis fancies she knows everything. Surely you noticed that."

So Julien hadn't told his family that he owed his life to me! My boyhood friend who had sought me out to help him and had pretended he wanted to return to France to be with me; who had always claimed to dislike his brother, Olivier, yet put his life at risk to save his son; for whom, apparently, the most important thing in the world was to insure that the heir of the Counts d'Airelles lived to carry on the family name. And who was I compared to them? Their servant, and afterward a revolutionary, and therefore their enemy. I had served my purpose; he no longer needed me; I could be forgotten. He had looked on me as his inferior from the beginning. What else could one expect from an aristocrat? But the enormity of his ingratitude was staggering. I felt betrayed.

We crossed the Pont Neuf and found Le Mousquet Rouillé, where Jacques, Armand and their women were waiting for us. Lucie realized at once that Josette and Élodie were tarts and our café was not the most respectable in Paris. She sat down with a show of dignity and smiled politely, but I could see she was offended. She asked for a glass of wine, which she drank slowly in tiny sips.

The atmosphere in the café was raucous, and my friends had already drunk more brandy than they could handle. They shouted to hear each other over the din, and Josette and Élodie doubled over in high-pitched laughter at everything they said. Everyone had proposed a toast, and Jacques insisted we do so too. I raised my glass and said, "To the Emperor!" We all drank. Then Lucie raised hers and said quietly, "To friendship!"

Josette laughed. "Friendship? To love, rather! Aren't I right, Jacquot?"

I jumped in to keep the conversation from turning bawdy, and at the same time attempted to pay attention to Lucie. Everyone agreed that she was very pretty, and Élodie complimented her dress, which she called "very distinguished, almost a gown." Lucie blushed, more because she had been singled out by low-life tramps than with pleasure. I seized the opportunity and made some comment about the latest fashions, which didn't interest Jacques and Armand, but it drew the women's attention away from what their men were saying, and they stopped fawning over them so blatantly.

All three agreed that we were well rid of the gaudy colors, the puffed out look, and the elaborate coiffures of the Old Regime, though Josette and Élodie regretted the magnificence of the jewelry. Nor did they miss the drab colors of the Revolution. They praised the whites and pastels of the current fashion, its simple elegance and the much more comfortable footwear. But when Josette and Élodie went into raptures over décolleté, Lucie demurred. Then Josette and Élodie started quibbling over plain bonnets, bonnets with flowers, and bonnets with feathers. They asked my opinion. Having none, I said that the choice of bonnet depended on the dress it complemented.

A fight broke out in another part of the café. Jacques and Armand ran to join in, and Élodie and Josette clapped their hands in excited amusement. I hustled a terrified Lucie out the door without saying goodbye.

We walked at a brisk pace. When we reached the corner, I saw that Lucie was fighting back tears. I told her not be frightened; we had left the brawling safely behind us.

She reproached me for having brought her to such a place and expecting her to share a table with a batch of profligates. I told her that Jacques and Armand had been my friends in Egypt, and I had only met their lady friends that evening. To make it up to her, I offered to take her to dinner at a real restaurant. She was miffed, but she reluctantly accepted.

I had thought to take her to the post relay where Laurent and I had worked for a year, but on our way we passed a more elegant restaurant called Le Jeune Phébus. Inviting aromas wafted from the kitchen, and I suggested we eat there. Lucie's dress would not be out of place among the more richly outfitted clientèle, and I, of course, was in uniform.

Over dinner we talked seriously together for the first time. I told her about how I had felt trapped as an employee of the Tribunal, about my time in Saint-Lazare, about Italy, and about the alien but strangely beautiful land of Egypt. She told me about her peasant upbringing and how she came to work at the chateau, about her astonishment at the press and bustle of Paris when she followed Berthe, and about her loneliness in Holland, where no one of her station spoke French. She said she had never spoken of herself to anyone before, how kind I was to listen to her nonsense when I had seen so much of the world and led such an exciting life, and that it made her feel close to me. She called herself a simple country girl. I told her no, her manners were very refined. "That's from living with the Baroness," she said modestly.

It was dark out, and I escorted Lucie to her door. Walking home, I thought how unwelcome it was that Lucie had attached herself to me with as much determination as Sandrine, though without the possibility of intimacy before marriage, and how shamefully Julien had treated me. Laurent's jealousy seemed trivial in comparison. I was more attentive to him than usual when we made love that night. I covered him with kisses and caresses, and grazing my lips and fingertips over his body excited me. Here was a man's body, with a flat stomach and narrow hips, whose flesh responded to the pressure of my hands with resisting firmness and didn't mash like a rotten orange when I squeezed it. On his chest, instead of flabby orbs flopping from one side to the other, I felt the solid bone of a rib cage and sternum that enclosed a beating heart. The low moans of pleasure from deep inside his chest, soothing to the ear, bore no resemblance to the hysterical shrillness that issues from a woman's throat when you make love to her. When I lowered my face to his groin, it filled my nostrils with the sharp scent of musk, not the sour odor of curdled milk or the stench of rancid lard. Sweet sap oozed from the tip of his cock and trickled down his shaft. I savored his size and hardness, and it never occurred to me to compare them with another's. This man loved me; he yielded himself to me and held nothing back; and in return he asked only for love. How easy it was to love him!

That night I didn't think of the deep emotional ties, older than memory, that bound me to Julien, nor of my frenzied couplings with Akmoud. Our lovemaking was subdued and soothing, and the brief convulsion of our orgasms satisfying. He nestled peacefully into the cradle of my arms in its wake, smiling contentedly. We didn't speak. The fullness of our union left nothing to say.

THAT night set the pattern for our lovemaking for as long as Laurent and I remained together, and his fears were assuaged, but the following month he and Thibaud were mobilized and sent to Boulogne to swell the ranks of the forces the Emperor was gathering for his planned invasion of England. Since I worked in the military bureaucracy, I knew about it before they did. After he left I gave up sex, convinced he was the love of my life, and for entertainment I adopted Lucie as my chaste companion. Once a week we would meet near the Châtelet and lunch together at a restaurant, then visit a museum or admire the art in one of the Paris churches, and sometimes we attended the theater or a concert in the evening. When the warm weather returned, we went for strolls or had a picnic or window shopped. One afternoon I hired a fiacre and drove her to Le Bresson for lunch. The food was excellent and the atmosphere unpretentious.

Sometimes I had Lucie meet me at the print shop. Adrienne remembered her. If I had some business to attend to, I might arrive late, and they had time to chat. Adrienne took a liking to her, and they became close friends. After that she always met me at the shop. Once Adrienne asked me if Lucie was my fiancée. I told her I would never leave Laurent for a woman and had no intention of marrying.

THE Emperor abandoned his projected invasion of England when his efforts at sea proved unsuccessful. Instead the troops stationed at Boulogne moved east to fight the Third Coalition, and Thibaud and Laurent were reintegrated into General Mortier's division. Toward the end of November we received a letter from Laurent saying that Thibaud was severely wounded at Dürrenstein. He was felled by a bullet to the shoulder. Laurent ran on ahead, unaware that he had been shot. Then a shell exploded behind him and knocked him on his face. It had landed close to Thibaud, and the fragments shattered his kneecap and tore up his face and hands. When Laurent turned to look for his friend, he was unconscious. They carried him to a field hospital and treated his wounds, then sent him back to France. By the time he arrived in Paris we had already learned of our great victory at Austerlitz and were expecting Laurent to return soon as well. The scars on Thibaud's face stayed with him for the rest of his life, and he walked with a limp.

Laurent returned a month later, in January, after the Treaty of Pressburg. (Napoleon had abolished the Republican calendar, and starting in 1796 our days were same as in the rest of Europe except Russia.) I continued to see Lucie. Eventually Laurent calmly asked if I was going to marry her, as if it were a matter of total indifference to him. He might have been asking about the weather.

"Lord, no. She's just a friend. I thought that would be obvious."

"Does she know that?"

"How could she not? Our most intimate contact is when she takes my arm in the street. We haven't even held hands."

"But does she know she won't find a husband in you?"

"It would surprise me if Adrienne hasn't told her. She asked if Lucie was my fiancée when I introduced them. I made it clear that I didn't see myself ever getting married. You know she wouldn't want to see Lucie hurt, and neither would I. We go out together because we enjoy each other's company. Lucie isn't one to harbor empty hopes."

"Unlike Sandrine."

"Exactly—unlike Sandrine."

He smiled. "Who you promise never was your mistress." I could detect no jealousy, no insecurity, in his voice, but he did add, "Are you sure it's all right that I won't fuck you?"

"Would a woman fuck me? Yes, it's all right." I thought a bit and told him that it would be nice to have a little anal stimulation when he sucked me. "Do you think you can do that?"

"I don't see why not, if that's what you want."

That Laurent could see me with a woman and not go mad with jealousy proved to me that he felt secure in my love and didn't feel he had to tie me to him. What had I done to bring on this sudden change? Or was it that he could sense the change in me? Had it been so obvious that another man, Julien, had been living locked in my heart? Apparently it was to him, and now he saw that this vain ideal I had clung to had gone, and there was a place there now for him. I took him so gently that night, showering him with kisses and hoping he would feel my love in every thrust, and he kissed my fingers and sucked them softly with his lips.

He was not in Paris long. Toward the end of spring his orders came to rejoin his regiment, which was reassembling outside of Strasbourg. Laurent asked to be reassigned to serve under General Davout, whom he considered our greatest general after Napoleon. Certainly no general in the *Grande Armée* was more devoted to the Emperor, and after Napoleon's final defeat and exile he proved himself the most upstanding and least self-interested of them all.

Laurent's request was granted. To Adrienne's horror, Thibaud said he would follow as soon as he could walk without the aid of a cane.

The War of the Fourth Coalition was about to begin. On the eastern front we would face the armies of Saxony, Prussia, Russia and Sweden. I petitioned to be released from my bureaucratic duties and take my place as a fighting man, and was given command of a battery under General Lannes. I was unlikely to meet up with Laurent at the front, but I wanted to share in his danger.

Although the Prussians had mobilized first, the lack of any clear order in their chain of command had kept them from developing a unified strategy of attack, and we advanced northeast toward Prussia via Saxony, intending to deliver them as crushing a defeat as the Austrians had suffered at Austerlitz. That we did. Two decisive battles, fought within twenty miles of each other on the same day, removed them from the Coalition, freeing the Emperor to concentrate on the Tsar's armies.

October found my battery in Thuringia, in the front line facing what we believed to be the entire Prussian Army on the plain north of Jena, with the divisions of Generals Augereau and Ney ranged behind us, and Soult, Murat and the Emperor on the other bank of the Saale to our east. Generals Davout and Bernadotte were to proceed south from Naumberg and attack them from the rear, but Davout encountered the bulk of the Prussian forces outside of Auerstedt and would have to break through to join us. The Prussian troops we fought at Jena were only a single detachment. Although Bernadotte, less than three miles away, had a clear view of Davout and his men engaged in combat with an enemy more than twice their size, he continued on his route south to Jena, where he arrived after we had already won the battle.

As I mentioned earlier, my luck changed the day I was stabbed in the streets of Cairo. From then on I never came through a major battle without having sustained some serious wound. In each case it came swiftly, within an hour or so of the first shots fired, so I developed a reputation for heroism without having played a particularly active role.

My battery was stationed on the left flank so we could turn our guns against General von Rüchel, whom we expected shortly to arrive from the west. Prince von Hohenlohe gave orders for his hussars to swoop down on us, one of General Lanne's squadrons rode in to defend us, and we found ourselves engulfed in a cavalry battle. One of our gunners was struck down, and I seized the ramrod he was holding to load our cannon just as a Prussian hussar rushed me. I swung the ramrod and knocked him unconscious to the ground, then grabbed his saber, jumped onto his horse and joined the fray, slashing this way and that. I performed admirably for a man with no experience fighting on horseback, but a Prussian saber sliced through the muscle of my left arm from shoulder to elbow, scraping the bone, and I collapsed on my horse's neck. It was a miracle he didn't sever my arm. A hussar, Lieutenant Jeanville, seized my reins and galloped to the medical station, where a surgeon managed to close my wound before I died from loss of blood. I had saved my battery, but my left arm was useless, and I sat out the rest of the battle. I watched from the sidelines and realized that it was General Lanne's cavalrymen who, in the very first engagement, had assured our ultimate victory. I was proud to have been one of them, if only for five or ten minutes.

Although it saved my battery, playing at cavalryman proved to be a rash and foolish act, and not only because of my injury. As will soon become clear, it marked the end of my career in the artillery and led to my transfer to a branch of the service for which I was quite unsuited. I liked being an artilleryman. Despite the grueling physical labor, soldiers in the artillery have a merry time in battle. Though we face the same danger of being killed at any moment by a shell or stray bullet or cannonball as the rest of the army, we seldom have to confront the enemy directly and almost never engage in one-on-one combat. Instead, we are busy every second loading, firing and repositioning the heavy guns. We constantly talk to each other and make jokes, and the prevailing mood is as a rule light-hearted. Soldiers in the infantry and cavalry joke before and after a battle, never during one.

WHEN we received word that Davout's Third Corps had defeated the Prussians at Auerstedt, the Emperor was incredulous, and remarked that Davout needed to have his eyes examined. (He did, in fact, suffer from impaired vision.) But it was true. As many would say later, on that day Napoleon's Army defeated a division and Davout's division defeated an army. Needless to say, the Emperor did not begrudge him his victory, but he was furious with Bernadotte.

Of course it was imperative for us to verify the accuracy of the report as soon as possible. Except for my left arm, now expertly sewn up and bandaged, I was unharmed, and it would be several weeks before I could fight again. Anxious to learn if Laurent had survived what must have been a terrible battle, I volunteered to ride to Auerstedt and confirm it. General Lannes proposed that I be sent and praised my heroism and my horsemanship, and the Emperor, who owed him his victory, acquiesced.

I found General Davout's weary but elated troops bivouacked on the field of battle and celebrating their victory. Contrary to his reputation as a stern disciplinarian, the General, seeing I was wounded, told me to remain with him for a day or two and get some rest, and sent another messenger to Napoleon to let him know I had arrived and the news of his success at Auerstedt was one hundred percent true. I went in search of Laurent, and, stopping at the first campfire I came to, inquired as to his whereabouts. Did they know where I might find infantryman Laurent Pavot?

"Why celebrating, of course!" And where exactly might that be? "In his tent. Where else?" they answered, laughing, and told me how to get to it. A few paces from his tent, I called out his name, and he recognized my voice. "Gérard?" I entered the tent and found him lying on his stomach under a blanket, and, on top of him, Thibaud, who had reached Auerstedt on the eve of the battle. I felt no jealousy and understood at once why he had felt none over my relationship with Lucie.

Thibaud invited me to join them. I did not hesitate, but I had to be helped out of my uniform. "You've been wounded!" Laurent exclaimed.

"A scratch," I replied, "thanks to which I get to spend two whole days with you, though I fear I may not be able to perform with the vigor you are accustomed to."

They had me lie on my back and went down on me together, my first experience of having two men service me at once, Thibaud greedily sucking my cock while Laurent's mouth seemed to be everywhere at once—my lips, my neck, my nipples, my belly, my balls and my thighs—rushing about like the bride's mother at a wedding. He could hardly wait to feel me inside him again, and we obliged, Thibaud and I filling his ass and mouth in turn. We changed places repeatedly; the dear boy was in ecstasy. Nor did Thibaud and I neglect each other. I had not seen him without a shirt since he'd been wounded. His chest heavily scarred was not a pretty sight, but the patterns fascinated me, and I traced the lines with my lips and tongue. He could feel my mouth on them only vaguely, and he expressed the desire to find out for himself exactly what sensations drove Laurent wild. Over five years had gone by since I had last felt a dick in my ass, and I promised Thibaud that if he fucked me first, I would return the favor.

Laurent sat cross-legged beside us and played with himself while he watched. Thibaud lifted my legs and entered me easily. His French dick was no match for Akmoud's Egyptian engine, but I was glad to have him in me, and he knew how to fuck a man, having practiced the art on Laurent on numerous occasions. When it came his turn to bottom, Thibaud said that the pleasure far exceeded his expectations. I knew he would be tight, and I entered him slowly, waiting until I had reduced him to moans before I went at him full throttle.

We had thought the merrymaking outside would drown out our sex noises, but we emerged from the tent two hours later to the applause of their fellow soldiers who had seated themselves in a semicircle in front. We slept on our sides one behind the other that night, Laurent always in front and Thibaud and I switching places to have a turn at him and at each other. In the morning we lay sucking in a head-to-crotch triangle till lunchtime.

THE Emperor arrived in Auerstedt before I had left. Despite their exhaustion, he wanted Davout and his troops to accompany him to Berlin in reward for their valor. My playtime with Laurent and Thibaud cut short, I returned to Jena, where I discovered that I had been transferred to the cavalry and made a commandant on General Lanne's recommendation. As the General did not wish to pass over his own men in replacing the commandant who had fallen at Jena, I was assigned to Marshal Mortier, who was less than pleased to find himself saddled with a new officer who had no idea how to lead a cavalry charge, though since I would be in no condition to assume my duties for some weeks, he would have time to train me. Those few weeks were not enough, as we discovered four months later at Eylau. When we made our first charge, a bullet struck my right shoulder and toppled me from my mount. It fell on top of me, breaking my leg and pinning me beneath it, and I spent the rest of the battle lying on the ground.

Although I had made a complete botch of it and much to Mortier's disgust, the Emperor saw my name on the list of wounded and remembered the lavish praise Lanne had bestowed on me and that he had recently promoted me for heroism, and he made me a colonel. No doubt he was distracted; no one would call our victory at Eylau brilliant. I suspect he had forgotten that I was only a commandant, and he needed someone to replace Colonel Chabert, who was killed that day. (I am convinced that the man who showed up several years later in Paris with the intention of passing himself off as Hyacinthe Chabert was a fraud.)

Chapter 6

By THE beginning of May I was well enough to travel, and I returned to Paris slowly, via Vienna, arriving two weeks before Laurent and Thibaud, who remained in Poland until the Tsar had signed the Treaty of Tilsit. The reasons for my detour were many. Austria had not joined the most recent Coalition; we were nominally at peace with her, and I wanted to see the lands that would one day compose the French Empire, and most particularly Vienna, for I knew from having worked in Napoleon's military bureaucracy that he considered the Danube central to his eventual conquest of the European heartland. Furthermore, I had learned from Berthe that Jeanne lived there. I was quite certain that she would not remember me, and though no friend of Napoleon, she would receive a colonel of the *Grande Armée* who was acquainted with her sister and could give news of her. It was not unlikely she would offer me hospitality. Most of the higher ranks in Napoleon's army came from the upper class, and she would not discover I had been her father's gardener until after my departure. I relished the slap in the face to Julien's family.

Finding her took me a day and a half. My inquiries about the *Vicomtesse de Vigneulles-Hâtonchâtel* were met with total incomprehension. Even those I asked who spoke passable French were unable to make the connection between that name and *die Gräfin von "Fick-Noyless"*, which left me little doubt that it would give her untold pleasure to hear the French language spoken with a faint trace of the regional accent she had known as a girl.

She received me graciously and asked how recently I had arrived in Vienna and how long I intended to stay, addressing me as *Monsieur le colonel* or *Monsieur de Vreilhac*, though I had not ennobled my family with a "de" when her major-domo announced me. As I had only visited the Hotel L'Envol once since their return to Paris, I had to rely on what Lucie had told me and freely invent the rest. It did not take long to realize that the *Gräfin von Fick-Noyless* would take me for a member of her sister's intimate circle of friends if I looked down my nose at the Baron.

"The Baron has petitioned several times for the return of the Hotel L'Envol. Unfortunately for your sister, I don't think he'll succeed. The Baron remains a merchant at heart, and he did not do well in Holland. He has little to offer the Emperor in return for such a favor."

"Yes, my sister writes that they are living on one floor of a residence and haven't much room for themselves."

"The house they live in is nice enough and in a good neighborhood. Except for the lack of space, I don't believe they're uncomfortable there. Still, it isn't what she's used to. But you, Vicomtesse, have you not thought of petitioning for your chateau? I believe the Emperor would receive it favorably."

"Oh, I'm well enough off here. I'm a widow, you know, and I don't suppose many of my old friends have returned to Lorraine. I should be quite lonely there."

"But for your children's sake, surely…?"

"Napoleon would not hesitate to return our estates and title to Sebastien if he approached him, but as *Vicomte de Vigneulles-Hâtonchâtel* he would have to join his army, and his allegiance, I'm afraid, is to Austria. As for Annette, her husband is no more inclined to fight for Napoleon than Sebastien. But she has married well. A property in France is of little interest to her husband."

"But you, *Vicomtesse*. You could sell it and use the money to buy a hotel in Paris, or stay here and live on the income from the estate." I mistakenly assumed the prospect of humbling herself before Napoleon held her back.

"I have thought about it, of course, but from what I hear, life in Paris is far less agreeable than in Vienna, and I assure you I am well provided for. The Emperor Franz granted me a most generous pension in recognition of my late husband's service to Austria."

Indeed, Jeanne did appear to live more comfortably than Berthe, and from what I had seen of Vienna, its streets were cleaner and wider than ours.

I stayed on as her guest for ten days. She invited her children, now well into their twenties and married to Austrians, to dine with us in my honor. They spoke German among themselves and execrable French to me. Sebastian von Fick-Noyless (he now spelled and pronounced his Christian name with an *a*) wore the uniform of the Austrian Army. He struck me as spoiled and effete, and I estimated it was lack of ambition, not pride or loyalty to Austria, that kept him from reclaiming his chateau in Lorraine. Of course I took care not to praise Napoleon too highly. Truth be told, being a republican at heart and one who saw no reason for the French to own all of Europe, I was of two minds about our Emperor. Despite that, I could not help but feel devoted to him—the man inspired absolute devotion—and joined in the cheering whenever I saw him.

When I left Vienna, the *Vicomtesse* gave me miniature portraits of herself and her children as a present for her sister in Paris. I called on Berthe soon after my return. Lucie came to the door, and her jaw dropped open at the sight of me in my colonel's uniform. She exclaimed, "Oh, Monsieur Gérard!—*Monsieur le colonel*, I should say—I don't imagine you will take notice any more of a mere lady's maid such as myself."

"Nonsense, dear Lucie. My new rank has not turned my head. I shall go on living with my old friends Adrienne and Thibaud and shall continue to see you on your afternoons off. I have no desire to frequent the salon of the Baroness de l'Envol and rub elbows with the highest society." Although Lucie was painfully aware that her mistress no longer enjoyed the status and esteem she had had before the Revolution, my sarcasm went straight over her head. "My only purpose in coming here is to convey to her the greetings of her sister, Madame de Vigneulles-Hâtonchâtel, whom I saw during my stay in Vienna."

I HAD not had sex since my threesome with Laurent and Thibaud. As a colonel in Napoleon's *Grande Armée*, I would have been ill-advised to solicit men for sex in the back streets of Vienna. However, until my friends returned I freely indulged my taste for other males in the streets of Paris. I would rent a room above a restaurant for the afternoon, change my outfit so as not to call attention to myself, and go out and prowl.

In two short weeks they were back. Laurent resumed his place in my bed, and Thibaud in Adrienne's, who was none the wiser as to how we had spent our day-and-a-half-long reunion in Auerstedt. I collected a colonel's salary, over twenty times more than what Thibaud's printing business brought in every month, and I insisted on paying for Laurent's room and board as well as my own. Neither of my friends received a penny from the Army except on active duty. I did not have to work and was free as a bird, but I seldom went out on my own, preferring to spend my time at the print shop. With Laurent back in Paris I had all the sex I needed and more.

For the sake of my lover's reputation, I advised him to follow my example and find himself an in-name-only mistress. This was no easy matter. Laurent's boyishness aroused a woman's motherly instincts, but they sensed instinctively that a eunuch would do as well as a potential husband. I asked Lucie to find a chaste partner for my best friend (I explained he was very shy) so we could go out as two couples together, and she introduced him to Valérie.

Valérie was a petite, very feminine brunette, and quite as shy as Laurent, though anyone could see he attracted her. She would gaze lovingly at him and on our strolls would hold his arm with both hands. She was the youngest of us four (Lucie was the oldest) and, I suspect, was too naïve to sense his lack of physical interest. On the whole we made a singularly ill-matched foursome. A *fantassin* in the company of two simply dressed girls was a common enough sight. True, the Emperor had begun his military career in the artillery and ever since Toulon his brilliant positioning of artillery had probably played a more decisive role in his victories than any other aspect of his strategy, but in spite of that most people looked on cavalrymen as the most romantic part of any army, and I wore a colonel's uniform. So although people turned to look at us, they accepted our association as understandable, if unusual, because the ladies were pretty.

OUR stay in Paris lasted almost two years. The war in Spain dragged on, but the Continental System had given us an alternative to warfare as a way to deal with Great Britain. We countered their blockade by imposing a trade embargo to isolate them from the rest of Europe. I thoroughly approved of this strategy and hoped we had seen the last of the fighting. England, however, did not; Austria had grown tired of licking her wounds, and the Emperor suspected she would soon seek to avenge the shameful defeats we had inflicted on her. In the Confederation of the Rhine we already had a significant force in Bavaria under Marshal Berthier. Fearing that Austria planned to take back Italy, Napoleon concluded that the inevitable confrontation would center on the Danube and set about mobilizing the rest of the Army. This caught us unprepared, because they launched their attack on Bavaria, and earlier than he had supposed. Berthier proved himself an incompetent commander, and we entered the war at a disadvantage. Fortunately, we only had to fight the Austrians.

Marshal Mortier categorically refused to have a Cavalry Colonel as unfit as I serving under him. I requested to be assigned to Davout along with Laurent and Thibaud. In his ignorance, the General accepted me, and the three of us left for Bavaria via Strasbourg, falling in en route with some ten thousand other men heading for different divisions in the Rhineland. In Strasbourg we learned that Davout had fallen back on Regensburg. Our armies had to shift position repeatedly, so our soldiers were ever on the move, marching this way and that for no apparent reason. We could not count on halting in towns where we could find lodgings for the night beyond Strasbourg, so we purchased a small tent for the three of us. We had to squeeze into it, but we didn't mind pressing up against each other—or into each other, for that matter.

When we reached Ingolstadt, we heard that Davout had abandoned Regensburg and was moving south toward Neustadt. We met up with him in Ratisbon the same day, two days before the tide turned in our favor on the twenty-second of April at the Battle of Eckmühl.

We were in heavily forested and very hilly country, which led the Emperor to misjudge the disposition of the enemy forces. He transferred over half of General Davout's Third Corps, Laurent and Thibaud among them, to support General Lannes, who he imagined would engage the main body of the Austrian Army. As it turned out, it was our depleted divisions that faced them. Luckily, he realized his error and sent reinforcements, who arrived in the nick of time.

We managed to capture the bridge and Eckmühl castle, after which the main attack was entrusted to the cavalry. We were ordered to charge the enemy artillery under heavy fire, and in the end our cavalry did reach them with drawn sabers and slaughtered their gunners. I, however, did not get that far. My showing at Eckmühl was identical to how I had performed at Eylau. I had neglected to train for the cavalry during my three years in Paris, and the men in my command had no respect for me. My horse was shot out from under me in the first hour of the engagement, and I again found myself pinned beneath it and the same leg broken and a dislocated elbow. I fell with my left arm extended, and as my own troops galloped past, one of their horses trod on it, crushing my wrist. I lay there until the following day, when after the battle Thibaud found me unconscious and had me carried to the hospital tent. They splinted my fractures and put me in a wagon, where I was bounced up and down in excruciating pain for two days until we reached the hospital in Ulm. My years of war had come to an end, but it would be another six years before my country was finally at peace. In fact, I would not see Laurent again until after Napoleon's ignominious retreat from Moscow.

I was still in hospital when we won the Battle of Wagram, and I remained in Ulm until after the Treaty of Schönbrunn in mid-autumn. I had had no news of my friends since Eckmühl, nor had I been conscious when Thibaud found me, nor had I woken up until after he left me with the surgeons. It was they who told me who had saved me. I hoped that he and Laurent had survived and we would see each other in Paris, but they remained with the Army, for Napoleon had set his eye on Russia, because the Tsar showed little enthusiasm for our Continental System and cooperated minimally.

IT WAS a bitter disappointment not to find my friends in Paris, but at least I knew they were alive. Adrienne and her daughter, now twelve years old, lived alone in the same house. She had sold Thibaud's press, dismissed her workers, and closed the shop, the demand for printers having diminished to almost nothing. For the moment she was living on the money she had got for the press, but she would soon have to find another source of income. I presented myself at the War Ministry and resigned my commission after collecting my accumulated salary, a very substantial sum, and put off seeking employment for the time being.

I took up with Lucie again, only now when we went out I had four women in my entourage—Lucie, Valérie, Adrienne and Lisette. I continued to wear my uniforms on such occasions and must have cut a very dashing figure indeed. But at thirty-six I was very much in my prime, and my desire for sex was as keen as ever. Laurent and Thibaud had each other, and I had a city full of men to choose from. Of course I dressed in my civilian clothes when I went out to hunt for one. At first I enjoyed as many as I could, whenever I could. The sight of a good-looking man inevitably whetted my curiosity to see him naked. I had felt no such curiosity during my military training or with the soldiers in my regiment. I would give them no more than a cursory glance when they undressed, as most men do, and once I had seen one of them I did not feel the need to look again. This was different. It was not just their penises that interested me, but a passion for the male physique in its entirety. I thought it the most beautiful thing in the world, and I still do. I do not mean to imply that getting them out of their clothing satisfied me. I made my evenings a veritable feast of cocksucking and butt-fucking. Adrienne was the only member of my little harem who knew of my debaucheries, which went on uninterrupted for nearly a year.

The public at large, however, used to seeing me in the company of four unattached women, took me for a ladies' man. (At forty, Lucie would have been considered an old maid, but she looked and dressed much younger.) I daresay my sexual partners, all of them male, thought I was a Lothario as well as a sodomite. It's a fairly common phenomenon. Eventually my number of female companions increased to five, for I ran into Sandrine, who had not given up her hopeless love for me. She may even have heard about me and tracked me down; I had become a bit of a celebrity. This caused more than a little friction, because she and Lucie saw each other as rivals. Sandrine's persistence put me in an uncomfortable position. Lucie, hitherto content simply to go out with me once or twice a week, followed her example, and the two women became an annoyance. Since Adrienne was her friend, Lucie expected she would side with her, but Adrienne realized the futility of both their positions and kept out of it. On the other hand,

Sandrine got on well with Valérie, who worked for a seamstress and had ambitions of opening a shop of her own one day.

I BECAME a little less promiscuous after I met Stéphane Chambron. He noticed me from his seat in the corner of a wine bar where I often went to pick up men. He caught my eye, raised his glass, and with a glance invited me to join him at his table. He was about ten years my senior and seemed a well-to-do, respectable gentleman, not at all the kind of person you'd expect to find in those surroundings. He told me he was "slumming", which he sometimes did, though he rarely invited anyone to go home with him, fearing he might have taken up with a thief, a blackmailer, or worse. He recognized me from having seen me in my officer's uniform escorting a bevy of well but modestly dressed young ladies and felt he could trust me, so he invited me home with him. Although he attracted me less than many other men there, I accepted, perhaps because his words reminded me that I often had been less cautious than I ought to.

Stéphane lived a fair distance from the wine bar, in the Faubourg Saint-Antoine, so we walked to the Quai des Augustins and found a fiacre to take us to his lodgings. When he asked if he should have the driver wait an hour so I'd have a coach to bring me home, I told him that the night was mild and I'd rather walk. I foresaw that our activities would not provide the stimulation to which I was accustomed and thought I had a good chance of meeting a more satisfactory playmate if I returned on foot.

I realized that I had fallen in with a man of wealth the instant I entered Stéphane's drawing room. His first-floor apartments were spacious and tastefully appointed with furniture imported from Italy, Austria and England. Many fine paintings hung on his walls, and expensive curios lined the shelves. "Since we didn't ask the driver to wait, we've no need to hurry," he said. "Why don't we take some time to get to know one another before we proceed to... to your reason for coming here?" he added after a moment's hesitation. He offered me cognac and sweet biscuits, and we chatted amiably for about half an hour before turning to the business at hand, which we took care of in the drawing room. He did not invite me into his bedroom. As I had anticipated, Stéphane was not the most exciting partner. He had a below-average endowment and an above-average paunch, and the thought of anal intercourse disgusted him; we limited our activities to mutual masturbation and sucking cock. In other ways, however, we got along splendidly, and I continued to see him, only seeking out other men when I felt an overwhelming urge to fuck or be fucked. I thought of the risks I had been running, both of disease and discovery, we enjoyed each other's company, and having fewer partners made me feel less guilty about Laurent, who I hoped would come back to me in the near future. The Tsar would not attack our armies unprovoked, and Napoleon evidently felt that controlling Poland provided sufficient containment of that vast nation. As far as I know, Stéphane had no partners besides me after our first time together.

In time he asked to meet my harem. He enjoyed the company of women everywhere but in his bed, and he feared his employees had grown suspicious of his sexual tastes. For the sake of his image he wanted them to think he had a mistress. When I finally introduced them, my lady friends thought him charming. Sandrine and Lucie in particular were relieved to discover that I had been spending my time away from them with a male friend. I told Stéphane and we laughed at their foolishness. Not that we only met to have sex; sex made up a relatively small part of our relationship. We dined together regularly. We played chess and talked politics. I confided in him that my harem was only for show, that I was intimately involved with none of them, and he replied he suspected as much. Many men who had the same tastes as we used their friendship with a woman to keep their preferences secret. He, too, had once had an in-name-only mistress whom he saw as little as possible until she got tired of waiting for him to propose and sent him packing. For my part, I complained that I needed time away from the women who monopolized the greater part of my life. I was spending far too much time with the fair sex and missed the company of other men. Stéphane, who had numerous connections in the business world and a good deal of money as well, obligingly found me an adequately paid position as head clerk in a bank. To Lucie's relief, I began to lead a more regular life. She had feared that I was seeing Sandrine while she was fulfilling her duties at the de l'Envols' and may have suspected we were sleeping together.

Stéphane soon proved himself useful in other ways, and again Lucie saw herself as his chief beneficiary. Her career as lady's maid came to an end a few months after I had introduced them. The Baron de l'Envol died in 1811 on Christmas Eve, and his widow was free to realize her girlhood dream of entering a convent. Berthe did not lift a finger to secure positions for her servants in the households of her acquaintances. She gave them a modest sum as a parting gift and said she would leave the rest of her property to the Church, so Lucie found herself unemployed and with no place to live. Naturally, she turned to me, and I turned to Stéphane. He owned three or four houses in Paris where people rented rooms, and made her head concierge. She would have her own lodgings in the nicest of them and have no work to speak of; she had only to make sure that the concierges under her kept the buildings clean and in good repair. He had offered the same job to Adrienne a couple of months earlier, but she did not want to give up her house. "I'd sooner take in washing," she declared, and by the time the Emperor abdicated, she had.

For now Adrienne was hoping for her husband's return, much as I yearned for Laurent's, but I was less optimistic. "Napoleon controls all of Europe," she argued. "Surely the *Grande Armée* has served its purpose. What's left for him to conquer?" But in the spring Russia withdrew from the Continental System, and the Emperor made up his mind to invade, confident of crushing the Tsar's Army as swiftly as he had defeated Prussia and Austria. They were poorly armed and had only one-third the manpower we did, and he had made careful preparations. Thibaud wrote that he would soon see Moscow. Something Laurent had once said came back to me: "The Austrians meet us head on, and we crush them every time. The Russian generals have more sense. When they see we have the advantage, they withdraw. It isn't that they're cowards. They retreat; they don't run away like the Prussians."

When Napoleon crossed the Niemen River into Russia's Polish territories on the twenty-fourth of June, no one anticipated that it would result in the near-destruction of his entire Army.

Chapter 7

AT FIRST the news was more than encouraging; it was excellent. Our forces advanced quickly into the interior of Russia. The great Battle of Borodino ended in a stalemate, but when it was over General Kutuzov withdrew his troops, leaving Moscow undefended. Thibaud wrote us an ecstatic letter from the Russian capital dated 14 September, the day our troops entered Moscow. It told of golden domes reflecting the sunlight, stately pastel palaces, and an unearthly quiet in the streets. It was the last letter we received. No one we knew with a relative in our Army in Moscow heard anything. Wild rumors began to circulate in Paris.

In November news reached us that our troops had withdrawn from Moscow, and two weeks later that apparently the *Grand Armée* would leave Russia altogether. Nobody could guess what it all meant. Surely we had won the war, since we had taken Moscow, but we heard nothing about a peace treaty or a Russian surrender. Then, at the beginning of January the Emperor returned to France alone, clearly dissatisfied with the results of his expedition, and in early spring the first starving, frost-bitten remnants of his once proud Army staggered into Paris. Laurent and Thibaud were not among them. Those who had survived the Russian invasion told stories of harassment on the part of the Austrians, of massive desertions among our Prussian and German troops, and of tens of thousands of French soldiers who perished on their way home.

We had no news until the beginning of summer, when we received a letter from Laurent, who never wrote. He had managed to get as far as Pilsen, but he was suffering from pneumonia and could go no farther. He had nowhere to stay and could not afford to buy medicine. He barely had enough money for food. He begged us to send some before he starved to death. His letter made no mention of Thibaud. I immediately procured a horse and set out to bring him back to Paris. I told Stéphane where I was going. Knowing that Laurent was the love of my life, he gave me twenty gold napoleons from his purse. I stopped along the road only to eat a hasty meal or catch a few hours' sleep. My horse collapsed a few leagues before I reached Nürnberg, and I made the rest of the journey by coach.

After much searching, I found Laurent lying on the straw under a horse blanket in the stables behind an inn. He was dressed in rags and burning with fever, delirious and coughing up blood. I demanded the innkeeper give us his best room, paying a week in advance, and had him light a fire in the stove and heat a basin of water while I carried Laurent upstairs and put him to bed. Then I had him bring a steaming bowl of beef broth and sent him for a doctor. I cut Laurent's tattered uniform his body and burned it in the stove, and then sponged him with water from the basin. I wept when I saw his body. He was so emaciated you could count every rib; his skin covered with eczema; the hair of his groin crawling with lice; the blisters on the soles of his feet had become oozing sores, and he had lost three toes to frostbite; but to my tear-filled eyes he was the most beautiful man in the world. While I was washing him, he woke, recognized me, and smiled weakly. His gums had receded and a few of his teeth were rotten. Then he began to cry. He said he was happy to see me once again before he died. I promised I would make him better, but I had little faith I could.

At last the doctor arrived. He said there was still hope and prescribed a small fortune's worth of medicines. He said the beef broth was good, also eggs, warm milk, and stewed fruit. I got Laurent to swallow half the broth. I asked the innkeeper for strong lye soap and sent him to find some clothes to cover my friend. When he left, I scrubbed Laurent's scalp and pubic hair. I briefly fondled his penis to reassure him all was well, but it stayed as limp as an eel when you've chopped off its head. Then he took another sip or two of broth and fell asleep while I kept watch in a chair by his bedside.

I awoke in the middle of the night, sensing something had gone wrong. Laurent had been seized by a violent fit of trembling. I undressed, crawled into bed beside him, and held him in my arms to keep him warm.

The fever had not abated the next morning, but he felt calmer. He wanted to tell me about the retreat from Moscow. "That can wait until you're better," I said.

"Thibaud's dead."

"I know. You can give me the details later. In the meantime I'll write to Adrienne and let her know, and that I found you and am nursing you back to health."

It took all summer before Laurent was well again. We waited a month until his gums healed and he could eat solid food. The sores on his feet closed over, the eczema went away, and he put on some weight, but his cough persisted. It had gradually abated and he no longer spat blood, but he had frequent relapses that shook his frame and left him exhausted. For the rest of his life his breathing was labored. He was anxious to get home and asked how much longer we would stay in Pilsen. "When you're strong enough to make love again," I answered.

My money ran low, and I wrote Stéphane to send what he could spare. He responded with a letter instructing his banker in Prague to allow me to withdraw whatever sum I wanted from his account. Stéphane had a bank account in Prague? Did he have other accounts in other cities? How rich was he? He dressed simply and his apartments were not ostentatious. Who was this man, and how far did his financial network extend?

I left Laurent in the care of the innkeeper for two days and returned with a letter from the bank in Prague promising their branch in Pilsen to make good on any amount I withdrew. My seemingly inexhaustible flow of cash amazed Laurent. I told him about Stéphane, assuring him he had no cause to be jealous. "Jealous of Stéphane?" he replied. "Why, the man is our savior."

Little by little I learned the story of the retreat from Moscow. Remembering the horror of those days upset him, and I would not let him tell me all at once. "Now let's talk about the good times," I'd say, "like our stay in Saint-Lazare." He'd laugh, and we'd reminisce about the happy days we lived together in Paris and our nights of passion.

Moscow had never formally surrendered. Any other nation would have made peace after we took Smolensk, yet the Tsar ignored every overture Napoleon made to negotiate, and now we occupied the capital. Yet they had no allies to speak of: the British were on the other side of the continent, the Austrian Emperor had married his daughter to Napoleon, and Prussia and Saxony had also become our allies.

"It was a crazy situation," Laurent said, "unprecedented." Nearly three-quarters of Moscow's inhabitants had fled the city. Only the very poor, foreigners, brigands and lunatics remained within its walls, and only because they had nowhere to go. Fires broke out and looting was rampant. They had come all that way for nothing.

The return (or withdrawal—they didn't call it a retreat at first) began well, but the troops fell into disarray after the Russian Army attacked them at Vyazma, and from then on it was more of a rout than an orderly retreat. The Russian winter set in early, and they lacked warm clothing to keep out the bitter cold. It was nearly impossible to find food. They ate grass, carrion, and the leather of their boots. The Russian Army had burned everything in its path on its retreat beyond Moscow, leaving nothing but scorched fields and abandoned farms. Laurent's eyes widened in amazement as if he saw the devastation in front of him. "Who would have imagined that a nation would destroy itself sooner than surrender," he exclaimed, "like a scorpion that stings itself to death! I tell you, Russians are a different breed!"

Thibaud had died on the road along the Dnieper River. His limp had grown worse in the snow and ice till he could no longer walk without leaning on Laurent's shoulder. The Cossacks harried them, keeping their distance when they returned fire, and picked off those who lagged behind. Finally, Thibaud could go no farther. He sat on the ground and wouldn't budge, telling Laurent to go on without him. Laurent refused to leave. The other men in their unit would not wait. They argued for hours, until they could no longer keep their eyes open. In the middle of the night, the sound of a musket discharging woke Laurent. "Cossacks!" he thought. But there were no hoof beats. Thibaud had dragged himself a few yards away and shot himself in the head. Laurent snapped his bayonet trying to dig a hole in the frozen ground to bury him. When morning came, he took his boots, coat, scarf, gloves and ammunition, and left him to the wolves. He made me promise not to tell Adrienne. As if I would have otherwise!

Laurent made the rest of his journey alone. He might fall in with a group of stragglers for a few days, but if they came to an abandoned farm or burnt-out village, he would stay there and rest for a day and leave the others to plod on. He instinctively knew how to conserve his strength. He taught himself to make a hollow in a snow bank to sleep for the night. He forded or swam across half-frozen rivers. He lived by scavenging on the dead. (I dared not ask if he had tasted human flesh.) This weak, effeminate, boy-like man had a will of iron; this man who had served six years in the infantry, never promoted, never recognized for heroism, had succeeded unaided where thousands had failed; this man whom, when I held him in my arms, I felt I could crush like a flower, the rigors of the Russian winter could not crush, nor the pangs of starvation, nor a thousand weary miles on foot. Knowing what he had endured, I thought back on the night I had sponged his broken body, and realized he had come through it all virtually unscathed.

Somehow he lost his way and ended up to the south of the retreating army, which may have been to his advantage since our so-called allies turned on us in our defeat, and had he been part of a regiment they might have been attacked. On the other hand, the terrain was less flat and more wooded. His road became easier when he passed into Moravia. People there took pity on him and would give him a crust of bread or even a bowl of soup, but he had already worn himself out. When he arrived in Pilsen he was deathly ill and his strength had just about given out. He had the good sense to stay there and write us for help.

Not surprisingly, Laurent thought our defeat total and permanent, but Napoleon did not. He mustered troops and went on the offensive to preserve his crumbling European Empire, and in late August he scored a major victory in Dresden. Our innkeeper brought us the news and then stood by eyeing us coldly as if he expected us to call for champagne to celebrate.

"Do you think we came here to hang banners from your windows when Bonaparte marches into Pilsen?" I asked. "Or maybe you think we've hidden a regiment under the bed. We haven't. See for yourself."

The innkeeper left, annoyed by my sarcasm and at the same time relieved that we, at least, had no designs on his country.

"So France isn't dead yet," Laurent said, his eyes glowing.

"No. None of our enemies want to annex us," I answered dryly.

We would keep France, but I knew we could not hold on to the rest of Europe. Our enemies knew now that Napoleon was not invincible. More importantly, our troops knew it, too.

LAURENT'S interest in sex had begun to return. He nuzzled up to me at night and gave and asked for caresses. He became more responsive. He played with my penis and got an erection when I fondled his. We used our mouths, too. When he asked when I would fuck him again, I answered, "The night before we leave."

He became more insistent, and the first week of October I gave in. I took him very gently and did not try to hold back my orgasm to make it last longer, thinking him weaker than he was. The next day I began to make arrangements for our return to Paris. We would travel by coach, in easy stages, and dress like noblemen so people would take us for *émigrés* returning from exile. We crossed Germany followed by the slower-moving French forces as the advancing armies of the Sixth Coalition pushed them inexorably back toward France. We arrived at the end of the month. At the end of January the warring armies crossed the French border, the border we'd had before Napoleon became Emperor.

Adrienne had taken in lodgers. She did their laundry, cooked their meals, and cleaned their rooms once a week. She had taken Lisette into her own room, but she had saved ours, and she would not accept payment for it, knowing I owed Stéphane a large amount of money, though I had not lost my job at the bank. In return, we undertook to do some sorely needed repairs on her house.

I introduced Laurent to Stéphane. Laurent thanked him—we both thanked him—and they shook hands. As we were leaving, Stéphane whispered to me, "He's lovely. Treat him well, and be happy. He's all yours now; there's nothing that can take him away from you. The Empire is struggling to catch its last breaths."

As usual, Stéphane was right. The Russians entered Paris the last day of March. Soon soldiers from all nations flooded the capital. The Emperor abdicated a week later, and our former King's younger brother returned to France as Louis XVIII and took up residence in the Tuileries. We were once again a monarchy. The King promised us a new constitution but would not honor our old one, which he ripped in half standing in front of the Senate. He promised that those who had owned property confiscated by the Revolution would be compensated for their losses.

On 13 April Napoleon went into exile.

THE next ten months slipped by in relative calm. How could they have seemed otherwise after two decades of almost uninterrupted warfare?

However, the calm masked an uncertainty that agitated every French heart. The Congress of Vienna set to work redrawing the map of Europe, which Napoleon had turned into a hodgepodge of republics, duchies, principalities, confederations and God knows what else. France's pre-Revolution boundaries would be left intact, no doubt as a favor to the new King. That allayed our fears somewhat. On the other hand, every French citizen was of two minds with regard to our current situation. We had had enough of war and were glad that was over, but some longed for the Republic, others the Empire, the proposed constitution displeased the constitutional monarchists, and the royalists rejected the idea of a constitution altogether. Nobody was satisfied, and all regretted our past glory.

None of this uncertainty perturbed Stéphane. "I learned long ago not to put all my eggs in one basket and to let history take its course," he told me. "Nothing we do can change it." He explained that since the end of the Terror he had made a fortune lending money to both sides, little by little founding banking establishments in every country in Europe, including England and Russia, which meant his financial empire covered a larger area than Napoleon's at the height of his power. "And I'm careful not to call attention to myself," he said. "That would be fatal. One must operate behind the scenes to stay out of danger. Besides, I have simple tastes. I never cared much for luxuries. Give me good friends, quiet times and the basic comforts, and I'm content."

Good friends, Stéphane said. When we went out now it was always in a group of eight: myself, Laurent, Stéphane, Adrienne, Lisette, Lucie, Valérie and Sandrine. One day Stéphane proposed an excursion in the country. I suggested Le Bresson. Everyone was pleased with the honest fare and the attractive setting, and we made it a tradition to dine there once a week for as long as the weather held.

I was convinced—we were all convinced—that after twenty years of near-constant warfare that had followed upon the heels of the Revolution we would have a lasting peace; we could ask for nothing better. It was a noble experiment, I thought, our Revolution, whose day would surely come in time, and if I didn't live to see it, so be it. It made me happy that my days of separation from Laurent had reached an end, and I counted my blessings—or thought I did. During that all-too-brief interlude I took our time together for granted, and though I loved him as much as ever, we lived our love less intensely than when the wars had kept us apart. We had been lovers for almost twenty years, but had lived as a couple for less than five. Sometimes I wondered what would happen if Julien returned to Paris. I couldn't imagine I loved anybody more than Laurent, but what if I still loved Julien without realizing it? That kind of soul-searching didn't bother Laurent.

NEWS of the growing dissatisfaction in France reached Napoleon on Elba. A man like him does not accept that his Empire has slipped through his fingers forever; he cannot believe that he has been forgotten by multitudes who used to worship him and they do not long for his return. And in fact, many did; they were prepared to follow him in an instant. He escaped from the island, landed on the coast outside of Antibes, and with a band of a few hundred followers marched over the mountains toward Grenoble. People flocked to join him, and his band swelled to an army. His reputation was unsurpassed, his speeches stirring, and his charisma irresistible. Entire regiments of the King's infantry went over to him, including the royal forces stationed in Lyon. Louis fled Paris, and Napoleon entered the city in triumph at the head of an army some twenty thousand strong less than a month after he left Elba. The Empire was reborn.

Napoleon's swift and stunning return to power took the Allied Nations by surprise. I need hardly say that they distrusted him and expected he would re-embark on his career of conquest if allowed to stay in power. That to stand idly by and allow him to brush aside the conditions of the Treaty of Fontainebleau would seriously diminish their own prestige and encourage him to flout them further was an equally compelling reason to get rid of him once and for all. England, Austria, the Netherlands, the German States, Spain, Italy, Prussia and

Russia united against us. However, Napoleon had caught them unprepared. Feeling secure in their victory, they had disbanded the greater part of their armies, while his seemed to grow from one day to the next. Napoleon saw that his advantage would not last long. He called for a general mobilization, ordering all soldiers who had served in his *Grande Armée* to return to their units, and went on the offensive.

Not every man heeded his call. Most were sick of war, and many sick of him, but by the end of May he had tripled the size of the French army and was able to lead nearly one hundred thirty thousand men north into Belgium to engage the Duke of Wellington's and Field Marshal von Blücher's slightly smaller numbers in the final decisive battle of his career.

Of course I ignored the call. I folded up my colonel's uniform and packed it away at the bottom of a chest. The injuries I had received at Eckmühl, from which I never fully recovered, would have in any case excused me from service, but more than that, I was a staunch republican at heart and the legend of Napoleon Bonaparte had long ceased to enthrall me. I was dismayed when Laurent announced he was determined to go. I cannot say whether he wanted to make good the inglorious ending of his military career and the futile sufferings of his last campaign or if he was dazzled by the Emperor's miraculous resurrection, but there was no dissuading him. I argued with him, pleaded with him, did everything in my power to keep him in Paris, all in vain. Napoleon thought himself invincible, had infinite faith in the loyalty of the French, and openly mocked the courage and fighting abilities of the British and Prussian armies, and Laurent and many others believed him.

I tried to hold on to him till the day he left. I cannot count the number of times I said, "Laurent, I beg you, don't go. Don't risk your life in a crazy venture that can only end in disaster. We will have accomplished nothing even if we win. Nobody will know the difference if you stay in Paris."

"Do you wish to live under a monarchy?" he asked.

"No, but I don't wish to be governed by an emperor either, and most of all, I want to live and I want you to live."

"Does your duty to your country mean nothing to you?"

"France will be better off if she accepts the inevitable. We will remain at war with the rest of Europe as long as Napoleon is in power. The Empire was an empty dream."

We made love the night before he left. (But we made love almost every night.) I wrapped my arms around him when I fucked him and clung to him desperately, as if by so doing I could keep him with me. I bathed his neck and shoulders with my tongue and my tears, and when my orgasm exploded inside him, I felt as if my very life were emptying into his soul.

I withdrew from him and slid off his back beside him onto the mattress. He turned to kiss me. "Why, you're crying," he said. "I'll be back."

I shook my head and bit down painfully on my lips, my shoulders as stiff as the knotted lump in my stomach.

"Silly," he said, and kissed away my tears.

I SHALL not write about a battle I did not witness and about which so many have written. Everyone knows what happened at Waterloo on the eighteenth of June 1815, and men will argue over the necessity of its outcome for as long as the earth endures. Would we have won if he had attacked earlier, if the weather had been clear, if Field Marshal von Blücher had arrived later or not at all? Vain speculation, all of it. The end was inevitable, if not at Waterloo, then elsewhere. But the Battle of Waterloo put an end to more than just Napoleon and his ambitions. Some thirty-five years have passed, and we have not had a war in Europe since. For that I am thankful.

Napoleon returned to Paris three days later hoping to muster more troops, but few rallied to him. The Senate demanded his abdication, and he surrendered to the British. The Allies exiled him to Saint Helena on the other side of the world, and there he died. He lay there in his grave for a quarter-century; then ten years ago they brought his remains back to France. They are now building him a magnificent tomb in the Invalides.

I waited for Laurent to come back to me, knowing in my heart he wouldn't. We had lost close to fifty thousand men. I pored over the list of the dead looking for his name, but I didn't find it. For a while I hoped he might be among the seven thousand taken prisoner, but when their names were made known, his was not among them. To this day some fifteen thousand men remain unaccounted for, and we shall never know how they died, only that they died and where they died. Laurent Pavot is one of those men.

I locked Laurent away in my heart and made myself a solemn vow never to sleep with another man.

PART III:

My Years of Comfort

Chapter 1

WE HAD a new map, and Great Britain emerged as the dominant power, not just in Europe, but in the world. This tiny island now controlled the seas, and her possessions covered the globe from Australia to India to Egypt to North America—a virtual empire. In France, the Restoration of the Monarchy brought with it many changes, and not all of them what we had expected. As promised, we had our constitution, or Charter, as it was called, and the nobility returned. That is, many nobles did, but it was not the same aristocracy we had once known. Neither they nor the King set the social tone for the rest of the country; they followed the lead of the highest ranks of the bourgeoisie. Whereas before the Revolution the richest members of the middle class had sought to find a place among the nobility, their salons were now the most important in Paris, and the returning *émigrés* had to fit into a social structure that had taken hold during their absence. Of course the rich bourgeoisie welcomed them and basked in the prestige of their titles, but they had lost their prerogatives, privileges and also their estates, and the wealthy propertied classes saw themselves as their equals and acted accordingly.

Among the first to return was Olivier de la Motte, Count d'Airelles, and his English wife. Lucie told me he'd come back. She had learned of it quite by chance and had presented herself to the new Countess in the hope she would take her on as a chambermaid, but the lady rebuffed her. Olivier would not intervene on her behalf, a way, Lucie believed, of slighting his sister Berthe. He had come to France to seek compensation for the loss of his chateau, only to learn it had never been confiscated and still belonged to him. Olivier, however, did not want to bury himself away in the country; he wanted to live in Paris and had set his eye on the Hotel L'Envol. Berthe was among the few who had managed to reclaim her property in order to sign it over to the Church, which dashed the Count's dream of securing it for himself. Instead of taking their place at the very pinnacle of society, the de la Mottes found themselves decorative hangers-on in the salons of the lion-hunting bourgeoisie. The news delighted me.

Stéphane grasped the significance of the new social climate and stepped out of the shadows. His business interests demanded that he take his place in the most prestigious salons. With this in mind, he purchased a hotel in one of the finest sections of Paris and turned his thoughts to marriage. Sexually, women left him cold, but he needed one to accompany him on his visits. His other option would have been to enter the Church, which would surely have taken control of his finances; nor did he have any religious convictions. He turned to me for advice. Though he and his wife would not sleep together, he would have to live with her, so compatibility was his primary concern, and after that, finding a woman who could move easily in the highest social circles. He had hit on the idea of proposing to Adrienne.

I thought him unrealistic. "Nobody would take Adrienne for anything other than a working woman," I said. "She would stand out in a salon like an elephant in a herd of goats."

"Indeed, I could not present her to Mesdames Porcigny or Tournedos, but Lisette is young and pretty, and her manners are more than adequate. She would charm everyone, and no one would consider it unusual for a man my age to go about accompanied by his stepdaughter."

Lisette at nineteen was as fair and fresh as a day in summer. Her laughter reminded me of gentle rain on a spring morning, she moved with the grace of an autumn leaf falling from a tree, and her curly hair was as dark as the sky on a winter's night. Her skin seemed to glow with an inner light, and her grey eyes sparkled like jewels behind their long lashes. Passers-by turned their heads to gaze at her. She was so lovely that, despite her full figure, I thought she looked more Laurent's daughter than Thibaud's, though of course the very idea that Laurent might have fathered a child was inconceivable. She would grace the arm of any man in the most fashionable salon in Europe.

"She could go with you whether or not you married her mother," I said.

"People know I'm unmarried. If I went about in the company of a young lady her age, they would think she was my whore."

"But would Adrienne want to marry you? She knows you like men."

"That is, of course, the question. We are good friends, we enjoy each other's company, I can offer her security, a good home, fidelity..."

"Fidelity?"

"I am not a philanderer, and if I ever do want to be with a man... Well, my indiscretions will be irreproachably discreet."

"They always have been. And, mind you, I will not get involved with Adrienne's husband under her very nose even for half an hour." (I did not count Thibaud and me fucking each other at Auerstedt as "under her nose".)

"No, no, of course not," he said.

I had not had sex with Stéphane since I had brought Laurent back to Paris, anyway. I had with others. My needs were more pressing than his, and despite my vow, I had not given up sex altogether. I excused my disloyalty to Laurent's memory on a technicality: a quick blowjob or jack-off did not constitute "sleeping with" someone.

"Adrienne has never asked anyone to support her," I went on. "If she were to marry, I think she would be looking for something else."

"I suppose you're right," he sighed, "but it can't hurt to ask."

To my surprise, Adrienne took his proposal seriously, asked for time to think it over, and accepted. She was not an ambitious woman and cared nothing for the advantages of living in luxury and not having to work. She made it clear that she would go out with him to a restaurant or the theater if Lisette came with them, but she would feel uncomfortable socializing with his rich friends. She would only make a fool of herself, and they would snub them both. If she agreed to marry him, it was for her daughter's sake, so she could marry well and have an easier life than her parents.

Monsieur and Madame Chambron were quietly married in one of the smaller churches in Paris. After a simple ceremony, we celebrated with a luncheon at Le Bresson, our first time there since Laurent had left for Waterloo. Stéphane invited Valérie and Sandrine to join us. Laurent's absence hung like a cloud over what ought to have been a happy affair, and when the owner of the restaurant inquired after him, the women started crying.

It was, I believe, the most unconventional wedding party in history, for after each of us had toasted the bride and groom and made a little speech wishing them health and happiness, Stéphane proposed a toast to our "deeply missed and regretted friend" Laurent, and gave a much longer speech recalling the good times we had had together and asked me and Adrienne also to say a few words about him. Then he raised his glass to Thibaud, whom he had never met, saying that he knew he would never replace him in Adrienne's heart, but he would do his best to make her a good husband. Moreover, instead of us buying presents for the newlyweds, Stéphane, who was many times wealthier than all of us put together, had bought us all fine clothing for the occasion, and announced over lunch that he was giving us gifts in honor of his marriage. One would hardly call them gifts, they were so generous. He had arranged for my promotion to assistant bank manager, although I knew next to nothing about banking. Sandrine and Valérie were ready to open their own dress shop. One of his houses was located on the edge of a part of Paris that was rapidly becoming fashionable, and he was in the process of making improvements to it. The largest apartment had a separate entrance on the street and another into the courtyard. It would make an ideal location for their new business. He would build an inside staircase to the apartment above it so they could live there. Though the building Lucie lived in was very nice, the neighborhood was not. She would move into new lodgings at the back of the courtyard when the workman had finished the repairs. She would be more comfortable there, and safer and less lonely.

THE women had to wait four months until the building was ready, but I assumed my new position at the bank immediately. Most of the additional salary I was to earn in the first month went for new clothes as befitted my higher status. I asked Stéphane if I might wear my colonel's uniform instead, but he said, "Not until you become the director. You should have it altered, though, for you will wear it when you appear in society."

"Am I to frequent the salons, then?"

"Absolutely. Retired army colonels and bank managers are not only welcome there, they are very much in demand. You shall go as my guest, and afterward I assure you you will not lack for invitations."

"But I served under Napoleon!"

"If that made a difference there should be no military men at all in any salon in Paris. It will be a mark in your favor that you did not rejoin him after he escaped from Elba."

"But who on earth will I talk to? And what about?"

"About anything at all except Bonaparte, and take care not to seem too radical. Republican convictions are fine, in moderation. Also, under no circumstances are you to neglect the ladies. They decide who will be received and who will not. Gallantry comes naturally to you; you know how to turn a woman's head. Lucie's and Sandrine's, for example."

I made my entrance into society at a soirée hosted by no less a personage than the Marquise d'Espard. She received me most graciously and pressed my hand warmly when Stéphane told her I was Lisette's godfather, which I was not. Lisette, it appeared, had become quite the darling of more than a few middle-aged society ladies, and a number of the men were likewise very attentive, though as far as I could tell none of them saw her as a possible match. As for finding people to talk to and appropriate subjects of conversation, Oreste Orville, a fellow soldier at the siege of Mantua, recognized me, and Jacob Lavandier, a former corporal in General Lanne's cavalry, remembered my heroism at Jena. They took me under their wing, and before long I felt myself very much at home. I spent most of my salon evenings in conversation with them. A certain Captain Ramballe, a pompous individual who liked to philosophize, often joined us. He had fought as an infantryman in the Russian campaign, but I never asked if he had known my friends Thibaud and Laurent, because he would have bored them as much as he did me.

I had grown up in the shadow of the very highest society—my closest childhood friend had been the son of a Count—and I had lived on its outskirts when there was a high society to live on the outskirts of, so it flattered my ego to be considered one of them. Nevertheless, I enjoyed my quiet evenings with Stéphane, Adrienne and Lisette infinitely more. They were my family. Lucie, Sandrine and Valérie often joined us. Stéphane preferred their company, too. For him, frequenting the salons of the rich was above all a matter of business.

Notwithstanding the pleasant evenings I passed at Stéphane's and having been accepted into a social set far above my wildest dreams, those first months were among the dreariest of my life. I still had the room I had shared with Laurent, and with Adrienne and Lisette gone, I found living there oppressive. It eventually became unbearable, and I asked Stéphane if there might be room for me in the house where Sandrine and Valérie had opened their dress shop.

"God forbid!" he exclaimed. "Better to feel gloomy than to be constantly surrounded by three women who have a crush on you! Yes,

Valérie, too, has fallen under your spell. Your presence there would cause endless squabbles. Find yourself some other place to live, for their peace of mind if not for yours. But now that you've become a habitué of the Paris salons, you should procure yourself a more suitable dwelling."

"I don't have the money to buy one, much less furnish it, nor can I afford servants."

"That shouldn't be a problem. I—"

"Don't say another word. I refuse to accept any more from you than you have already given me. I've taken too much already."

"Do let me finish. I was about to suggest that you apply to the War Ministry for a stipend. After all, you are a colonel."

"Was."

"Precisely. If you were still a colonel, you'd have a salary, not a stipend."

"I can't imagine that—"

"Inquire, and you'll find out. It will add immeasurably to your prestige if you're on their payroll."

"I should feel like a fraud. I didn't earn my rank. Promoting me to colonel—and in the cavalry, no less!—was the stupidest thing Napoleon ever did."

"Stupider than invading Russia?"

"Yes, just not as grave an error. I didn't belong in the cavalry. I had no training and wasn't suited for it."

"You were a good artillery officer."

"Good enough, but even there I owed my promotions to having outlived my commanding officers. And when I think of Laurent, who was a model soldier and went sixteen years without a promotion or a single decoration…"

"But surely you know why."

I assured him I did not.

"Because he had sex with men and didn't hide the fact. I'm surprised no one beat him up. They must have found him an agreeable comrade and respected his courage, but medals and promotions...? Which reminds me, you ought to follow my example and find yourself a wife. As a retired officer, you could more acceptably go on living as a bachelor than I, but it's always to one's advantage to appear in society in the company of a woman. It would also excuse you from the necessity of carrying on an affair." (Almost all men were having affairs, married and single alike.)

"Me? Marry? That would be more dishonest than collecting a colonel's pension!"

"Why? Are you afraid you won't be able to perform?" he asked with a twinkle in his eye. "You used to have sex with women when you were young."

"I haven't in nearly twenty years, but I'm certain I could in a pinch. But you know my natural inclinations favor men."

"I see no reason why you should have to forgo that pleasure. I haven't. Your wife won't think it unusual if you have a mistress. She doesn't have to know she's a man."

STÉPHANE had given me sound advice. The Ministry of War allotted me a lump sum for "services rendered"—services, I supposed, which I had rendered by hardly having served at all, and certainly not in a colonel's capacity, and by having made a very poor showing when I did—and on top of that granted me a modest but very adequate yearly stipend. I used the lump sum to set myself up in a spacious second-floor apartment on the rue de Varenne, which Lisette helped me to furnish like a gentleman.

Stéphane kept pressuring me to marry. I did not take his suggestion seriously, but neither would it go away. I was forty-five years old and did not relish the prospect of living out my last years alone. I had far more space than I needed; even with my manservant, housekeeper and cook, my apartment seemed empty, and I spent as little time there as possible. It had all the comforts one could wish for, but it did not feel homey. What he had said about a wife providing an excuse for me to beg out of an unwelcome liaison made sense, too, and I had always felt pride when I appeared in public with a woman on my arm. My arm, however, was as close as I wanted her to get. And what if I should fall in love again? Ridiculous! It took less than a second to dismiss the possibility that anyone would ever take Laurent's place in my heart. There remained the vow I had made him. Again, I shoved it aside on a technicality: the person I was sleeping with would not be a man.

I went on the prowl that evening to test myself: did I find men really all that indispensible? My adventures of that night remain etched in my memory with the same clarity as my nights of passion with Laurent, Akmoud and Julien.

I went back to the wine bar where I had met Stéphane. The atmosphere was more genteel than I remembered it, and the clientèle younger, but the kind of place it was had not changed. I saw no familiar faces.

One man in particular caught my eye, about half my age, slim, with shoulder-length, wavy auburn hair—a bit of a dandy in a short, light blue frock coat and matching breeches, with a frilly white shirt and bright pink necktie, and a ring with a large pink stone on the index finger of his delicate hand. He wore shiny black leather boots that came halfway up his calf. I saw him in profile as he stood at the counter talking to a much older man whom I took for the owner of the establishment, who must have noticed me and said something, because my dandy turned to face me. He had a charming face: eyes the color of his coat, a cute turned-up nose, lightly rouged lips, and a dimple on his chin. He was quite handsome, though nowhere near as beautiful as Laurent.

He smiled and approached my table, taking his glass with him. "May I sit here?" He sat without waiting for an answer and extended his hand. "Roubaix."

I quickly made up a name for myself. "I don't remember seeing you here before," he said.

"I used to come here frequently. Long ago."

"Long ago?" He laughed. "You make yourself sound like a grandfather."

"Well, it's been over five years."

"I didn't know the place had been in business so long. I mean its current business." He smiled knowingly and pressed his knee against mine under the table. I returned his pressure.

"I'll be waiting in the street," he said, leaving his half-empty glass on the table. "Don't be too long."

I finished my wine and stepped outside. He nodded to me to follow him. He turned into a narrow passage between two buildings and gestured that we should move back into the shadows. When we reached a spot where nobody could see us from the street, he took my hand and placed it over his cock. It was very hard but no bigger than average. "You like?" he asked.

"Not here, not outdoors," I said.

"In your lodgings, then? No, I suppose you're married. They have rooms over the bar you can rent by the hour, but I'm not paying for one."

"That's all right. I'll pay for the room."

"I'll get the key from the proprietor so you won't have to feel embarrassed. Just leave a franc on the counter when you pay for our wine."

"A whole franc for one hour!" I was so startled I didn't notice he'd said "*our* wine".

"As a favor to me… for services rendered. Whenever he asks." In case I hadn't understood, he drew his thumb across his lips and sucked in between his teeth with a sound that suggested a kiss. "The usual price is a franc in addition to the cost of your drinks."

"How is my paying less a favor to you?"

"Men sometimes balk at the price. Don't change your mind. I fancy you. What's a franc to a gentleman like you?"

I nodded my agreement and we went back to bar. The proprietor lit a candle for him and opened the door to the back rooms. I followed him up a dark staircase, which ended at a landing on the third story with four doors giving onto it. He opened one of them and used his candle to light three more, stubs already burnt most of the way down with wine bottles for candlesticks, that sat on a dusty dresser next to a small open jar of lard, a bar of soap, and a ewer of water. The room was not much cleaner than the alley he had led me to, its only other furniture an unmade bed with dirty, rumpled sheets, a chair and a bidet.

"We have a bed," he said, opening my breeches, "so we may as well undress all the way."

"We shan't be using the bed." I was thinking of my vow to Laurent.

"I'll brace myself on it when I bend over. You see, I'm holding nothing back. I fancy you."

He didn't dawdle over the preliminaries. I wouldn't call him businesslike; straightforward, rather. He reached into my breeches, sliding his hand underneath my balls, and pulled out what I had inside. He looked at it appraisingly and said, "God was good to you. I like that. You'll fill me up all the way." He retracted my foreskin. "And clean, too! I'm afraid I'm not, but it won't take long to fix that."

He took off his coat and undressed from the waist down, folded his discarded clothing on the chair, and with total nonchalance emptied the ewer into the bidet and squatted over it to wash. Then he stood up, looked about the room for a towel, and, finding none, dried his backside and privates on the bed sheet. Next he opened the window and poured the water from the bidet into the courtyard below. His shirt and short coat rode up, giving a view of the splendid little round ass I would get to fuck. Finally, he sat in the chair on top of his clothes, beckoned me over, and pulled my breeches down around my ankles. "Let's see how big this thing gets," he said, closing his mouth around my cock.

He did a very good job, and it got very big. He beamed at it and said, "I knew you wouldn't disappoint. I can always tell. This is going to feel wonderful inside me."

He gestured to the pot of lard and leaned over the foot of the bed, holding on to the frame with one hand and hoisting up his shirt with the other. I coated my dick with a dollop of lard and dabbed some more on his hole, slowly working a finger inside.

"Not like that," he said. "Slap my cheeks. Hard. And when you've made them all warm and pink, shove it in all the way without stopping."

The spanking was new to me. I remembered the time Akmoud brought me a stick to cane him because he'd broken the glass. I thought I'd let Roubaix have it as long and hard as I used to do in Egypt but finish in under an hour so I wouldn't have to pay another franc.

When his buttocks had turned bright pink, I put another dab on the outside of his anus and drove my cock into him up to the hilt. He grunted loudly and fell over the bed frame. After ten minutes of pumping, my back started to ache from leaning over him. I pulled him to a standing position and went back to fucking him, reaching around his waist to grab his shaft. It was sticky from the copious amount of precum that had oozed from the tip.

Another ten minutes and he said his legs were about to give out. I flipped him onto his back, raised his legs, and plowed into him. His eyes glazed over and rolled back into his head. I thought he would faint any minute. I exploded inside him. He tightened his anus to milk every drop of my semen.

He staggered to his feet and said, "Whew! You're no grandfather. Nobody's ever fucked me like that before." Then he asked for twenty francs.

"Twenty francs, when I've just given you the time of your life?"

"I don't deny it, but you had fun, too, and you came and I didn't."

"Then I'll suck you off, and we'll be even."

"A blowjob isn't worth twenty francs."

"Neither is a fuck. I'm as good a cocksucker as I am a top. I'll buy you another glass of wine downstairs afterward."

He shrugged and accepted my counteroffer, probably out of curiosity to sample my oral talents. Although I knew now he was a professional, I believe I taught him a thing or two.

I had had more fun fucking Roubaix than with anyone except my long-term lovers. It made me realize what scant and fleeting pleasure I had with the men I picked up when I went out in search of relief and how ungratified it left me. And Roubaix had expected me to pay him. It would happen more and more often as I got older. I made up my mind to marry.

I was not about to go out and scour the salons for a prospective mate. If she hadn't married Stéphane, my most obvious choice would have been Adrienne. She was my closest friend, man or woman, and she knew my sexual tastes. I looked on Lisette as my own daughter. Valérie was still young enough to find a husband who would be a real husband to her. That left Lucie and Sandrine. Sandrine would be more fun in bed (probably more fun than any of them), but that didn't even appear on my list of reasons to get married, and it also meant she would make the most demands on me. Sandrine was prettier; Lucie's hair was turning grey and she had grown stout. On the other hand, I could no more present Sandrine to a duchess than I could Adrienne; in fact, she was less presentable, because Adrienne possessed a natural dignity that Sandrine could never hope to emulate. Lucie had been the Baroness de l'Envol's lady's maid for most of her life, and her bearing was impeccable. Since Berthe seldom entertained, there was little risk anyone would recognize her. She understood titles and had a fairly extensive knowledge of the noblest families in France. She had her roots in the same part of France as I. Sandrine and Valérie were happy running their dress shop and were thick as thieves. Lucie's job as chief concierge was little more than a sinecure. In short, she was the poor relation of our so-called family. I proposed to Lucie.

Chapter 2

OUR wedding was as quiet and unobtrusive as Stéphane and Adrienne's. I arranged to have the ceremony in the same church, followed by a luncheon at the same restaurant. To make sure there would be no toasts to Laurent, I invited Orville and Lavandier. Stéphane and Lisette they knew from having seen them in the salons and were surprised that the other women present, including Stéphane's wife, were members of the lower class, though I daresay they, too, were of humble origins. The innkeeper, pleased to cater a second wedding party for us, inquired if any of the other "charming couples" were planning on getting married in the near future. Sandrine blushed with pleasure at the thought of landing one of my friends, but if either of them showed any interest, they directed it at Valérie. Indeed, the next time I saw him, Lavandier asked where he might find her.

The bride sat stiffly in her place, ate sparingly and blushed at the bawdy jokes Orville and Lavandier felt obliged to make. They didn't faze Lisette, who must have heard more shocking repartee in the salons, but Adrienne looked on disapprovingly, relieved that no strangers had been invited to *her* wedding. I thought how much happier I would be if I had married Laurent and his cheeks were flushing bright pink at their jokes. Then I remembered Roubaix's buttocks, and I wondered if I had made a mistake in marrying Lucie.

Lucie had never seen my apartments. Despite her familiarity with the lavish residences of the aristocracy, the thought of living in such a place as mistress overwhelmed her, and when I presented Clarisse to her, whom I had hired to be her chambermaid, she seemed embarrassed. We had separate bedrooms, an arrangement which she took for granted, but she asked shyly if I would be visiting her that night. I answered, "Yes, my dear, and shall on many nights to come."

I had not given thought to the frequency of our conjugal unions. Two or three times a month seemed to satisfy her, and since I invariably left her bed unsatisfied, it more than satisfied me. She was ashamed when I saw her naked, and my nakedness terrified her. We kissed but seldom touched except to hold hands, and our couplings were perfunctory. I estimate that I had recourse to other outlets twice as often. I thought of looking for Roubaix, but paying a franc for an hour when I could rent a cleaner and more comfortable room for seven or eight francs a month was reason enough to put him out of my mind. Unless I rented such a room.

Lucie's principal function as a wife was to attend fashionable salons with me, so we had Sandrine and Valérie make ten gowns for her and bought jewelry to go with each of them. I believe Sandrine was more jealous that Lucie had become a lady than that she was sleeping with me. Having more than three dresses in her wardrobe bewildered Lucie, though for years she had seen to several armoires full of her Baroness's gowns.

At the salons I would go sit with the men in the smoking room and leave Lucie with the women. They could not fault her toilette or her manners, but they treated her as a non-entity because of her conversation. She blended in with the walls. She had little fashion sense, had not read the books they discussed, and took no interest in politics. Since she had no close friends there, she could contribute nothing to their gossip. Nor did she wish to. Their gossip appalled her, and she often complained of it. After our first visit to a salon she told me that the women talked about each other the way servants talk about their mistresses. She dutifully accompanied me, and she always behaved graciously and feigned interest, but she did not enjoy herself unless our hostess had planned an evening's entertainment, such as a musician, a famous actor, or a poetry reading.

I HAD begun to make sense of the world of banking and understand its inner workings. In preparation for my eventual promotion to manager, Stéphane sent me to our branch in Brussels, which internal squabbles had put in disarray, to assess how we might put things right. Lucie and I had been married for several months. It mattered little to her that people spoke French there; Belgium was still the Netherlands, and she did not want to go with me. I looked forward to a week away from her and the possibility of sex with men every night, but I did not look forward to traveling alone. Perhaps if I took a companion with me? The first person who came to mind was Roubaix.

I returned to the wine bar to look for him. He wasn't there. I asked the owner how to get in touch with him, and he answered that if I proposed a day and time for us to meet, he'd see to it that Roubaix was there. "Would three days from now be too soon?" I asked. He said no, three days would be fine. I had forgotten the made-up name I had given him and identified myself as "a gentleman he wouldn't mind seeing again".

Of course Roubaix recognized me. His face lit up with pleasure, although I hadn't paid him for his services—or perhaps it lit up with anticipated pleasure. "Monsieur Laguiole! I never thought to see you again," he exclaimed.

He was disappointed that I didn't want to go upstairs with him, but he listened carefully to my proposition. "And what benefit do I get from all this?" he asked.

"Your coach fare, the chance to visit a foreign city, your meals and lodgings, all the Belgian beer you can drink, and…"

"And?"

"Your entertainment."

"It will mean more than a week without income. I have rent to pay."

"How expensive could your room be? Surely a week and a half of free meals will cover it."

He wasn't used to letting a man have him for nothing, but I had set a precedent and the offer was tempting. "Very well," he said, "I'll go. When do we leave?"

"In five days. It will seem odd if we share a room and I address you as Monsieur Roubaix."

"My name is Anatole."

"And I'm Gérard."

We left in the morning before sun-up. A light snow began to fall outside of Senlis. It did not get very deep, but it slowed us down and we did not arrive in Saint-Quentin until late that evening. Anatole complained his legs were stiff with cramp. He was delighted that our room had a fireplace. In spite of the cold, it was stuffy inside the coach, and our clothing was damp with perspiration. I asked the innkeeper to draw us a bath. He had a servant bring a copper tub to our room, half fill it with water, and hang a cauldron over the fire. He asked if he should return to pour it for us. We said we would pour it ourselves, but would he please serve our dinner while we waited for it to boil. We would eat in our room.

He returned with towels for our bath and also laid a cloth on the table and set out knives, forks and plates. We were very hungry. I ordered four dozen oysters with a crusty country loaf, fresh butter, and champagne, followed by a *vol-au-vent*, leg of lamb, roasted root vegetables, a generous slab of the local cheese, and a bottle of red Burgundy wine. Anatole's eyes bulged at the copious fare, but he had no trouble cleaning his plate. "Will we eat like this every night?" he asked.

"Only if we're this hungry every night. We should eat a hearty breakfast, too, for we only stop an hour for lunch."

"I shouldn't have let you eat half the oysters. They increase virility."

I made a sign he should watch what he said, and he grinned sheepishly. The servant was standing by to clear our plates after course. When the water in the cauldron came to a boil, he swung it away from the fire. It would stay hot for as much as an hour. He collected our dirty plates and left us to bathe and finish our wine and cheese.

"Well," I said, knowing how the discussion would end, "which of us gets to bathe first?"

"You're paying for all this, so I defer to you."

"I'm the host, and I say we bathe together. That way we can scrub each other's backs."

"Only our backs?" He was eager to try any new sexual game.

I had my own plans for our first night. I thought that if his legs were still cramped, I would massage them for him. I felt sure my fingers could reduce him to moans, though I had never done it before. Akmoud had often massaged my feet till they felt as if I had never walked on them before, and the feeling was exquisite. Then, once Anatole was totally relaxed, I'd fuck him blind. We could skip the spanking. It didn't arouse me, anyway; Anatole aroused me; his lovely bottom aroused me, no less in white than in pink. Covering his buttocks with kisses, burying my face between them, and kneading them with my hands would give me infinitely more pleasure than slapping them.

We undressed for the bath. He noticed my battle scars and asked if I had been a soldier.

"In the artillery and then the cavalry under Napoleon. My military career ended when I was wounded at Eylau."

"Do they still hurt?"

"My shoulder and wrist—a horse's hoof crushed it—in cold, damp weather. Otherwise I scarcely notice them."

"It's cold and damp here."

"Not in a hot bath in front of the fire."

We stood in the tub facing each other, attentively soaping each other's genitals, getting to know them by sight and touch until they were as familiar to us as our own. I asked if he would want me to spank him every time we had sex.

"Every time? No. It does excite me, though. You should try it some time."

"No thank you." When we were boys, Julien used to slap me when I made a mistake in Latin, and it humiliated me.

"I also like being tied up, but I don't dare with a stranger. You I can trust."

"Do you ever fuck other men in the ass?"

"I do whatever my clients want, and most of them want that, but I like it more when they fuck me."

"I like both, especially with the same man."

"Really? The way you fucked me last time, I thought you always took the active role. It was fabulous."

"Do you kiss?"

"Not often. It has to be someone special."

"Am I special enough?"

We kissed, and I whispered in his ear, "By the way, do your legs still hurt?"

"They feel a little sore."

"Then I have a treat in store for you."

I had him lie on his back and sat at the foot of the bed with my legs crossed. I placed his feet in my lap and massaged each of them in turn, slowly working my way up his calves. Until then, sex had always been something he did quickly; you got down to business, got off, and that was that. He knew how to suck cock and bend over, but the other things we did on that trip were new to him. "This is heavenly," he said. "Is there anything you don't know?"

"I've been around a lot longer than you. That doesn't mean I know everything. I'm sure there are things we'll discover together."

As I moved up his thighs closer to his groin, my mouth joined in to help my hands. I licked my way up the inside of his legs, over his balls and onto his shaft, then down again and gave his balls a thorough bath, and lower, reaching my tongue into his crack. I had him turn over, and I pulled his cheeks wide apart and traced circles around his hole with my tongue and probed as far deep inside it as I could reach. He sighed and wriggled his hips in response.

"You want me to shove it in all at once, right?"

"Please."

I did. He gave a short cry; then he slowly released the air from his lungs in a rumbling sigh that resembled the lowest note of a pipe organ. I gripped his upper arms firmly and fucked him, biting so hard into his neck and shoulders as to leave marks, until his hole tightened around me and he ejaculated onto the sheet. A few moments afterward, I came.

In the room over the wine bar we had had sex; in Saint-Quentin we made love. We curled up in bed pressed close to one another like two spoons. Not until I was about to drift into sleep did I realize that I was breaking my vow to Laurent.

I did not think of Laurent our next night on the road—because we stopped at the post relay in Valenciennes, the same inn where I had stayed with Julien. The innkeeper did not recognize me. Since we were traveling at the bank's expense, we took the best room. I remembered how I had fucked Julien night after night for a few weeks before he disappeared from my life forever some twenty-odd years ago, and he hadn't fucked me even once. It was a crazy idea, but to make it up to him I asked Anatole to fuck me, and I rediscovered a pleasure I had not known since Thibaud took me in Laurent's tent at Auerstedt.

Anatole had never left the country before, whereas I had followed Napoleon halfway across Europe and as far away as Egypt. To me, Brussels resembled the cities of Northern Picardy and Hainault; to him everything looked different. It amazed him to hear people speaking Flemish in the streets alongside oddly accented French, and he thought Dutch men extremely attractive. I reminded him that he belonged to me for the duration of our trip.

OUR branch in Brussels seethed with resentment, old grudges and jealousy. I spent two days figuring out what lay behind it and another negotiating a temporary truce. That evening I wrote Stéphane a long letter explaining the situation and detailing what I thought we should do to fix it. I told him that the strain of trying to deflect so much animosity had exhausted me, and I would stay on in Brussels another two or three days to settle my nerves. I spent those days exploring the city with Anatole under a uniformly oppressive grey sky. We consumed vast quantities of steamed mussels, fried potatoes and beer. I bought a large box of chocolates as a gift for Lucie, but Anatole and I polished it off that night as part of a silly sex game we invented, and I had to buy another. We invented many silly sex games that week, and I did spank him one night and tie him up another. The spanking was actually rather fun, because I turned him over my knee and played with his ass between slaps.

After we had made love our last night in Brussels, Anatole asked if I would be coming back to the wine bar to look for him. I told him I didn't care for the room.

"If you're a regular—say, once a week—Jacques will let you have it for half price, and I won't ask for anything, not of you."

"No, not there."

"Then maybe in my rooms?"

"Maybe. Don't worry; we'll see each other again."

"How do I know you're telling the truth?"

"Will you believe me if I tell you my real name? It's Vreilhac. And I'm a colonel. There, now you can blackmail me."

"I may be a whore, but I'm not a scoundrel."

"I didn't mean it as an insult. I said it so you'd know you have my complete trust, as I hope I have yours."

"I let you tie me up, didn't I?"

We lingered an extra two days in Brussels, so instead of stopping on the way back to Paris, we rode through the night. Anatole slept with his head on my shoulder as the coach swayed and bumped along the rutted highway. I stayed awake thinking of us as a couple. Could we become one? I was happiest when I had one man to love and make love to. No two of my long-term partners had been alike, and the relationships I'd had with them had also differed. Julien and I had been friends all our lives before we became lovers. We were adolescents, and the sex we had was adolescent sex, an initiation, a time to experiment and of self-discovery, passionate, spontaneous and playful. Technically speaking, I was his servant. Akmoud *was* my servant; he felt I had the right to his body; as he understood the world, it was perfectly natural that I should have that right, and he was totally devoted to me. At the same time, it was he who set the pattern for our sexual encounters. He belonged to another culture, and a wild, uninhibited, distinctly un-European exoticism pervaded our lovemaking. Laurent was more like my wife. Our relationship lasted over twenty years, though near-constant warfare kept us apart more often than we were together. With the passage of time it matured and the emotional bond between us grew stronger. He always took the woman's role, yet neither of us saw me as the dominant partner. Had he lived, we would still be together.

A relationship with Anatole would be just as different. He was a male prostitute and young enough to be my son. If Laurent had been like a wife, Anatole would be like a mistress. I would find lodgings for him, take care of his household expenses, and buy him presents. I would visit him regularly, at times arranged in advance. It would not upset me if he hired himself to other men when I wasn't there. I had no doubt he would agree to the arrangement, but I was not yet ready to make that kind of commitment. In the meantime, I would go on seeing him from time to time and leave the door open.

I SLEPT all day after we got back to Paris and gave my report to Stéphane the next morning. He was very pleased with the letter I'd sent and said that my talents as a peacemaker would prove invaluable. Later in the week, Lucie and I attended a concert hosted by the Marquise d'Espard—an opera singer and harpist. An acquaintance of Berthe's, the Duchesse de Langeais, also came to hear them, and Lucie sat as if frozen to stone while they played, terrified the Duchess would recognize her. No doubt she did but was too well bred to let on. Ladies of her station do not go out of their way to embarrass people. Nonetheless, it was three months before I could convince Lucie to return to the Marquise's salon. I had to lie and tell her that the Marquise had inquired after her and asked if she were ill. Lucie promised to attend a soirée there with me the following Saturday.

We had been there but five minutes when the footman announced the Count and Countess d'Airelles. Lucie fled to the ladies' sitting room. Knowing that for Olivier it would go against the grain to associate with me, I resolved to engage him in conversation.

I waited until he was alone to approach him. "I don't know if you recognize me, *Monsieur le Comte*," I began, making my smile at once smug and affable.

"I recognize you, Vreilhac. You've come up in the world." His manner was cold, but he could hardly snub me. He did not, however, offer to introduce me to his wife.

I asked for news of Julien. "He also took refuge in England. You must have seen a lot of each other."

"We saw each other… on rare occasions."

"I hear he's married."

"Yes, to the daughter of a schoolmaster he'd taken in to care for his bastard son. He refused to say who the mother was, so she must have been some trollop he shacked up with when he felt the need. But there's no doubt whose the bastard is. He looks just like his father."

So Julien had fathered an illegitimate child in London and married a woman so he'd have someone to look after it. "At least he recognized him as his own," I said. "What's the boy's name?"

"I wouldn't call man of twenty-five a boy. And can you imagine? Giving his spawn a name like Phébus!"

"Phébus?" I couldn't believe I'd heard him right.

"I would have left the brat in Paris," Olivier sneered.

Then Julien had kept the child and not told his brother whose it was. But why? I tried to cover my amazement and asked, "Will he be returning to France eventually?"

"I doubt it. He's become thoroughly Anglified. He owns a business in London, and he has no prospects here."

"Would you be so good as to convey my greetings to him if you have occasion to go to London?"

"I will, but I don't expect he'll accept them after the humiliation you put him through getting him out of France. Dressed as a woman and pretending to be your wife!"

"Very few slipped through the nets of the Terror in its final months," I replied, restraining my anger but not hiding it. "I did what I thought necessary, and it worked. Would I have done better to disguise him as a dancing circus bear and lead him on a leash from village to village until we reached the border?"

He answered with a show of dignity. "We would do best to put the past aside and not stir up old resentments. We all have too much to reproach to too many. We have lived through times of hatred, and nobody wishes to see their return. The insult was not to me." He made an almost imperceptible bow and went to take his place at the gaming table. Lucie had been watching us from the door to the sitting room. The moment he left, she beckoned to me and begged me to take her home.

"How could you have faced him so brazenly?" she asked in the carriage.

"Brazenly? I'm a colonel, Lucie, and this is not the Old Regime."

"But what could you have possibly had to say to each other?"

"I asked for news of his brother."

"Oh, I should not at all have minded meeting Monsieur Julien!"

I had no reason to believe Olivier would tell Julien he had met me, nor was I sure I wanted Julien to have news of me. The next day Stéphane and Adrienne came to lunch with us. Lisette stayed home to practice a keyboard sonata. Madame Porcigny had asked to hear her play. Lucie told them how she had seen her former master the evening before and how much it had upset her.

"The Count d'Airelles?" Stéphane said. He sounded surprised. "His brother is one of the more important clients at my bank in London. He goes by the name of Lamott."

"Julien?"

"Do you know him, too? But of course you must, since you were a gardener at his father's chateau."

"I knew him quite well, in fact, though I haven't seen him in a quarter of a century. My mother was his wet nurse. We were friends, to the extent that an aristocrat can be friends with the son of his father's gardener. He taught me to fence, and I taught him to swim."

"Then I shall certainly look him up and tell him I know you when I'm in London. He has his own firm, a very successful exporter of Scotch whisky and woolen goods. I should like to make his acquaintance, and I was planning a trip there in the next month or so. Now that Great Britain is the most important power in Europe, our London branch has become the focus of our financial interests, and I have yet to meet its Board of Directors. At the rate we're going, we shall soon all have to learn English. I'd have asked you to come with me, Gérard, but it seems everybody there gets on splendidly. Instead I want you to look after Adrienne and Lisette in my absence."

It relieved me to know I would be staying in Paris, because Stéphane would have expected me to come with him to see Julien, and if what Olivier had said was true, our reunion might have proved very awkward indeed.

Chapter 3

I GOT together with Anatole once before Stéphane left for London. After he left, Lucie and I spent every evening in his apartment, except for one night when I escorted Lisette to a literary evening at Madame Porcigny's and Lucie stayed home with Adrienne. The evening after he got back, Stéphane invited us to an "intimate dinner of close friends", where he would tell us about all the wonders of the English capital.

We had expected the other close friends would be Valérie and Sandrine, but when I entered the drawing room I saw a familiar figure standing by the fireplace, blond, fine-featured, youthful and handsome, exactly as when I had last seen him over a quarter-century before, but dressed in the latest men's fashion.

"Julien!"

A friendly chuckle drew my attention to an armchair by the window. "Did you think me ageless? Alas, no. I've changed more than you have, it would seem, but not nearly as much as my son, Phébus."

"Then this must be Gérard," the young man said in heavily accented French. "Everyone says I look just like my father when he was my age. Now I know they must be telling the truth."

"The resemblance is remarkable. Isn't it, Lucie?"

"Oh, yes. They look exactly alike. I, too, thought he was *Monsieur le chevalier*."

"I remember you very well, young man, though you couldn't possibly remember me," I went on.

He laughed. "Indeed not, but Father has never let me forget that I owe my life to you. And now I get to shake your hand."

"You didn't tell me half of it when you said you knew him," Stéphane said, "but Monsieur Lamott filled me in on everything. Honestly, Gérard, you are far too modest. As soon as I told him I knew you, he treated me like a long-lost friend, and I didn't have to repeat my invitation to get him to accept."

"Father had been meaning for me to get to know my country of origin since Napoleon's defeat. I kept asking him when we would make the journey, but he kept putting it off. Monsieur Chambron's offer of hospitality and the prospect of seeing you again was all he needed to get the lead out of his feet."

Julien rose from his chair and stepped out of the shadows, a bit stouter, his hair grey and cut short, and there was something English in the way he held himself, but I would have recognized him in spite of that. I extended my hand.

"So long a separation calls for a warmer greeting than a handshake," he said, and he embraced me. "I can't tell you how good it is to see you again, Gérard."

"I thought you had forgotten me."

"Forget you? You asked me not to write, remember? You said a letter from me would put you in danger. Then I heard that the Committee of Public Safety had arrested you. What was I to think? I almost fell off my chair when your friend here informed me you were alive, a retired cavalry colonel, and received in the most fashionable salons of Paris. Compared with yours, my life in England is humble and undistinguished."

"I went to see your sister Berthe after she returned from Holland. Didn't she tell you?"

"I would not have expected her to. That was when you became friends with your future wife, was it not?" He turned to Lucie. "I am very happy to see you again. You're a very lucky woman to have Gérard for a husband."

Lucie, who had always been afraid of meeting well-to-do people who had known her as a servant, blushed with pleasure. "You were always very kind, *Monsieur le chevalier*," she said.

"I ceased being *Monsieur le chevalier* when France became a republic. She's a monarchy again, but I'm just Monsieur Lamott. As the wife of my dearest friend, you may call me Julien, and I hope that by the time my visit ends my host will also call me by my first name."

"I shall as of this evening, provided you, too, drop the formality of 'Monsieur'. But you two have a lot of catching up to do, and we are in the way. Do retire to my cabinet and get reacquainted. We shall have no trouble amusing ourselves in your absence, and dinner will not be served for another hour."

Lucie concurred. "Yes, do, Gérard. You were such close friends, not at all like master and servant. It's obvious how happy you are to see each other. You must have every opportunity to renew your friendship."

"That Gérard was my servant was an accident of birth. We went through the motions so as not to scandalize my family, but I never thought of him as anything other than my friend."

"What my father says is true," Phébus said. "He used to speak so often and so warmly of his friend Gérard that I came to consider him one of the family. I was stunned when he mentioned one day that he'd been one of the household servants."

"How long will you be staying in France, *Monsieur le...* Julien?" Lucie asked.

"Two or three weeks, I think. Maybe a month. I want Phébus to know his roots. He'll be the Count d'Airelles one day, after all. I suppose you don't approve, Gérard, you being an ardent republican."

"If a blacksmith's son can be a blacksmith and an upholsterer's son an upholsterer, why shouldn't a count's son be a count?"

"Nephew," Phébus corrected.

"Son, nephew, what's the difference? Besides, titles of nobility have become as much a commodity as a distinction. Look at me—a colonel! If I can be a colonel, why shouldn't your son be a count? The Emperor gave out titles right and left for service to the Nation, though he clearly felt that members of his family served the Nation more than others."

Stéphane cut in. "Let's not waste time standing around listening to each other say things we already know. Off you go, my friends. I'm sure you have a lot you want to tell each other. One of us will come get you when it's time for dinner."

I had little to tell Julien. My escape from the Terror had most likely been an oversight, and my performance in the cavalry less than sterling, but we had a good laugh over my promotion to colonel. My non-military experiences in Italy and Egypt interested him, and he asked many questions. He did not ask about my love life, and I didn't tell him about Laurent and Akmoud, nor did I say how I had met Stéphane. He said his life had been much less colorful than mine, but there were many things I wanted to know, most of all how Phébus came to be his son.

"I didn't think Olivier deserved the boy. I went to see him the moment I arrived in London. He had been married for half a year to the daughter of a wealthy baronet whose sole ambition in life was to be called Lady Anything and live in London. As soon as he'd heard Marie-Catherine had been arrested along with our parents, he considered her as good as dead and saw no reason to wait to get his hands on the dowry. He didn't even notice I had an infant in my arms. I said, 'This is Phébus,' and he answered, 'Oh? Where did you get him?'

'He's mine,' I said, and he has been ever since. Now Olivier will die childless, Phébus will become the Count d'Airelles, his real father knows it and is livid that a bastard will inherit his title, and I bite my tongue and enjoy the irony. I shall take him to see the chateau before we leave. Will you and Lucie come with us?"

"I should like that very much. Lucie has been dying to see it again."

"Olivier owns it, but he hasn't gone back. I hear it's fallen into disrepair. What he wants is Berthe's old hotel."

"But she donated it to the Church. They've turned it into a seminary. Hasn't he given up?"

"Olivier never gives up. He's utterly despicable. I'll tell you later what he said to me. But Berthe still owns the Hotel L'Envol and allows the Church to use it as a seminary. It's hard to believe, but he went to see Berthe in the convent and demanded—demanded, mind you—that she give—give, of all things!—him the hotel. She told him she was a humble bride of Christ and had left all her worldly possessions behind and would not reclaim the Baron's property. He made a scene and refused to leave when the Mother Superior asked him to. He threatened to take the whole convent to court if Berthe didn't 'clear out the clerics'. She answered him in language that must have kept her on bread and water for a month and stormed back to her cell. His wife had come with him. She didn't speak a word of French and had no idea what was happening."

"You have the story from Berthe, I assume."

"No, from Olivier. I found it incredible, so I wrote my sister and received an answer from the Mother Superior. So I know both versions of the story."

"And what did Olivier say to you?"

"I told him how you helped me escape from France, and he said I had disgraced the family name by dressing as a woman."

"He said the same to me. I asked if I should have dressed you as a dancing bear."

"Good for you."

"I believed him, though. I thought you were angry with me and that's why you never wrote to me."

"I rather enjoyed being your wife. Then I thought you were dead, and I remarried, so to speak." He laughed loudly. "I suppose that makes me as much a bigamist as my brother."

"I enjoyed being your husband."

"Oh, the things we did when we were young! I don't regret them, but we're grown men now, aren't we? The Church would never have recognized our marriage, anyway."

"Does Phébus know all this?"

"*All* this? Lord, no. But he knows I got out of France disguised as your wife."

"And what did he say about it?"

"I've raised Phébus to be a decent person. He thought it was very funny and said that in that case I was really his mother and you his father. But I haven't finished telling you about Olivier. He called me a coward and said he was ashamed his own brother had stooped so low to save his wretched life. At that point I almost told him I had done it to save his son. Instead I said I had done it to save mine, which proved I was less of a coward than a man who would run away to save his skin and leave his wife behind to face the executioner. He threw me out."

"Tell me about your wife. Why didn't you bring her to France with you?"

"Oh, Anabel is a good soul. She's given me two daughters and has been a devoted mother to Phébus. But she's very timid. It frightens her to go more than a few miles from our house, much less all the way to France. Besides, she has no breeding and doesn't speak French, though I've tried to teach her, and I brought Phébus here in the hope he would eventually take his place in society."

"He'll have to improve his French first."

"That's why I'm leaving him here with your friend Stéphane, to learn the ins and outs of Paris society and to conduct himself like a Frenchman. I'll go back to London in a week or so, after I've taken care of my business here. My place is with my wife and daughters; Phébus is ready to strike out on his own."

He saw my disappointment and said, "Never fear. I'll be back to visit my son. Phébus and I are very close." Then he went on where he had left off. "I always intended that Phébus would return to France, but to live alone? I certainly would not have entrusted him to his uncle. When I met Stéphane and found out you were here to keep an eye on him, too, I thought I'd found the perfect solution. We discussed my son's living with him and settled the matter in under an hour. My family was surprised I came back with him instead of waiting a couple of months to make proper preparations. I wanted to see you."

Clearly Julien was fond of me and had never stopped being my friend, but I couldn't tell if he loved me. I had the impression that for him sex with men was a thing of the past.

STÉPHANE insisted that Lucie and I join them for dinner every night until Julien left, without Valérie and Sandrine. I had accepted an invitation from the Marquise d'Espard for one of those nights. I wrote her that a very dear friend whom I had not seen in years, an *émigré*, was in Paris for a few days and I wanted to spend as much time with him as possible. I was sure she would understand. She wrote saying I should bring him with me. I wrote back asking if the Count d'Airelles would be there, since he and my friend were not on speaking terms. I showed Julien her reply.

*If your friend wishes at all costs to avoid meeting
the Count, he can only be his brother, Julien. I should
be delighted to make his acquaintance. He need not
worry. The Count will not be present.*

"I see nothing has changed in France," Julien said. "Everybody knows everything about everyone else. We cannot possibly decline her invitation."

I wrote back promising we would be there and asked if Julien might bring Lisette inasmuch as I would be coming with my wife. The messenger I sent it with returned in half an hour with a short note: *Mademoiselle Chambron is always welcome in my home.*

In the meantime, Julien had accomplished a lot. He had announced at dinner one evening that he had been to see Berthe and she had agreed that if Phébus remained in France and married a Frenchwoman, she would let him have the Hotel L'Envol. "My dearest wish is that Olivier lives long enough to see it happen," Julien told me after dinner.

"I'm astounded you were able to convince her."

"I'm sure she's only doing it to spite Olivier. Holy Orders haven't changed her. It isn't just his behavior at the convent she holds against him. You know it was Olivier who talked Father into insisting she marry the Baron."

It was the first I'd heard of it.

Julien made himself as English as possible the night of the Marquise's salon, perhaps to let everyone know that he was a man who faced facts and had made a life for himself abroad, unlike his brother, who had sat brooding in London, waiting for the British army, in which he hadn't fought, to clean up the mess in France so he could go home and live in the luxury he had known before the Revolution. There were other *émigrés* present who had behaved like Olivier, and one could tell by their faces that they disapproved. But the Marquise was graciousness itself. She had little love for the Count and detested his wife. She introduced Julien to everybody, praising his good sense and industry.

"We need more men of your stamp here, *Monsieur le chevalier*," she said. "May I ask with whom you're staying in Paris? Is it with the Colonel?"

"No, I'm the guest of my banker, Monsieur Chambron."

"With Lisette's stepfather? You're very wise to entrust your money to his firm. Your brother's dealings with Nucingen will land him in the poorhouse. But there I go speaking of your brother. There's no love lost between you, I understand. I don't suppose you'd lend him money if he asked for it."

"He wouldn't stoop so low as to come to me, nor would I give him any if he did. I'd bend over backward for his children," he said, winking at me, "but for Olivier, not a farthing." He used the English word.

"A *farthing*? And what, pray tell, is a farthing?"

"Four times what you'd give a beggar."

"Shame on you, *Monsieur le chevalier*! Not that he deserves any more. Will you be staying the whole time in Paris, or do you intend to see a little more of France? Our country has changed a great deal since you were last here."

"As matter of fact, I shall be making a short trip to the Chateau d'Airelles to show it to my son. We leave tomorrow, and *Monsieur le Colonel* and Madame Vreilhac are to come with us. We would have left sooner were it not for your kind invitation."

"Is your son here, too? Had I known I would have invited him."

"Oh dear, no, *Madame la Marquise*. This is the first time Phébus has been to France. I should have been very embarrassed if people heard him speak French. But no doubt he will improve quickly."

"In a week, *Monsieur le chevalier*? You son must be unusually gifted."

"He is already comfortable in our language, *chère madame*. I only wish he spoke it better. But he will remain in Paris for several months. I'm determined that he come to know and love his father's native country. I'm afraid he's grown up to be your typical Englishman."

"I think my friend does not realize how very English he himself has become," I said in jest.

"Well, when you deem Monsieur Phébus sufficiently polished, I insist he come here first so I get credit for having discovered him," the Marquise said, tapping Julien's shoulder with her fan. "You leave tomorrow, did you say? Your chateau—"

"My brother's."

"I promised the Colonel we wouldn't speak of your brother. I believe your *family's* chateau is in the Charente?"

"About ten leagues north of Angoulême."

"I don't know the region, but I hear it's lovely at this time of year."

Lisette expressed a desire to come with us to visit the chateau.

"If your stepfather allows it, you will be most welcome. Madame Vreilhac will be happier for your female companionship. Is that not so, Gérard?"

STÉPHANE let us have his coach and coachman for the journey, and Lucie's maid came with us to serve the ladies. We could get there in four days if we stopped only to eat, sleep, and change horses, unless the women found it wearying, which was unlikely since Lucie was anxious to see her old home and Lisette had more energy than all of us. Julien pointed out the many chateaux along the lovely stretch of the Loire between Orléans and Tours. He was shocked to see the state of disrepair into which most of them had fallen. We did not know if ours would be in a condition that would allow us to stay there, and there were no inns close by, so we had taken sheets and blankets with us, hoping there would at least be beds. If not, we would stay only one night. Since we could not count on finding food in the village, we also brought a large hamper, which we filled with food when we stopped for the night in Poitiers. The coachman could always drive to Angoulême for more if we stayed longer.

The coachman stopped in the village where Lucie had been born to inquire if the chateau were livable. Elegant coaches never stopped there, and everyone in the village came out to stare. They looked at us coldly. The people who lived on the d'Airelles estates had always resented their haughty ways. Julien, Lucie and I, who remembered the Terror, felt the tension and didn't hide our apprehension. Phébus and Lisette couldn't understand our fear.

Phébus stepped nonchalantly from the coach to stretch his legs, and an elderly woman cried out, "Why, it's Monsieur Julien!..." then, as if she'd seen a ghost, "...not much older than he was when he went away!" and she crossed herself rapidly.

Phébus laughed. "Monsieur Julien is my father."

As much as they hated the rest of the family, they had been fond of Julien, who had always been friendly and even hung around with one of the Count's servants. We got out of the coach and were recognized. Julien and I were still friends; a girlhood companion of Lucie's was still alive in the village; we were open and casual with them. The old folk started chattering, telling their children and grandchildren about the days before the Revolution, and everyone clustered around us. Had Monsieur Julien come back to live in the chateau?

Julien explained that Olivier owned the property, but he had no children and it would go to Phébus after he died. Was it still inhabitable? They looked doubtful. Was it fit for us to sleep in at least one night? Maybe. A half-dozen men from the village said they would do what they could to make it possible.

The grounds were overgrown with weeds, the steps leading to the main entrance had big cracks in them, and many windows were broken. Inside it was empty, not a rug or a stick of furniture. Mice scurried across the dirty floor, and a thick layer of dust and cobwebs covered the walls and windowsills. The upstairs rooms were just as empty, but the door to the top floor was locked. When the village men arrived, we all threw ourselves against it with all our strength, and it gave. Some of the old servants' rooms still had beds in them—two doubles and three singles, exactly enough if Phébus slept with his father. We also found a few chairs and two small tables. The men carried them downstairs, set up rooms for us, and sent to the village for brooms, rags and mops. A handful of women and children came to clean. To show our gratitude we shared our food hamper with them in a picnic on what used to be the lawn, and pretty much emptied it. We decided to stay three nights and sent the coachman to Angoulême to replenish our stores. We needed time to assess what repairs were required and put ourselves on a good footing with the local inhabitants.

Julien's coachman was delayed on the road and had not returned by mid-morning the next day. He was an avid outdoorsman when his duties allowed it, and had brought a fishing pole with him. Julien, Phébus and I set off for the river with it to see if we could catch some fish in case he didn't get back till evening. "Let's go to the spot where we used to swim," Julien said.

"You know how to swim?" Phébus asked his father. He sounded impressed. He had lived all his life in big cities, and he didn't know how.

"Gérard taught me."

"Will he teach me, too? Can I learn in one afternoon?"

"You can learn the basics," I said, "and we have two more days before we leave."

We stripped off our clothing and waded in. Phébus naked resembled his father no less than with his clothes on, and I got to feel his chest and stomach lying on my arms and had a close-up view of his backside when I supported him in the water. My gaze, however, rested on Julien, a man closer to me in age with a body I had loved that to me looked as beautiful as ever. I realized that I had never ceased loving him. His eyes must have examined me, too, because he noticed my battle scars, which were not all that visible, and asked about them.

After Phébus's lesson, he stood naked on the bank and fished while he watched his father and me horse around in the water. Of course all our noise and splashing about frightened the fish, and he caught nothing. Then we all stretched out on the grass to dry as Julien and I had so often done as boys. "I like being naked," Phébus said. "It's a good feeling. I have to start spending more time in the country. You can't go about naked in the city."

I laughed and asked if people wore nightshirts to bed in England.

"They do, but I don't. I imagine it's the one French habit I had before I came here."

"Don't think French people go running about outdoors with their clothes off," I said. "It's been years since I felt the fresh air and sunlight on my body."

"As I remember, Gérard," Julien said wistfully, "we used to run around a lot with nothing on. I knew exactly what I'd see when you took your clothes off."

Phébus pointed out that he'd know exactly what he'd see if any man took his clothes off. Julien ignored the remark and went on, "I suppose we still haven't grown up yet."

"Oh, we've grown up," I answered. "I sometimes wish we hadn't."

The coachman had returned while we were at the river, so it didn't matter that we returned empty handed. Over the next two days Lucie, Lisette and the servants spent their days in the village building good will. Phébus, Julien and I combed every inch of the chateau making a list of the most essential repairs and went for walks in the woods where we had played together as boys. Julien suggested we go riding now that we had the horses again. "No thank you," I said. "I've had two serious injuries from falling off a horse."

Julien smiled. "Nobody will be shooting at you this time," he said, but I declined.

Every day we spent an hour or so at the river to continue Phébus's swimming lessons, and the coachman tagged along with his fishing pole. It took him aback at first to see his employers prancing about in the water stark naked in front of him, but we were having so much fun he took his clothes off and plunged in. He was an excellent swimmer, and he took over Phébus's instruction.

Three days sufficed for us to assess the damage to the chateau. There was much to do; it would take months. Julien said we could hire workers and start the major repairs right away. Olivier wouldn't know what we were up to. On the other hand, it might be years before his son could take it over, so he advised we go about it slowly.

Phébus wondered if Olivier might not outlive us all.

"I'm twenty-two years older than you and fifteen years younger than my brother," Julien told him drily. "Your uncle is over sixty, almost three times your age. Your chances of not inheriting the chateau are next to nil."

Chapter 4

JULIEN returned to England a few days after our trip. The longer he stayed, the more deeply I had fallen back in love with him. Now more than ever I felt the need for a steady male partner. I found Anatole and asked what he would say if I bought him an apartment. I promised it would be a good one, an entire floor of a nice building in a nice part of Paris.

"You're asking if I'm willing to become your kept man."

"Are you insulted?"

"No, no, quite the contrary. I only wonder what prompted this sudden decision."

"Not all that sudden. I've had it in the back of my mind since Brussels."

"Something must have made you… how shall I put it?… take the plunge."

"I saw an old friend, someone I hadn't seen in many years."

"A special friend?"

"Very special."

"Then you don't love me?"

"No. Does it matter? You don't love me, do you? But I need to be with one man."

"I don't."

"I'm not asking you to. I'm not taking away your freedom. I ask only that you reserve one or two nights a week for me and not bring strangers to the apartment."

"That shouldn't be a problem. Jacques will let me have the room over the wine bar. And since you'll be like my father, I won't let anyone else spank me. Does that make you happy?"

"Then you accept?"

"Will I have my own manservant?"

"Yes. I'll find you a pretty boy you can play with whenever you want. Perhaps we'll all three play together sometimes."

"Will I have an allowance?"

"You won't need one if you go on working."

"And if I don't want to work?"

"Then we'll arrange something."

"What if you see your friend again?"

"Then you'll have a short vacation from me, and I'll come back to you very frustrated and very horny."

"I understand now."

"Well, what do you say? Shall I look for an apartment?"

"How can I refuse? I thought this only happened in fairy tales."

"Good. I'll take you out to dinner to celebrate and rent us a room for the night."

"What will your wife have to say when you get home?"

"I told her I'd be out late. What would you like for dinner?"

"Steamed mussels, fried potatoes, and beer," he grinned.

I found a comfortable apartment for him on the rue des Canettes, an easy walk from where I lived, and hired a housekeeper to come for two hours every morning and a full day once a week to give the place a thorough cleaning, but I had to conduct countless interviews before I found a suitable manservant. Toussaint had just turned seventeen and looked more like a girl than a boy. He had very short dark hair, was thin as a rail, and moved awkwardly, as if he had suddenly grown six inches overnight and was unaccustomed to his new body. He seemed very shy and had never been in service before. I told him that if I took him on, there were a few things he should know about his future employer.

"Then I shan't be working for you?"

"No, for a young friend of mine. He has tastes which most people consider peculiar."

He immediately understood what I meant. "I think I may have the same tastes," he said.

"'You think', meaning you aren't sure of what his tastes are or you aren't sure of your own?"

"I'm sure now," he answered. "We have the same tastes."

"Then you will be his new manservant. Mind you, your tastes are not the only reason I'm hiring you. If you don't fulfill your official duties satisfactorily, which include shopping for groceries and cooking his dinner, you will be let go."

"Might I ask my new master's name?"

"Anatole Roubaix."

I TOLD Lucie that I would come home late one night a week and be gone all night on another. I would do my best to set a regular schedule so she would know when to expect me for dinner. She assumed I had a mistress, which was not entirely false, but she did not protest. She believed the old wives' tale that men, no matter how old, have pressing needs, and women lose interest in sex as they grow older. (As if she had ever had any.) She wanted to know when I would be gone next. I named the day when Anatole was to move into the apartment. "All night?" she asked, and I told her yes.

Anatole had spent every day at the apartment for a week, waiting for the workmen to deliver the furniture and telling them how he wanted it arranged. He went back to his old room to sleep, or else to the wine bar. I had chosen the furniture but had no idea where he would put it. He wanted to surprise me, as I wanted to surprise him and was waiting until he moved in to present the manservant I'd found him. He only knew his name and that he was seventeen years old. I had taken Toussaint to buy the clothing he would need as a manservant and sat through all the fittings, feeling the cloth and what lay below to see that it hung properly on him, so I knew that Anatole would be very pleased with him. On the afternoon Anatole took possession of his new lodgings, I met Toussaint with his small satchel of personal belongings at the tailor's to pick up his new clothes, then took him to dinner.

Anatole gave us a tour of the apartment. Toussaint seemed awed by the comfort in which he would be living and said he liked his small room very much, but most of all he couldn't take his eyes off Anatole. I had not described him to Toussaint, and he must have pictured someone my age, though when I'd hired him I had referred to his future employer as "my young friend".

Anatole told Toussaint he would not be needed that evening and sent him to his room to put away his things. We drank a bottle of champagne together and retired to the master bedroom. "Tonight is your first night as my papa," he said, "and I want you to spank me." He pointed to a chair. "Other men just slap my bottom while I'm standing up. The way we did it in Brussels is much better."

I sat, and he pulled down his trousers and lay across my knees. "I know you enjoy this," I said. "I don't know why, but you do. One thing, though—don't ask me to cane you. I won't. I'll only use my hand."

"Cane me? God forbid! A cane leaves marks."

"And you have a very pretty ass."

He did have a pretty ass. If any part of him was pretty—and many parts were—it was his rump. I ran my hand over it, caressed it, traced the line of his cleft, squeezed his cheeks between my fingers. He wriggled his bottom in anticipation of the coming slap, but I made him wait for it. Then, whack!—I brought my hand down hard. He gasped, caught his breath, and whimpered softly. He had one pink buttock and one white. My hand burned. I could only imagine how his ass must have felt.

I played with his ass, alternating slaps with caresses, until his buttocks were hot to the touch and as pink as a sunrise, his hard cock pressing into my lap. "Have you had enough?" I asked.

"No, please go on. This so much better than an ordinary spanking. I love the way you mix the petting and the pain."

"Then it does hurt."

"Oh, yes. Awfully."

"And you like it?"

"Awfully."

"You'll tell me when to stop?"

"I promise."

I had wet two fingers with spit and had been running them up and down his crack while I questioned him, slowly separating his cheeks as I did. Now I carefully worked a finger deep into his hole and swirled it around his pleasure lump. He lifted his hips to get more of it, but I pushed him roughly down so my finger popped out and landed a wallop on his rear that echoed through the house. I felt his cock twitch and a warm wetness soak into my breeches.

"Now see what you've done! Couldn't you have warned me?"

"I couldn't help myself. Punish me. Bring tears to my eyes."

I did—not as a punishment, but to have done with it quickly. I had grown very hard playing with his ass and was itching to put it in him. If he hadn't come all over my lap, my own leaking would have left as big a stain. I stopped as soon as I saw the first tear drop to the floor. I asked him to let me dry his tears and carried him to bed to make love. The spanking had been exciting, and the chance to gaze on and play with his ass an unmitigated delight, but sex that was three-quarters hugs and kisses was what I wanted most from him.

I left at dawn. Anatole lay sprawled naked on the bed, looking very drowsy. "You'll be here on Tuesday, right?" he asked.

"Yes, but just until midnight."

"And again next Thursday, for the whole night?"

"Oh, dear. I've been so busy setting this place up and outfitting Toussaint that I forgot to tell you. I'll be away for two weeks, to Marseille. I'm looking forward to it. I passed through there when I was in the army on my way to Italy and again when I sailed for Egypt. Provence is beautiful."

"Two long weeks!"

"And a half. I really must spend a little time with my wife when I get back."

He yawned, stretched, and rubbed his belly. I leaned over to kiss him goodbye. "Will you knock on Toussaint's door on your way out and ask him to draw my bath?" he asked.

I THOROUGHLY enjoyed my visit to Marseille—the blue skies, the salt air and spicy food, the seemingly endless procession of good-looking sailors to ogle from my café table by the port. I did not attempt to lure any of them to my hotel room, since I had a permanent partner in Paris, taken on at no little expense precisely so I would not have to pick up men, though I would very much have liked to catch a glimpse of them with their clothes off. I had the chance one day for more than a glimpse. I had hired a horse and ridden to the *calanques* outside Cassis for a day at the beach. I had not been swimming since my afternoon skinny-dip at the chateau with Julien and Phébus. I stripped, dove into the clear water, swam the length of the *calanque* out into the ocean, then back again, and lay down on my blanket to dry off in the sun.

Shouting, loud laughter, and feet crashing through the bushes catapulted me into a sitting position. A dozen or more sailors came rushing down to the shore. I was uncertain as to how they would react, coming unexpectedly on a naked man, but they just waved merrily, tore off their uniforms, and ran into the water. They were a rough-and-tumble lot, wrestling, splashing and ducking each other under the water, diving deep below the surface and coming up suddenly to surprise anyone so lazy as to grab a few moments' rest floating on his back, climbing up the rocks to dive off the cliffs. I swam out to the rocks for a closer look. Every one of them was strongly built, every one good looking, and every one manly. I feasted my eyes and enjoyed the Provençal scenery more than I ever had before. I returned to the *calanque* before I left Marseille, hoping to see more, but there was nobody there all day but myself.

BACK in Paris, I spent one evening with Lucie and our friends before rushing off to spend the night with Anatole. I sent a note so he would expect me and not go out for an evening at the wine bar. Toussaint served us a light supper and disappeared into his room before clearing the table. I jokingly asked Anatole if he had made a bundle of money in my absence.

"I haven't been out at all," he said, "not even once. I've been getting to know Toussaint."

"Should I be jealous?"

"I thought you'd be happy to know I've been faithful."

"You have an odd concept of fidelity. Just remember, I hired him to be your manservant. I set you up here to be my lover. One kept man on the premises is sufficient."

"He undresses me. Isn't that what a manservant's for?"

"So do I."

"And I'm teaching him things."

"I'm sure you are."

He suddenly became very intense and serious. "I have something to ask of you. A favor. Promise you'll say yes."

"What is it?"

"Say yes first."

"Oh, very well. Yes."

"I want Toussaint to watch you spank me."

"So he can spank you too?"

"Absolutely not. *You're* my papa. So I can spank him."

"I'm glad that at least there's *something* you haven't tried with him."

"Then you agree?"

"I said yes, didn't I? No threesomes, though. He only watches."

"But we'll have one someday."

"I don't see how I can avoid it."

Toussaint came running the second he was called. "Do I—" he began. Anatole nodded before he could finish his question. He followed us into the bedroom. I pointed to an armchair in the corner and told him sternly he must keep to his place and not join us. He asked if he could open his pants and play with himself while he watched. "You can take them off, for all I care," I answered. "For all I care" was a fib. I very much wanted him to take them off.

I repeated the spanking of three weeks before almost stroke for stroke. This time Anatole didn't come on my lap, but my breeches were just as wet. Toussaint had left a puddle on the rug long before we finished. "Must I leave now, or can I stay and watch the rest?" he asked. I said he might as well see it all.

Anatole and I ripped off our clothes and signaled Toussaint to fold them neatly on the chair we had vacated. Then Anatole got on his knees and sucked me until I could no longer stand the wait. Then he leaned over the foot of the bed and I fucked him while he yelled out his delight. Toussaint stood next to me watching intently, and when his jism shot onto Anatole's buttocks, I smeared it around and gave him a few more slaps. I came, pulled out, and told Toussaint it was time to go.

We curled up next to each other in bed. "Isn't he lovely?" Anatole asked. "And his cock is almost as big as yours."

"Has he fucked you?"

"Need you ask? Will you let him join in next time? I want to watch you spank him."

"Yes, you'll have your threesome, but don't expect to make it habit. And I won't spank you every time, either."

"I don't think I'll be ready for another for at least a month. My poor bottom is on fire." In fact, it was three months before he wanted another, but he made me spank Toussaint when we had our threesome.

WHEN Lucie and I were not going out, which we did less and less frequently, we usually spent my evenings away from Anatole at Stéphane's. Valérie and Sandrine joined us there once or twice a month, and sometimes Lavandier came with them. We tacitly understood that Valérie was his mistress. At least three nights a week, though, there were just us six: Lucie and I, Adrienne and Stéphane, and Lisette and Phébus.

Stéphane had bought Phébus a small library on French history and geography, on her noble families, and on her many regions and their traditions, from which he read aloud to perfect his diction, but one could see it would be impossible to remove all trace of an accent. He required him to read our literary classics and the popular novels of the day. Every evening over dinner we quizzed him on his reading and lectured him on politics, Stéphane and Adrienne doing their best to tone down my republican convictions, but most of all we made him speak. It was essential for him to learn to discourse at length on a variety of subjects and frame his arguments elegantly. For ten minutes every evening we pretended none of us knew the others so Phébus could practice etiquette. On top of all that, Lisette said it was important he learn to dance, and she undertook to teach him. The poor boy said that if he didn't write his stepmother a letter once a week, he would forget how to speak English.

"And your father?" I asked.

"Father makes me write in French and sends my letters back covered with corrections."

"That's because it's essential you learn to write, too," Stéphane said.

We never stayed past ten o'clock. Lucie said all the serious conversation exhausted her and made her head spin. She tired easily, and went to bed early when we stayed home. Sometimes I sent her home in the carriage and walked to Anatole's. Eventually I stopped leaving at midnight on Tuesdays and often stayed for breakfast, too, so I didn't get home until after work the following day. Sometimes I went three nights a week. I never neglected to send word to Lucie, and she took it in stride, as though she had expected it to happen sooner or later.

MONTHS went by, and Julien never came to visit. It was hard, seeing the man I loved day after day and knowing it wasn't him. When I inquired after him, Phébus would say that his father was doing well but the import-export business left him little time to travel. Stéphane added that he sent regular reports, and Julien did not feel the need to check up on his son. He was very satisfied with his progress.

"As he should be," Lisette chimed in.

On my way to see Anatole late one afternoon, I passed Lavandier standing idly outside a bonnet shop, smoking a cigarette. He asked where I was going.

"To see a friend. He lives a few streets from here."

"I'd ask to come with you—you can't imagine how bored I've been all afternoon—but Valérie is inside the shop choosing a bonnet. She's been more than an hour at it."

"Then she *is* your mistress."

"One of them. Keeping one mistress is too expensive. You have to rent a nice apartment for her, pay for her wardrobe, furnishings and servants, and Lord knows what else. When you have several, you only need to buy them gifts. I suppose a wife is cheapest of all," he added laconically.

"Then why don't you marry?"

"Because I can afford mistresses. In the plural. But I see Valérie waving to us. She must want me to help her choose. I really wish I could go with you—if you really are going to see a friend and not your mistress."

"A friend, but I couldn't have asked you to come anyway. We have a matter of personal business to discuss."

"Then don't let me keep you. Will I see you Friday at the Chambrons'?"

"Certainly."

ALTHOUGH I had Anatole for my regular outlet, and sometimes Toussaint as well, I did not neglect my wife. I came dutifully to her bedroom about once a month so she would know I still looked on myself as her husband. I always returned to my bedroom after sex. I would not have had difficulty falling asleep next to a woman. In fact, on one occasion I did, and Lucie woke me so she could sleep alone. She claimed I was snoring, but Anatole said I never snored, and Julien and Laurent had also told me I was a quiet sleeper, and Akmoud, who snored louder than a desert sandstorm, never asked how to say it in French, so I have to conclude that Lucie could not fall asleep unless she was alone in bed.

In the middle of the spring of 1824, Lucie learned she was pregnant. We had thought she was past the age of conceiving. The doctor warned us of the dangers of a woman her age bearing a first child and told Lucie she must go out as little as possible and go to bed early. Above all, no parties, no dancing, no rich foods, and avoid noise. No, there was no harm in spending a quiet evening at a friend's house so long as she didn't stay too late.

Adrienne was happy for us, but concerned. Our other friends were certain that everything would go smoothly. What could be more natural than motherhood? My colleagues at the bank congratulated me and made jokes about my virility. What was the secret of my potency, or what had taken me so long? A man of fifty about to become a father for the first time!

I HAVE written very little about my duties at the bank because, although I was good at my job, I found the work unspeakably dull. The only aspect of it I enjoyed was the opportunity to travel. Stéphane, who had begun to feel his age, found traveling difficult, and he came to rely on me to visit his branch banks when some problem arose or just to let them know he was keeping his eye on them. I took Anatole with me when I would only be gone a day or two. One morning Lavandier saw my carriage in front of Anatole's building. He approached, saw me sitting inside it, and asked where I was going.

"Rouen."

"To Stéphane's bank?"

"Where else? I'll be back tomorrow to see Phébus make his grand entrance into society. Will I see you there?"

"The Marquise didn't invite me. Will his father be there, or is he staying in London?"

Just then Anatole came out the door carrying a small suitcase. Anatole seemed embarrassed. I had to introduce them.

"Monsieur Roubaix, my secretary. Anatole, this is my friend, Corporal Lavandier."

I wondered if Lavandier might be one of Anatole's clients. I asked him point blank after we drove away. "I've never seen him before in my life," he said.

"You appeared embarrassed."

"Because you were obviously talking to a friend. I've never met any of your friends before, and until you introduced me as your secretary, I didn't know who I should pretend to be."

"Are you sure?"

He looked me in the eye and said, "I wouldn't lie about this, Gérard. If I had one of your friends for a client and you didn't know it, it could put you in a very awkward position."

I didn't doubt his sincerity.

I RETURNED from Rouen to a flurry of last minute preparations for Phébus's début. Lucie lavished more attention than usual on her toilette, almost reducing her chambermaid to tears, and would not stop fussing with my uniform. In spite of all her rushing back and forth, we were ready two hours before Stéphane's coach came to fetch us, and we squeezed in beside the others and set out for the Marquise d'Espard's.

The Marquise had taken an interest in Lisette since they had been introduced, and she was similarly predisposed in Phébus's favor. Lucie and I were relatively unimportant, and Stéphane only held in esteem for his money, but Phébus had it all—wealth, an impeccable lineage, and an exotic foreign upbringing. She asked us to come early so that "our Englishman" would not be overwhelmed walking into a crowded salon filled with distinguished strangers. When she saw how dashing he was and how polished his manners and speech, she knew she had found a pearl.

"What was Monsieur Lamott (as he wishes us to call him) thinking of in keeping his son from us so long? Why, *Monsieur le chevalier* is more French than his father!" she declared.

"My father had to expend enormous effort make himself English and finds it difficult to relax and be himself," Phébus replied, kissing her hand. "I fear that if I appear very French, it is for the same reason."

I believe that at that moment she resolved to take him under her wing.

When *habitués* arrive at a salon and see a new face, they are most often reserved and show at best moderate interest in who this person may be, unless they have been forewarned of his or her importance. They wait for their hostess to present the newcomer to *them*, who have already made a name for themselves and proved their worth, though very few, of course, have proven anything of the sort. Phébus cut such a striking figure and so obviously had everyone's attention that they asked to be introduced and were ready to make fools of themselves in order to make a good impression.

The Marquise kept an eye on her new protégé, beaming as he moved easily from one group to the next with Lisette on his arm. She approached me where I stood with Lucie watching them from our spot near the window. "How handsome the youngest d'Airelles is!" she exclaimed.

"His father was no less handsome when he was young."

"And don't he and Lisette make a charming pair!" And she waltzed off to attend to more important guests.

"Do you think Lisette will marry him?" Lucie asked me.

"Who? Phébus? Whatever gave you that idea?"

"Honestly, all men must be blind! Haven't you seen the way they look at each other? I've been wondering about them for weeks. Wouldn't it be lovely, though, if they did marry, and we all went to live in the Chateau d'Airelles?"

"We all? Do you still imagine yourself a ladies' maid, my dear?"

She realized her error and said, "I meant we could visit often. Maybe stay for the summer."

Chapter 5

ISN'T it strange how deaths seem to come in waves? On the morning of 16 September 1824, in the seventh month of her pregnancy, Lucie went into labor. She died in childbirth a little before midnight; the baby survived another hour. The next day all France went into mourning. King Louis XVIII had died the same day as my wife.

We buried her as soon as we could, at Montmartre, because the streets would be thronged when they brought the King's body to lie in state at Saint-Denis. We need not have hurried; his body remained at the Tuileries for a week. His brother was now Charles X. He envisaged a coronation more sumptuous than Napoleon's, with preparations so elaborate that it would not be held until late in spring. I did not think that boded well for the constitutionality of our constitutional monarchy.

I sent Anatole a note to tell him my wife had passed away and he would not see me at his apartment for about two weeks. Not out of respect for Lucie; I had spent more nights with him than with her while she was alive, but I had many petty formalities to take care of related to her death.

Lucie was the only one of us who was sincerely religious. She had attended mass every Sunday without me; she went with her chambermaid. I asked the priest who had married us to sing mass for her. Then we went to the cemetery, where the grave was dug and the coffin waiting to be lowered into it—Stéphane, Adrienne and Lisette, Phébus, Sandrine, Valérie and Lavandier, the priest, and I. Another more elaborate and well-attended funeral was going on a few hundred yards away—Olivier's. His widow must have borrowed heavily to pay for it. I asked Phébus whether he oughtn't to pay his condolences to his uncle's widow. "I think not," he said. "I may have killed him. I paid him a call last week and told him that I'd decided to live in France permanently and Aunt Berthe would give me the Hotel L'Envol. I thought he would burst a blood vessel."

"But your Aunt stipulated that you remain permanently in France *and* take a French wife," I pointed out. "Do you plan to marry Lisette?"

"I've already proposed, and she accepted. Except for her, you're the first to know. I have yet to ask Adrienne for her hand."

"You don't expect her to refuse, do you? Have you set a date?"

"After the coronation. It will be a gala affair, and the new King wouldn't appreciate the competition. I don't have to tell you how vain he is."

"A very gala event. You're the Count d'Airelles now."

"No, Father is until he officially transfers the title to me. I hope he puts it off at least until summer so I'm not obliged to go to Reims for the coronation."

"Does he mean to be crowned in Reims?"

"So I hear—*and* anointed by the Archbishop. I doubt it's because he wants to cure scrofula."

"No, he intends to restore the Old Regime. We can kiss our Charter farewell."

The gravediggers lowered the coffin, the priest mumbled a short prayer, each of the ladies tossed a small bouquet on top of it, and the men each threw in a shovelful of dirt. No one made any speeches. Stéphane and Lavandier wandered off a ways for a smoke, and Adrienne and Lisette went to look for tombstones of famous people.

Sandrine must have imagined that with Lucie gone I would be in the market for another wife, and dropped hints to remind us she was available. "You will be very lonely living all by yourself," she said to me. "You've only lived alone once before, I believe, after Stéphane and Adrienne were married, and I remember how sad you were."

"Gérard has lived with loneliness for ten years," Valérie said quietly, "ever since Laurent died. He never truly loved anyone but Laurent. Did you really not understand that?"

Sandrine's stunned expression surpasses my abilities for description. Fortunately, she lacked the intelligence to put two and two together and did not realize that the Mademoiselle Julie whom I had helped escape was Phébus's father. How Valérie found out about me I do not know. Perhaps Lavandier suspected or their liaison had made her wiser.

Phébus was standing nearby and overheard her. He looked at me and nodded calmly. Had he figured out that Julien and I had been lovers? I decided to sound him out the next time we were alone together.

But we were never alone together. So a week later, I asked Phébus to come have dinner with me, just us two, for a serious man-to-man talk. Lisette and Stéphane looked surprised, but Adrienne understood. I had told her about my relationship with Julien long ago, when I lived in her house with Laurent. I have never met a woman more discreet than Adrienne; she had more tact than a duchess. She said, "Phébus can practice his French. There are things men talk about among themselves one doesn't discuss with ladies present."

I WOULD be totally alone with Phébus. When Lucie died, I had found another position for her maid and also my manservant. Most of what he did I could do for myself. Such tasks as seeing to my uniforms would not put an undue burden on my housekeeper, and the cook could bring my meals to the table. I had dismissed my coachman but kept my carriage. I could hire a driver at need. (The same groom saw to all the horses in my building and the one next door, and I continued to pay my share of his salary.) My servants had rooms on the top floor of the building. After the cook served me, she would leave the apartment until she came to clear the table in the morning. From eight o'clock on, I was alone in an empty apartment. I found the solitude calming; it suited my melancholy.

Over our wine after dinner, Phébus asked, "You want to talk about my father, don't you?"

I wasn't sure how to begin. "He promised he'd be back to see you. Years have gone by and he hasn't. Can you tell me why?"

"You want to know what I think, not what he says. I think he stays away because of you. He still loves you, but he's married and has other obligations he does not want to transgress."

"Then you know about us."

"I suspected. What you said just now confirmed it."

"It doesn't upset you?"

"If it upset me I should not have slept until I knew the truth. You see it hasn't kept me awake."

"But if Julien loves men, he must face similar temptations in England."

"I don't think my father is attracted to men; he just happens to be in love with you. He's always been a faithful husband and a devoted family man. My parents have always slept in the same bed, and I'm certain they make love often. Don't look surprised. I don't mean I overhear their lovemaking. My stepmother may be a pastor's daughter and a homebody, but I've never met a more uninhibited woman when it comes to sex. You may find it hard to believe, but she once delivered a lecture to my sisters on the pleasures of the bedchamber in my presence—and went into greater detail than I've read in any novel except de Sade's *Justine*! She told them that in choosing a husband, a man's ability to perform in bed was more important than his financial security and almost as important as his character. Then she turned to me and said, 'I hope your father has seen to *your* education, Phébus, and you'll satisfy your wife as he satisfies me.' My sisters stared at me appraisingly, and I thought I'd die of embarrassment. So I'm quite sure my father prefers women, unlike you."

"You know I love men and only men?"

"Of course. I heard what Valérie said about your friend Laurent."

"And it doesn't scandalize you?"

"Do I look scandalized? I wish you would tell me, though, whom you loved more, Laurent or my father."

"Loved or love? I loved your father in my youth, and I thought my heart would break when we parted. Then I thought him gone from my life forever, and for twenty years I loved Laurent."

"Have there been others?"

"One. Maybe two. But if you set any of them against Laurent or Julien, I wouldn't hesitate to say whom I loved more. It's different with your father and Laurent. How can I put it? Do you love Lisette?"

"I think I do. That is, yes, I do love her, but when I see the love between you and my father and my parents' love for each other, I'm not sure I know what love is. Is that what you meant?"

"Not exactly. It's not a question of comparing how one loves X or Y. Perhaps you're too young to understand this, but one simply cannot weigh one part of one's life against another. Do you think your father ever asks himself whom he loved more? It's enough to know whom you love now."

"And you, whom do you love now?"

"I can't say I'm in love at all. I loved your father when I saw him again, but perhaps I only wanted to be in love with him. It's hard to tell, when you know you won't be making love to a person."

"That's a very honest answer."

"I tried to be honest. It was hard to put into words, so I don't know if I said everything I meant. I believe I meant everything I said. I'm very glad we had this conversation, though I was apprehensive of having it."

"I'm glad too."

We shook hands. It was a strange feeling, confiding in a man so much younger than myself, but it was a good feeling. I still felt I had something left undone, however. Adrienne had known all about me and Julien for years, but Stéphane did not. She would not have told him; nobody kept secrets better than Adrienne. Phébus would not hide it from Lisette, so I thought he had a right to know, and it was my responsibility to tell him.

I COULD come right out and tell Stéphane such things in plain language. I had known him for years, and we used to beat off together and exchange blowjobs. "Julien and I were more than just friends," I said. "We had a relationship dating back to when we were boys, and when he escaped from the Terror by posing as my wife, he did more than pose."

"Was that the subject of your heart-to-heart talk over dinner with Phébus?"

"Yes, but I didn't go into details."

"I don't expect you to go into details with me, either. Do you still love him?"

"Still? That wouldn't be fair to Laurent. Rather say that I'm in love with him again."

"And do you think he still loves you?"

"Phébus says he does, but there's no chance we'll get together again."

"I believe I'm right to assume you have someone else, someone you've been with for quite a while. Do you love *him*?"

"No, but we get on well, and I'm happy."

"Except for Julien. Have you been honest with this other friend of yours?"

"He knows there was… is… someone."

"Is he a person I would like to meet?"

"No. He isn't like us at all."

"Is he very young?"

"About the same age as Phébus."

"Are you keeping him? Does he take money from you?"

"I pay for his lodgings and a servant."

"I don't like where this is going. I can only rely on your better judgment."

"Anatole is a man of principle in his own way. He's honest and doesn't take advantage of me and is extremely careful not to compromise me. I was apprehensive at first, but I know now I can trust him."

"Is he good in bed?"

"Very, and he's learning what it means to be a lover."

"Well," Stéphane said with a sigh, "now that you've got that off your chest, why don't we talk business? I've been feeling very poorly of late and mean to retire to the country after the wedding. I've already bought a small villa about a league south of Saint-Germain-en-Laye, so you see we won't be far away. Lisette and Phébus will live here until they can take over the Hotel L'Envol. Then we'll sell the apartment. His aunt is allowing the Church six months to acquire another building for the seminary, and then they'll still have to fix it up. I want you to take over the bank."

"But I have no head for figures at all!"

"One doesn't need a head for figures to be a figurehead. Monsieur Monceau will take care of the business side of things. But nobody knows him, while Colonel Vreilhac is a name that inspires respect."

"I'm not all that much younger than you. Why don't you put Phébus in charge? After all, Lisette is your rightful heir."

"Phébus knows even less about banking than you do!"

"What does it matter if Monceau is the real director? I'll be there to make sure everything is going as it should. The name d'Airelles would give the firm a far more distinguished cachet than Vreilhac. People will think it the most reliable bank in Europe."

"We are the most reliable bank in Europe. We've always been scrupulously honest in all our dealings. I stand on my reputation."

"Nobody knows that better than I. I still think Phébus should have the bank."

"Very well, but I'm counting on you to see he makes a proper job of it. So that's settled. Now to speak of something else, of course your friend Julien is coming for his son's wedding. Our house will be turned upside-down with last-minute preparations. You live alone, Lucie's old bedroom is empty, so I've suggested he stay with you. Actually, it was Phébus's idea."

"Will his wife and daughters be coming with him?"

"Phébus says the entire British navy couldn't drag his stepmother across the Channel. He'll take Lisette to London to meet them after they're married. Then they'll go to Scotland for a month's honeymoon.

He wants to hunt and fish. And would you believe Lisette wants to go hunting with him and has also asked him to teach her to ride?"

"Believe? I would have expected no less of her. She wants to spend their summers at the chateau, you know, and she won't sit at home waiting for neighbors who aren't there to call. How is work on the chateau progressing?"

"Slowly, and furnishing it will be an enormous expense. Your friend Julien wasted no time in transferring his title to his son. Did you know Phébus is now the Count d'Airelles, and Lisette will be a Countess?"

"Hard to believe, isn't it?"

"I doubt I'll ever get used to it. But the chateau won't be ready for at least two years. All that—the wedding, the honeymoon, setting up house—is months away, though."

STÉPHANE was right. The wedding *was* months away, but they flew by quickly. They were up to their ears in wedding preparations, and I saw little of Adrienne and Stéphane, but Lisette and Phébus I met at the salons, which they could not avoid attending. All France was abuzz with talk of King Charles's upcoming coronation. I expected no good to come of his reign. He had made himself extremely unpopular already by committing the State to indemnify the aristocracy for the properties they had lost during the Revolution and forcing the Anti-Sacrilege Act through both Chambers, making blasphemy illegal, so I could express a degree of guarded criticism, but I could only vent the full extent of my opposition to Toussaint and Anatole, with whom I spent every evening I was not at a salon. In fact, all we talked about was sex and politics. Toussaint knew nothing of the latter, and I soon turned him into an ardent republican.

I was hardly ever in my apartment. Toussaint joined us four times out of five, and almost every night was an orgy, but then he would go to his own room and leave Anatole and me to sleep as a couple. When we were alone together, we were gently affectionate. I teased him that he couldn't be making much of an income. "Why would I need an income when I have you," he said, and, although I could not keep track of how many times we had come that day, we made love again.

Anatole did go out and earn some money one evening, however. Toussaint said he would like to have me all to himself for once, and Anatole thought it a good idea.

"But you don't even have Anatole all to yourself anymore!" I protested.

"No, but you have, and you two get to have your fun together without me. Fair is fair."

I gave in but said it would have to be in his room.

As it turned out, it was I who made love to Toussaint. I explored every square inch of his young, almost hairless body. It was exciting, but I felt more as if I was with a male prostitute than I had with Anatole in the wine bar. He was almost entirely passive; there was nothing he wouldn't let me do. Anatole had trained him well, and he could look forward to a lucrative profession if he ever decided to leave his service.

AS COUNT D'AIRELLES, Phébus could not avoid going to Reims to attend the coronation. I let him have my carriage so that, the ceremony over, he could put in an appearance at the official celebration, do obeisance to the new monarch, and leave unobserved. He was back in Paris by morning. I knew he would give a deliciously cynical commentary of the spectacle, and I went to hear it.

I told Phébus he looked like a cross between an emperor and a fop in his ceremonial garb. "Don't I know it!" he answered. "If only wigs were still in fashion! I'll have to grow my hair out or stand all night bareheaded in a thunderstorm to get it back to normal. Now I can chuck this ostentatious outfit and concentrate on my wardrobe for the wedding. We only have three weeks."

Lisette thought that with a few alterations Sandrine and Valérie could turn it into something quite wearable.

"Yes," he agreed, "just the quantity of lace and ribbons would more than pay them for their work, and we can sell the diamond studs and use what we get to furnish the chateau from ground floor to attic. And I was one of the less elaborately dressed in the procession! Napoleon could have paid the salaries of his *Grande Armée* for a year on the silks and jewels that piled into the cathedral. You could smell the perfumes over the incense. Victor Hugo—"

"The young poet from Madame Porcigny's?"

"Yes, him. Copies of an ode he'd written to honor the occasion were circulating throughout the Tau Palace. Very polished verses, but more pompous than even an ode needs to be, and, oh, my God, the sentiments! The man is either the most fanatical divine right royalist in the nation or he's looking to be named poet laureate."

"A bit of both, I suspect."

"Tell me, Gérard, why is it that the common folk are so impressed with vain spectacle? I'm certain the crowd cheering him in the street was forty times larger than the one that escorted his uncle Louis XVI back from Versailles. The ranks of the Royal Guard were such that one would have thought the King meant to lay siege to the cathedral."

I was laughing so hard the tears rolled down my cheeks.

"Lisette, dear, if only we didn't have to be married in church and just signed a contract like simple folk. I could put up with being the center of attention for a day, but reception will follow reception for a week—longer than the coronation! Everyone will get to congratulate us five times at least, my arm will be sore from shaking hands, and your back will ache from making curtseys. But at least they will be social events. I swear, if it wasn't *you* I'm marrying, I'd break off the engagement. Why don't we just run off and have a quiet wedding in the country?"

"You know that's impossible, sweetheart. We'll have some time alone on our honeymoon."

JULIEN would arrive in Paris two days before the wedding and would have to stay a week after, for it seemed every hostess in Paris wanted to throw a party for their favorite couple. I told Anatole that my friend was returning for his son's wedding and that I wouldn't be able to see him for a week because I'd been invited to a party every night. "Then I know who your friend is," he said. "He's the father of the Count d'Airelles. I didn't know you moved in such exalted circles. It's a privilege to be your friend."

"Oh, much more than a friend," I said.

I hired a driver so there would be someone to carry Julien's luggage. I rode in the carriage to fetch him at the coach relay. "You came to meet me," he exclaimed. "I thought you'd be waiting at home."

"For old times' sake. Do you remember when we last saw each other here?"

"How can I forget? I was leaving Paris forever and posing as your wife. Phébus was with us, and now he's to have a wife of his own."

We drove to my apartment. "You live very well," he said. "This is much grander than my residence in London."

"Then you must see how it looks inside."

We climbed the stairs, followed by the driver carrying his luggage. I opened the door and pointed out where to leave his bags. "I've had Lucie's room made up for you," I said.

"Then I'll really feel like your wife again!"

"You probably don't want to hear this, Julien, but I have to be honest with you. I wish you were."

I stopped there, because the driver had returned. I tipped him, and he left. Then I looked at Julien, waiting for him to react. I expected a scolding, or at best a gentle refusal.

"I can be, for a week. I'll probably feel guilty for it, but I have to be honest too. I've missed you more since I went back to England than after the first time I left. I haven't been able to get you off my mind. Perhaps the only way to lay our past to rest is to relive it. If that doesn't work, we'll just have to accept that it will haunt us forever, because after this week, I promise, you'll never see me again. But not in your wife's room. Now, let's move my luggage to yours."

"No. Kiss me first to prove you aren't joking."

He wasn't joking. I melted in his arms and wouldn't let go of him.

"Whoa!" he laughed. "We have an entire week for that. Do we dine at Stéphane's tonight, or do we go there tomorrow?"

"Tonight. Tomorrow they'll be too busy. You won't see Phébus again until the wedding."

I think everyone at dinner must have known how we would be spending our time together, because we both looked radiant and kept glancing at each other. Adrienne would only let us stay a half hour after dessert, saying they had too much to do to waste time talking to old friends.

Later, while our eyes, hands and lips were engaged in a voyage of anatomical rediscovery, I whispered, "Take me."

"No. Remember, I'm your wife."

"No. I want you for my lover. You go first."

There was no doubt that after all these years I still loved Julien more than I could ever love Anatole. I thought my heart would burst from loving him when I felt his arms around me and him throbbing inside me and again when, my body covering his, I thrust repeatedly into him.

After, we lay facing each other, and I stroked his cheek. It was wet.

"You're crying," I said.

He raised his hand to my face. "You are too."

"From happiness. And also from sadness, because I know that for one short week our love has flared up for the last time, and neither you nor I will ever blow on its embers again."

"That's why I'm crying, too."

We were up and dressed before my housekeeper arrived, but we made no attempt to hide the fact that Julien hadn't slept in Lucie's room. We stayed home all day, cuddling, holding hands, exchanging confidences, and had sex again that night and every night until he left Paris.

LISETTE and Phébus were married at the Hotel de Ville. I hadn't thought its galleries could hold so many people. Adrienne wore a pink silk gown, a gold and sapphire brooch and six strings of pearls for what she said would be her one venture into Paris high society. Sandrine, Valérie and Lavandier must have been outside somewhere in the throng, but it was pointless to look for them. Half the notables in Paris formed a parade to accompany the couple to the religious ceremony at Notre Dame, where the other half were waiting in the pews. Although I had a place in the front row, I couldn't hear a thing for the noise, and when the great organ blasted out the chorale prelude I couldn't that hear that either. Then the parties started, and we were all run ragged. Stéphane joked that Phébus should wait to consummate the marriage; he would have plenty of time when the parties were over. But I have no doubt that his stepmother's views on sex in marriage had sunk in, and by morning Lisette knew the pleasures she could look forward to for the rest of her life.

The last party of the week was held at the Hotel Tournedos. Everyone was in a silly mood, as if a week of partying had exhilarated them instead of exhausting them. In the ballroom, the musicians played without a break, people spoke at the top of their voices to be heard over the conversations around them and laughed loudly at whatever anyone said, and boisterous gaiety filled the house from cellar to attic. Julien and I stood by the buffet table, drinking champagne and feeling melancholy. At eleven o'clock Phébus sought us out and said, "So, there you are! Take Father home now. He has a tiring journey ahead of him."

"So do you and Lisette."

"Yes, but we're young. Now thank our hostess and go home, you two. Get some rest, or stay up and unwind. But for God's sake, get away from this hubbub!"

Julien's bags were packed and his clothes laid out for the journey. We kissed when the apartment door closed behind us, gently at first, but our lips remained pressed together and our kiss fervent, until I thought our bodies would merge into one. "The last time," I said as I slowly unbuttoned his vest.

"Our last time. Do you know what I want to do, Gérard? I want to make love on the floor, just like the first time we made love under the eaves of the chateau."

"It was also a wedding that brought us together then. Go and bring the bedding from my room while I light a fire in the parlor."

It was the most tender lovemaking I ever experienced. I wanted to engrave every moment, every sensation, indelibly on my soul. When I buried my face between his legs, I thought, "This is the last time I will smell his scent"; when I took his penis in my mouth, "This is the last time my tongue will feel his hardness"; and when he came, I waited a long time before I swallowed, knowing that I would never taste his seed again. And likewise when I fucked him, and when he fucked me.

The fire died down to embers. "It's almost dawn," he whispered.

We dressed in silence, each of us watching the beloved body disappear behind a veil of everyday street wear. He left the evening clothes I had peeled off him as a keepsake to remember him by, and I gave him a ring.

Phébus and Lisette came for Julien in their coach as the sun was rising. We were waiting with Julien's bags in front of the building. I hugged him farewell while the coachman tied his luggage on top, and they drove off to Calais. I spent the day moping around the house and went to Anatole's after supper. "So," he asked, "have you come back to me frustrated and horny?"

"No, just very, very sad."

"I understand, and I'm happy for you. Now, let's see what I can do to cheer you up."

PART IV:

My Years in the Shadows

Chapter 1

TWO days after Phébus, Lisette and Julien left for England, Stéphane and Adrienne moved into the small villa he had bought in Saint-Germain-en-Laye, taking what furniture they would need and three servants with them. Stéphane left Lisette elaborate instructions on how the three vacant bedrooms—the newlyweds could share the largest bedroom until they moved into the Hotel L'Envol—could be converted into sitting rooms so they could receive large numbers of guests as befitted their station. He purchased a small, two-person carriage, had the coach which had driven them to Calais done over with Phébus's monogram in gilt over the d'Airelles escutcheon, and sent it to meet them when they returned from their honeymoon. Lisette tore up Stéphane's list and ignored his suggestions, saying she had no interest in starting her own salon and would wait until the Hotel was ready before hosting large parties. Why, it even had a room large enough for a ball!

Stéphane and Adrienne invited me to stay a few days in the country with them after they had settled in. The grounds were extensive, but the house itself was very modest—two drawing rooms, a dining room, and kitchen and water closet on the ground floor, four bedrooms above that, and an attic. There were two outbuildings, one for three times the number of servants they had and a coach house with adjoining stable for two horses. I told them they needed more servants;

a cook, a housekeeper and a multi-purpose man who served as everything from groom to handyman to footman to butler simply would not do. They ought at least to have a chambermaid, a scullery maid, a second male house servant, a groom—and definitely a gardener. I walked the grounds with them, showing them how I would lay it out. It was early summer, not too late to put in flowers and some vegetables. They had enough trees, but should plant shrubs in autumn. It occurred to me that I hadn't gardened in thirty-five years and that I missed it. I drove to the village and bought rakes and shovels, a spade, a watering-can and a wheelbarrow, ordered two wagonloads of manure, and spent the rest of my visit preparing the soil, promising to return a week later with seeds, bulbs, potted perennials and the gardener I would hire for them.

I returned in a hired wagon with seedlings—beans, cucumbers, Brussels sprouts, onions, beets—lettuce and radish seeds, and an assortment of flowers, but no gardener. I had made some inquiries but could find no one suitable. Stéphane thought I should look in the village. Adrienne thought she would enjoy raising chickens. I agreed it would be nice to have their eggs, but told her that chickens are loathsome birds. Better pigeons—or a pig, in spite of the smell. They had taken on a chambermaid who was willing to help out in the scullery and a groom to double as a footman. I taught him how to tend the plants I had brought until I found a gardener.

I did eventually locate a gardener, a Breton farmer who had joined the infantry when not yet twenty to fight the Fourth Coalition and had remained in Paris after the wars and was nostalgic for country living. I questioned him at length on agriculture and found him quite knowledgeable. He also mentioned that he had served under Davout. He had not been in Thibaud's unit, but he had met him and thought well of him. The news that the man he would work for had married Thibaud's widow was, in his words, "a pleasant surprise". It would also please Adrienne. He had never married, and the way he looked at me when I mentioned Laurent made me think that it was not impossible that, if he were so inclined, Stéphane might find other uses for him besides gardening. His name was Innocent.

So the next time I came to Saint-Germain I brought two surprises with me: a gardener and a puppy named Médor. Adrienne was thrilled that her new gardener had known her late husband, albeit slightly, and went out of her way to furnish his two rooms in the outbuilding comfortably. Innocent approved of how I had laid out the vegetable garden. He disagreed with me about the animals and said there was plenty of room on the grounds to build a chicken coop and a sty for a pig or two behind the outbuildings, which also made Adrienne happy. He knew next to nothing about arranging flower beds to make a formal garden entrance garden, however, so the front of the house remained my responsibility. I worked outside with him whenever I came to stay with my friends, but he did the heavier tasks.

NOW that I divided my time between my apartment in Paris and Saint-Germain-en-Laye, I saw much less of Anatole. When Lucie died, Anatole had asked if he would come live with me on the rue de Varenne. I told him no. I was not ready to accept our arrangement as permanent, nor did the idea of living with a man who peddled his body as a profession appeal to me. I was, after all, somewhat of a public figure. Besides, Toussaint came with the package. That they might have become full-time lovers and only put up with me for my money did not disturb me, but I felt some trepidation they might turn the lodgings I provided into a male brothel in my absence. However, when I spent the night there—and I no longer bothered to forewarn them when I did—I could detect no evidence that anybody made use of them besides them and, less frequently, myself.

I could make neither heads nor tails of their relationship. Outwardly, they seemed not only lovers, but best friends. However, Toussaint always used the formal *vous* with Anatole, and even during sex addressed him as "Monsieur". I asked Anatole if Toussaint spanked him, and he said, "Occasionally." I then asked if Toussaint called him "Monsieur" when he spanked him, and he answered, "Now that you mention it, yes, he does."

"Do you sleep together when I'm not here?" I asked.

"Never. Toussaint always sleeps alone."

"Does he go out and have sex for money?"

"Yes, sometimes."

"What does he do with his clients?"

"You mean, does he call them 'Monsieur'? I would imagine so. We all do."

"You call me Gérard."

"You aren't a client."

"No, I suppose I'm not. But I meant it quite literally. What does he do?"

"How should I know? We don't work as a team."

"Are you in love with him?"

"I'm not like you. Men like me don't fall in love."

"And Toussaint?"

"I don't imagine he ever will either."

LISETTE and Phébus returned from Scotland toward the end of July. Lisette learned she was pregnant not long afterward. Work on the Hotel L'Envol could not start until the seminarians vacated it at the end of the year, and they lived in the residence Lisette's mother and stepfather had vacated. They often visited them at their country villa; the older couple no longer came to Paris. I had enthralled everyone with my descriptions of Provence, Phébus wanted to see it, and it seemed to us all that they should make the journey before they found themselves saddled with a family—they planned to have three or four or more children—so it was decided they would winter in the south of France. They pressed Stéphane and Adrienne to return to the apartment so they would not find themselves isolated in Saint-Germain when the snows came, but Stéphane wouldn't hear of it. I promised Lisette to check on them regularly. If the snow was too thick to take my carriage, I could still ride.

No one but Stéphane knew he was dying. He had known for over a year; it was why he had bought the villa. His doctor had not expected him to live long enough to move into it, yet he had lived there for four months, and it was not yet apparent to us who lived with him, day in, day out, that he was ill when Lisette and Phébus left for Marseille in mid-October. However, his condition worsened soon afterward. We urged him to consult a physician; he brushed our concerns aside. When the new year came, we could see he was dying, but he refused to admit it and did not agree to write Lisette until February. He showed us his letter, and we learned that he had known he had cancer for over a year. He said that they must not leave Aix on his account (they had found the mistral in Marseille unbearable almost as soon as they got there) and forbade her to undertake the return journey until after the birth, for the sake of her unborn child and her own health. He hoped he would live long enough to learn if she had a boy or a girl. "Don't worry about your mother," he concluded. "Gérard will take care of her." By the time Lisette received the letter, he was gone.

We buried him in the village churchyard. Valérie and Sandrine came for the funeral and stayed overnight. Although she had remained friends with Adrienne, I had seen little of Sandrine since Lucie's funeral, and she greeted me coldly.

The women were quite taken with the villa. "Such a lovely house!" Valérie said. "How sad that you have to give it up!"

"Give it up? No, I shall stay on here," Adrienne told her. "Why would I want to go back to the noise and dirt of Paris?"

I told Adrienne she could not live in a small village on her own. She asked me why. We argued about it after they left, she promised to think about it, and in the end she agreed. But she would not go back to her old apartment. She would be in the way; Lisette and Phébus needed space for the baby. She would rent a small apartment, two or three rooms at most. When the children moved into the Hotel, then she would live with them.

"How would you be in the way? You could take care of it."

"Nonsense. They'll hire a nurse."

"Well, I shan't allow you to live alone. You will live with me until it's ready. I lived in your house for years; now you shall live in mine. Lucie's room is vacant, and you can bring your chambermaid and butler. As for the other servants—"

"The other servants will remain in the villa. I've decided that you will have it."

"What would I do with a villa?"

She smiled. "Why, garden, of course."

ADRIENNE came back to Paris with me. We stayed at home the first week and never went out. Then I realized that I hadn't seen Anatole in over two weeks. I wanted to sleep with him. When I told Adrienne I would be going out that evening and not return until morning, she asked, "Do you have a friend?"

"Well, yes, I do."

"Have you known him long?"

"About ten years."

"I thought so," she said. "Is he very young?"

"He was when I met him."

When I showed up at Anatole's, he and Toussaint were eating supper. "Where have you been hiding?" they wanted to know.

"My dear friend Stéphane died. I brought his widow to Paris to stay with me."

"Then you won't be going to Saint-Germain anymore."

"Not until spring. Adrienne has given me the villa, but there's little I can do there until the end of April."

"So now you own a country estate!"

"It's hardly an estate. You'll see for yourselves when I invite you for a week this summer."

"You don't intend to give up your apartment in Paris, I hope."

"No, I'll divide my time between the two. Winter in Paris, and the summer in the country."

From then on I spent half my nights with Anatole and half at home. He said he was happy to see more of me, that I'd been neglecting him. As he put it, he had missed his papa, although he no longer asked me to spank him, nor did he and Toussaint spank each other, at least not when I was present. Anatole's tastes had taken a bizarre turn, however, or else Toussaint's had and he went along with it. He would tie Toussaint spread eagle on the bed, and we would go to work on him, tickling him mercilessly with fabrics and feathers, or pour wine on him and lick him dry. Anatole also liked to pinch his nipples and squeeze and twist his balls, and Toussaint seemed to enjoy every minute of it. But after he went back to his room, Anatole and I would make love just doing the things that I imagine all male lovers must do in bed together. One night Anatole asked whether he might come to the villa whenever he wished.

"Certainly," I answered, "as long as my friends won't be there."

"Are you ashamed of me?"

"No, I'm ashamed of myself."

"That doesn't make sense. It amounts to the same thing."

It didn't, not as I saw it. I was ashamed to be keeping a man for my pleasure, not of the man I had chosen to keep.

THE COUNT AND COUNTESS D'AIRELLES take great pleasure in announcing the birth of their son, Laurent Thibaud Stéphane de la Motte, on the nineteenth day of March 1826 in Aix-en-Provence.

With the formal announcement Lisette sent a long letter saying they would return at the end of May. I spent the week before making the villa ready to receive them. They wanted to visit Stéphane's grave. They arrived in Paris with the baby and Beato, his nurse, a Provençale who spoke to him in her local dialect. After two days unpacking and setting up the room for the baby, they all came to spend a few days with me. Phébus had thought the child would go by the name Stéphane, but Lisette, Adrienne and I called him Laurent, and he was outnumbered. "We'll make Stéphane one of our second son's names, and *he* can go by that," Lisette told him, whereupon they started choosing babies' names, and naturally Gérard was high on their list. I objected that the child might not appreciate being named after his great-grandfather's gardener. Adrienne raised an eyebrow. Their eldest bore the name of his great-grandfather's gardener's lover. As it turned out, their next three children were girls—Phébus got tired of waiting and named the youngest Stéphanie—and Louis-Philippe was on the throne by the time Lisette gave birth to Paul Saint-Germain Stéphane.

She loved staying at the villa. She had developed a taste for the outdoors in Scotland and during their stay in Provence, and we unhitched the carriage horses so she could go riding with her husband. I often joined them. Although I was a cavalry colonel and Lisette had only recently learned to ride, they both sat a horse better than I did. She expressed her impatience to have the chateau put back in shape so they could spend their summers in the country.

After their visit, I alternated my weeks in Paris with weeks at the villa. In Paris Adrienne and I would go every evening to dine with her daughter and son-in-law and visit her grandson. One evening in three, I would leave early, drive the carriage back to my apartment and walk to Anatole's, and Phébus would have his coachman take Adrienne home. Anatole eventually asked when he could come stay with me at the villa. I suggested he not stay too long on his first visit in case country life did not suit him. He should come late the following week and drive back to Paris with me.

Not surprisingly, he came with Toussaint. They found me working in the garden. Anatole said I had become quite the gentleman farmer. Innocent laughed, and then corrected him. "Monsieur Vreilhac is a farmer who has become quite the gentleman," he said.

"Let me show you your rooms," I said.

"Our *rooms?*"

"Well, mine and Toussaint's." Innocent raised an eyebrow.

"Your gardener is one of us," Anatole whispered as we went up the stairs.

"Yes, I thought he might be."

"So you haven't—"

"No, nor will he. Don't pester me to send for him when we… to send for him this evening."

"I'm not interested in sampling your gardener. In fact, I was looking forward to three nights alone with you, but Toussaint wouldn't let me come without him. Your gardener… What's his name, by the way?"

"Innocent."

"Innocent is exactly what we need. Toussaint will go to his room tonight. Where is it?"

"In the outbuilding behind the house, second door from the right. Are you sure Toussaint will want to?"

"Won't you, Toussaint? You do understand there's no money involved, I hope."

Toussaint grinned at us and slept every night with Innocent. Anatole and I had three nights in a row of one-on-one lovemaking.

The day we were to return to Paris, Innocent asked if "Monsieur Toussaint" would come visit us again.

"Just 'Toussaint', Innocent, not 'Monsieur'. He's Monsieur Roubaix's manservant. And yes, you'll get to see him again. Often."

"He's a very pretty young man."

"That he is, and most accommodating, I'm sure."

Innocent blushed to the roots of his hair. I wondered what wild and wonderful activities they had engaged in.

WORK on the Hotel L'Envol would be finished in early October. The Count and Countess d'Airelles had invited at least a quarter of the Paris élite to a ball on Saint Martin's Day to launch their career among the foremost hosts in the capital. I asked if Julien planned to attend.

"Father will never return to France," Phébus said. "I thought you understood that. My sister Clarissa is to be married in spring. We shall go to London for the wedding so Laurent can meet his grandparents."

Adrienne said she hoped they would entertain no more than once a week, for she would keep to her room when they had guests. Phébus wouldn't hear of it.

"You will come to the salon and sit in a comfortable chair for everyone to pay their respects, and you will join us when we invite people for dinner. We'll have a new gown made for you, in a color that becomes a widow. Pink will not do. Your mother will look very handsome in a dark burgundy, don't you agree, Lisette?"

"*Maman* must have two gowns at least. Burgundy and forest green."

"I don't imagine anyone will have much to say to me, however many gowns I own. 'Good evening, *chère Madame*. I hope I find you in good health. Lovely soirée, is it not?' I can see myself sitting alone in my corner of the room all evening."

"I shall keep you company," I said. "I'll be sitting next to you, and people will sit and talk with us. They'll probably move on after a few minutes, which is all for the better."

"I suppose I shall have to make conversation," Adrienne said, "and smile benignly and keep my mouth shut when people go into ecstasies over our exalted and most benevolent sovereign. Honestly, Gérard, I don't know how you do it."

"Ours will be a liberal salon," Phébus said. "People expect me to favor a constitutional monarchy because I was raised an Englishman, and they expect Gérard to support Napoleon because he fought in the *Grande Armée*."

"You're too late," I told him. "Everybody knows my republican sympathies."

"So much the better. Adrienne will be able to speak her mind."

"Then you don't intend to curry the King's favor, Phébus."

"The d'Airelles don't curry anyone's favor."

"Ah, but they did. Your uncle Olivier bowed and scraped to royalty all his life."

THE COUNT AND COUNTESS D'AIRELLES had twice the household staff of Phébus's Aunt Berthe and her Baron, but they had to hire twenty more and two additional chefs for the night of the ball. The guests began arriving at five in the evening and stayed, I am told, until dawn. I was the first to leave, staying only for dinner after Adrienne decided she had had enough and retired at a quarter past eleven. By then I had resolved that this would not only be my last ball, but my last appearance in society altogether except for dinners at the Hotel L'Envol and Lisette's Friday afternoon salon.

Adrienne looked very distinguished in her dark green gown. We sat by the fireplace in the smaller of the two drawing rooms. Lisette dutifully brought all her most important guests to meet her *maman*—she couldn't possibly have introduced all of them—which kept me rising from my armchair and sitting back down until it felt as if I had spent all day doing the exercises I had been subjected to in military training. At length, when I had managed to remain seated for ten minutes, the Marquise d'Espard, who had arrived late, came up to us, and I had to stand up again.

"So this is our dear Lisette's mother," she said. "Lisette insisted on presenting me herself, but she is so busy being the hostess that I said I would do it myself if she told me where to find you. I am so very pleased to make your acquaintance at last."

I introduced the ladies and gave the Marquise my chair.

"Imagine," the Marquise continued, "little Lisette, no less a personage than the Countess d'Airelles! I'm absolutely delighted for her. What a handsome couple she and the Count make, and they're so very much in love! Far too many people get married nowadays who have little affection for one another. Don't you agree, Madame?"

"Lisette would not have married except for love. She had the example of her father's and my marriage, and also of my marriage to Monsieur Chambron."

"Yes, I've heard that you were a most devoted wife. How sad I was to learn of your late husband's passing! But why did you deprive us of your company all these years and never come with him when he visited his friends?"

"You are too kind, *Madame la marquise*. I'm a simple working woman who would have been quite out of place in society, as I'm sure you see for yourself."

"You wrong us, Madame. Paris society has its share of snobs, no doubt, but not all of us. Far from it, I assure you."

"You misunderstand me. I did not mean to fault fashionable people. I only meant that I do not feel at home with them. It is not my place to associate with the rich and famous. What would we say to each other?"

"Then you wrong yourself. You have excellent manners, very polite, and your bearing is beyond reproach. As for your conversation, we don't spend all our time talking about art and politics, you know."

"Madame Chambron can hold her own in any political discussion," I said. "Lisette's father had his own newspaper under the Republic, until the Committee of Public Safety closed it down and threw him in prison."

"How dreadful! Was your first husband a victim of the Terror? How foolish of me! He couldn't have died by the guillotine, since he was Lisette's father."

"I met Thibaud in Saint-Lazare, which is how I came to know Adrienne," I said.

"And it was *Monsieur le colonel* who introduced me to Monsieur Chambron," Adrienne added.

"After the Terror it started up again, and she ran it by herself for a while during the Directory," I went on, "while her husband was away at war. Madame Chambron knows more about politics than I do."

"Then she must be very well informed indeed. Of course, we women are entitled to hold political opinions, but we must not appear to know more than men. We discuss politics freely among ourselves but listen politely when men are present. Shhh... do you hear the music? The orchestra has struck up an *écossaise*. They play a waltz next, if I'm not mistaken. I promised *Monsieur le comte* I would be his partner. Do excuse me."

She rose and gave me her hand to kiss. "Why do *you* not dance, *cher ami*?" she asked me.

"I have not the agility, Madame. I was severely wounded at Eylau."

"Yes, I know, but I thought you had recovered. These last few minutes have been most pleasant, but I must hurry to the ballroom. Good evening, Madame."

Adrienne whispered as I plopped down on my armchair, "So you 'haven't the agility'. Liar! It doesn't keep you from working all day in the garden."

"I had to offer some excuse. The Marquise was very gracious."

"Indulgent, rather. This smile affixed to my face has given me a headache. I suppose I shall get used to it, but for now I only want to go to bed. Let's find Lisette and tell her I'm going to my room."

We found Lisette outside the ballroom at the center of a group of fawning admirers, male and female. Sooner than be drawn into the conversation, we waited near the doorway. She noticed us, excused herself, and came over. "But *Maman*, we haven't served dinner yet," she objected, "and you haven't eaten since noon!"

"Have the cook send up a bowl of consommé, a bit of fish, a small salad, and a glass of Riesling, dear. No more than that. If I stayed for dinner, I should have to have my burgundy gown altered the next time you receive. So many courses! Now kiss me goodnight and return to your guests."

Lisette turned to me. "But you will stay for dinner, won't you, Gérard?"

"For dinner, but just for dinner. I'm feeling weary myself."

The banquet lasted until nearly one o'clock. Late as it was, I went from the Hotel directly to Anatole's. I let myself in and woke him with a kiss.

Chapter 2

PHÉBUS had clearly taken his stepmother's instruction to heart. Lisette was expecting again and had begun to show when she and Phébus left for London at the end of winter. They decided to stay there until the baby came and took four servants with them: Beato, Lisette's personal maid, Phébus's valet and a footman. I remarked to Adrienne that it seemed the Count's salon would not remain the most liberal in Paris for long, and I wondered how Julien would react to his son traveling with so magnificent an entourage. She disagreed. Phébus knew his father's house and would not have brought them if it weren't large enough to accommodate them all, she said. He merely did not want to make extra work for his parents' servants, who would have enough to do at his sister's wedding.

"I don't believe Julien has had a valet since me," I said.

"Julien isn't a count. You will live here with me until I join them, I hope."

"You're going to London?"

"To be present at the birth. I missed Laurent's."

I went to the villa every other week with Anatole and Toussaint, the only times I saw them. Adrienne stayed at the Hotel and wouldn't come with me. I didn't go back to my apartment until a month before her granddaughter, Mélanie, was born. It remained empty all summer.

"You may as well sell your apartment and move to Saint-Germain-en-Laye," was Anatole's opinion.

"And where would I live in winter? I haven't given up my job at the bank, and I don't want to live full time at the Hotel L'Envol, where I used to be a servant. Nor will I live with you and Toussaint. All Paris would know of it."

"Can we live together when you retire?"

"All three of us? Do you really want to? We'll see when I do retire, from the bank *and* from society."

Our lovemaking had become more… shall I say standard? less unusual? When there were just the two of us, spankings and bondage were things of the past. I could envisage myself living with Anatole, but not until he stopped having sex for money, and not with him *and* Toussaint. He acted as if he had fallen in love with me, but he might have just grown used to the easy life he led at my expense. And could I be sure he wouldn't ask me to participate in some weird activity he'd read about in a novel by the Marquis de Sade if he didn't have Toussaint to fall back on?

MY TIME with Toussaint and Anatole was not 'round the clock sex play, though I may have given that impression. When we played cards we only occasionally bet articles of our clothing, and we did not always dips our cocks into the wine when we had dinner, nor did we have sex every time we swam naked in the Seine. We played with Médor, went for walks or drives in the countryside around the villa, and played tennis on the court Innocent built for me behind the house. While Anatole did not develop an interest in gardening, Toussaint did, perhaps because he enjoyed working alongside Innocent.

Our most frequent pastime, however, was conversation, and politics the most common topic. Toussaint, who was only three years old when Napoleon became emperor, listened avidly to my stories about the Revolution. I had already won him over to its principles, and he was predisposed to them. His enthusiasm for a real republic knew no bounds. He would go into raptures about the day when every man would be free to love whomever and however he wanted.

"Free to love or to have sex?" I asked cynically.

"Oh, to have sex, of course. Nobody can keep anybody from falling in love under any form of government."

"Dream on, boy. It will never happen."

"Why not? According to the *Declaration of the Rights of Man and the Citizen* there are no restrictions on our liberties provided we don't infringe on the liberties of others. All people are equal; not one of us is intrinsically better than another. The Supreme Being made us so, it says. He created me to have sex with men. I have worshipped their bodies and been enamored of their cocks and balls and bottoms since I can remember. Is there any drive more natural than to love and seek our pleasure in sexual union with the object of our desire?"

"I would have thought twice before giving voice to those ideas at the Jacobin Club."

"And after you thought twice?"

"I indulged my tastes more openly under the Old Regime than under the Republic. People closed their eyes to what went on in their neighbors' bedrooms, though it was their preferred topic of conversation. Compared to them, the Committee of Public Safety was a batch of prudes. In short, I would have kept those opinions to myself, as I did most other opinions."

"The Declaration states: 'No one should be disturbed on account of his opinions'."

"What you advocate, meaning the actions we engage in, goes beyond opinions. Not that it would matter. The Supreme Being you speak of also created people intolerant. There are hardly any exceptions. 'Law is the expression of the general will.' I can quote the Declaration as well as you."

"People will listen to reason."

"They will do nothing of the sort. What do you think, Anatole?"

"People are hypocrites. Nineteen out of twenty men who pay me for sex would clamor for anyone caught in their favorite act to be punished."

"Mercilessly. You did not live through the Terror, Toussaint. You have no idea how cruel people really are. It's the way of the world."

"Everywhere?"

I paused. "The cruelty? Everywhere. But men didn't have to hide their sexual activities with other men in Egypt."

"If in Egypt, why not in France?"

"Indeed, why not in France? But a republican government won't change anything. Not that way."

AT THE bank I read reports written by representatives in our subsidiaries. I was getting old, and traveling to visit them and see for myself how things were going tired me. I stayed close to Paris. I had never been to our branches in cities where French isn't spoken, and by the time the chateau d'Airelles was fit and furnished, I had given up all cities north of the Loire except Rennes, Tours and Rouen. I thought I would enjoy one final voyage before I retired, my last European tour, so to speak. It was 1829. I would go to Strasbourg, then on to Geneva, across Switzerland to Venice, visit our two other Italian branch offices in Milan and Genoa—I hadn't forgotten my Italian—then back to Paris via Marseille and Bordeaux, with a final rest stop at the chateau. I would take Anatole with me, provided he wanted to go. I wasn't certain I was strong enough to make the journey on my own, and it would help me decide if living with him permanently was feasible. He wasn't a youngster anymore. I might consider bringing him with me to the chateau and introducing him to my friends if the sexually irrepressible Toussaint wasn't with us.

"How long would we be gone?" Anatole wanted to know.

"A little over four months, I think. At my age I have to travel slowly and stop often. I can leave at the end of October and be back in March. That way I'll get to spend the worst of winter in the south. The question is, can Toussaint be left alone that long?"

"Toussaint won't be alone, you can take my word for it. But he should have some way of contacting us."

"The banks will know I'm coming. I'll give him an itinerary with approximate dates and he can write me there. But can he be trusted not to bring men home with him? If it were summer he'd be at the villa most of the time, gardening and doing other things with Innocent."

"I'm pretty sure he can."

"And you? Will I be enough for you? Italian men are gorgeous."

"Did you sleep with any when you were in the army?"

"I had a woman in Italy. But you haven't answered my question. We'll be together the whole time, and I won't have you going out at night to make a little money on the side."

"It's been three years since I've done that. Didn't you know? I'm almost thirty-five years old. No one will pay for my services except men in their sixties."

"I'm pushing sixty."

"In bed you could pass for my age."

"Don't flatter me, Anatole."

"That isn't flattery. Even Toussaint, who's under twenty-five, agrees with me. I want very, very much to go with you, Gérard. Will I go as your servant?"

"My assistant. The Count d'Airelles—he owns the bank now, you know—will lend me one of his coaches so I won't have to travel post. This is, at least officially, a business trip."

"How many coaches does the Count own?"

"Two. One in Paris and another at the chateau."

"Both with his coat of arms, I suppose."

"Yes, people will receive us like royalty, and there'll be just two of us in a coach that sits six comfortably, with cushions as soft as an overstuffed armchair."

"Will Joël be our coachman?" (Joël was my groom.)

"Yes, and our porter and anything else we need him for."

"Is he…?"

"No. Why? Are you interested in him?"

"Not very. He does know, though, doesn't he?"

"All my servants know. Are there any other questions you want to ask?"

"Will I finally get to meet your friends on the way back?"

"Perhaps, if you behave yourself. Mind you, if you misbehave, I will *not* spank you."

"I've outgrown spankings."

"Then maybe I shall… *if* you misbehave. You do have the loveliest thirty-five-year-old ass in Europe."

I DID not pack my uniform, thinking that few people outside of France would have any love for Napoleon. Our road to Strasbourg took us through Nancy, a short distance from Vigneulles-les-Hâtonchâtel. I told Anatole that Phébus's cousin might or might not own a chateau there. He asked if we would visit it.

"No. Sébastien is unspeakably dull. Anyway, he's probably in Vienna."

"Then you've met him?"

"A quarter-century ago, but Phébus hasn't."

From Strasbourg the easiest route, though not the most direct, was to go through Besançon to Lyon, where I paid a surprise visit to one of our largest branches, and from there to follow the Rhone to Geneva, where a letter was waiting for me from Phébus announcing the birth of their second daughter, Dorothée. By then winter had set in in the Alps, so our best bet to avoid a heavy snowfall was to continue along the Rhone to Brig and cut south over the Simplon Pass to Milan. "And from then on we'll have sunshine," Anatole said.

"Don't count on it, but we may be free of snow. The weather will get better when we reach the coast, but you can expect a lot of rain at this time of year."

"By 'reach the coast' you mean Venice."

"And Genoa, where we're more likely to see the sun. But I thought we'd linger in Venice and go to Genoa after Carnival. We're ahead of schedule, and I've never seen the city."

"The road to Venice takes us by Lake Garda, doesn't it? I'd like you to show me where you fought in the Italian campaign."

"I could show you Arcole. Have you seen Vernet's painting yet?"

"Of Napoleon on the bridge with the tattered *tricolore*?"

"Pure fantasy. He didn't cross the bridge till the battle was over."

"Are you sure?"

"I would have seen him if he had."

Luciana's village was just a few kilometers from the site of the battle. Chances were slim she still lived there. I would more likely run into her in Verona—almost anywhere—if she were still alive. I didn't think I'd recognize her, a plump old woman dressed in black, her grey hair in a bun. She wouldn't recognize me either, or if she did, she'd think she was mistaken. What would her Geraldo be doing in a nobleman's coach?

At Arcole we stood in the center of the bridge over the Alpone and I pointed out where and how the armies were arrayed and described what had taken place during the two-day battle in more detail than I have in this memoir. The countryside around us was so peaceful and free of devastation that I had to shut my eyes to hear the cannons and smell the gunpowder. Only the wooden crosses in the churchyard with French names etched on them remained to tell the story. I looked for familiar names but found none.

"One of these names could have been yours," Anatole murmured.

"You don't have to tell me that. Let's go see Venice."

THE men of Italy hadn't impressed Anatole much... until we got to Venice. Then he drooled over them, especially the gondoliers moored by the Piazza San Marco. "Tired of me already?" I asked.

"I'm just looking. Wouldn't it be fun, though, to get one of them into bed for a threesome?"

"Only if *you* pay for it."

"Then I get to choose our man."

"You have the money?"

"Did you think I came with an empty purse?"

"As long as you don't empty it. If it's just once, I'm game. I spent a year in this country and didn't get into the pants of even one pretty boy."

"That's because you didn't try. But we'll wait for Carnival. Everyone will be drunk then and more easily talked into it. Let's go buy our costumes. You should go as Harlequin, in tights to show off that big dick of yours. We'll see who eyes the bulge and recognize our man."

"And I'll give Joël a handful of *lire* so he can buy himself a piece of ass. To reward him for his patience.

Of all the men who eyed my bulge—and many did, as Anatole had predicted—the cutest was called Giuseppe. We noticed him staring at me just as the sun was setting. "Him?" Anatole asked. I nodded. He kissed me on the lips and winked at Giuseppe, who followed us, eager as a puppy dog.

My Italian was deficient when it came to parts of the male anatomy. "*Francesi?*" Giuseppe asked, and filled in the gaps in my knowledge. He swore I had a superb *cozzo* and hoped he'd get his share of it where he liked it best. "*Qui*," he said, rubbing his bottom in case we hadn't understood.

That was all the invitation we needed. Within seconds we had pulled off his costume and our mouths fell to devouring him. He had savory skin. The poor fellow didn't know which way to turn, so I helped him out by turning him over.

Giuseppe enjoyed himself *viva voce*. He must have yelled every word in his vocabulary except "*Basta!*" "They'll hear him over the carnival," I said. Anatole's cock made an effective gag. The fellow was getting it from both ends and loving every thrust. Soon Anatole's cum was running down his chin and mine was shooting up into his ass. He caught his breath while I fucked Anatole, and then they both fucked me, and we went on to more of the same.

I couldn't say how late the three of us dozed off. One o'clock? Two? The merrymakers were still laughing, dancing and singing outside our window. At dawn Giuseppe crawled out of bed and dressed quietly so he wouldn't wake us. He kissed us both goodbye—on our dicks. My eyes fluttered open; I nodded and smiled at him. I could still hear people in the street, but their noise was subdued. Giuseppe tiptoed out. I had fallen asleep before the door closed, so it stayed unlocked. At noon Joël came into the room and found us sprawled naked on the bed and was terribly embarrassed.

"So now you've seen," Anatole teased. "Sodomites look exactly the same as other men."

Joël blushed a deeper red. "Better," he said. Anatole immediately perked up, but he added, "If you're into that sort of thing."

"I know you aren't, my good man," I said, "and I trust you had as much fun as we did." He grinned to let us know he had—or thought he had. "Now you sit right there and wait for us to get dressed, and we'll all go have lunch together. You shall sit at table with us."

We stayed in Venice another week. Anatole hoped we'd run into Giuseppe again and that he was a gondolier. As luck would have it, we saw him in his gondola one day near the Rialto Bridge. He waved to us and said if we'd meet him at the same spot that evening at nine, he'd give us a free moonlight gondola ride. "Everything free this time," he promised.

"We won't turn him down, will we?" Anatole asked.

"I said only one three-way."

"But in a gondola—it's the chance of a lifetime! You know you want to."

"What if we capsize?"

"We won't. I'm sure Giuseppe has done it before."

"As a trio?"

"Maybe even as a quartet. Please. I've been a good boy. You haven't had to spank me once. Think how disappointed Giuseppe will be if we don't show up."

"All right, but we leave Venice the day after tomorrow."

TOUSSAINT had written me at the bank in Genoa asking for money. I have kept the letter.

> *You know I have never asked you for any money beyond my salary, but with you gone it is not enough to feed me unless I make some on my own in the usual way, which I shall not be able to do for some months to come. I find myself bedridden with three broken ribs, a broken nose, four fewer teeth, and covered with cuts and bruises from head to toe. I am not a pretty sight.*
>
> *It's entirely my fault; I should have listened to you. I never told either of you that I joined a republican club. Well, like an idiot, I opened my mouth and spouted my views on a man's right to love other men. I was shouted down. They called me names I would rather not repeat, and half a dozen men attacked me in the street after the meeting and left me there unconscious and bleeding. I woke up in the doctor's office the next morning. He had me brought home and asked if I knew any friends who would take care of me. I had him send for Innocent. I didn't think you would mind my having him in the apartment, but I need money for his food as well as my own. We have enough to last for a while, but not until you're back in Paris.*

I showed the letter to Anatole, who showed less concern than I felt. "I thought you said Toussaint could take care of himself," I said reproachfully.

"No, I said he wouldn't be alone and, as you see, he isn't. Innocent will look after him. Look, at least he's alive," he said. "He's lucky they didn't rape him. It wouldn't surprise me if some of those ruffians have sex with men." He winced. "I'm sure they kicked him in the groin—hard—but Toussaint wouldn't tell us that. How much will you send?"

Anatole thought Genoa more scenic than Venice and its architecture more impressive except for the Ducal Palace. However, he was anxious to get back to France, so we only stayed a day or two. It rained every day until we reached Ventimiglia, where the magnificent coastline begins, and from there we had sunshine all the way to Nice. We stopped briefly on the Gulf Juan on the way to Marseille to see where Napoleon had landed when he escaped from Elba.

WE SAT in a café in the port at Marseille and watched the sailors saunter by, as I had done ten years earlier. Anatole thought them handsomer than the Italians. I wagged a finger at him and said, "I said only one three-way and we did it twice, remember?"

"Mind reader! They do have nice asses, though."

"When I was here last, I went swimming in a *calanque* and got to watch a dozen sailors in the buff."

"When was that?"

"Don't you remember? Right after I set you up in the apartment. You had two whole weeks to get to know Toussaint outside and in."

"What are we waiting for, then? Is it far?"

"No one will be swimming at this time of year."

"It's worth a try, isn't it?"

We set out early and brought blankets for sitting on the beach. Joël stayed with the coach, and we hiked three or four miles to the *calanque*. The sun was dazzlingly bright and the cliffs protected us from the wind, but no one came to swim.

"I've never made love with you outdoors," Anatole said, "except in the gondola."

"We'll freeze!"

"No, we won't. We have the blankets. Have you ever made love outdoors?"

"Once in Egypt, in a tent at the foot of the pyramids. That doesn't count, I suppose. Have you?"

"Lots of times. In the alley by the wine bar."

"That only counts as sex, not as making love."

He had already begun to unbutton me, talking all the time. "You're such a darling! Letting you have your way with me for free was the smartest thing I ever did as a whore."

"I've spent a fortune on you since then."

"And I was worth every centime."

When he had me undressed from the waist up, I lay back on one blanket and he covered me with the other. Then he pulled off everything I had on below the waist and got naked. He had covered my face, too, so I only heard him taking off his clothes. Then he knelt between my legs and licked and sucked me for what felt like half an hour. It was exquisite, not being able to see where he would put his mouth next, and I had only a blanket to muffle my squeals.

Just as I was approaching orgasm, he sat up and said, "I'm cold. Lie on top of me and fuck me to warm me up again."

He was very cold, but not where I licked between his buttocks so it would be nice and wet when I slid my cock into him. Then I covered my body with the blanket and his with mine and gave him what he wanted. He thrashed about so much he got as much exercise as I did, and his yelps of delight echoed off the cliffs.

"Quiet! You'll scare the fish."

"Fuck the fish."

"Later. Right now I'm fucking you," I told him (as if he didn't know!), and I came a few minutes after that.

"That was heavenly," Anatole said. "Now I'm going for a swim." He ran into the water up to his thighs, dove in, and ran back out, his teeth chattering and his penis shriveled to a stump. He wrapped himself in a blanket, dried himself with it, and started getting into his clothes.

"Don't you want to come, too?" I asked.

"Tonight, in the hotel, after my balls have had a chance to thaw."

"Don't say I didn't warn you. But I'll give you an extra nice blowjob tonight since you missed out on one here."

Joël grinned at us when we got back to the coach. He took one look at our disheveled hair and rumpled clothing and knew why we'd been gone so long.

BY THE time our coach rolled into Bordeaux we were ready to head home. I had come to regard Anatole as a permanent and exclusive lover, whatever he might do with Toussaint when I wasn't there. (Anatole swore he did not, and I half believed him.) I decided the time had come to introduce him to the Count d'Airelles and his family. "If you dare embarrass me, I'll give you a spanking you'll never forget," I warned him. We both knew we were done with spankings and I could tease him about them.

I filled him in on the d'Airelles family history on our way to the chateau, how I knew each of them and how they had met each other, including my brief relationship with Stéphane, which he promised to keep a secret. He thought Phébus's read like high adventure and Lisette's like a fairy tale—a printer's daughter marrying a count. I told him about my boyhood at the chateau, about walks in the woods with Julien and teaching him to swim in the river. "It's too cold to swim now," I said, "but we'll visit them again in summer. If not this summer, then the summer after."

"Won't they be in Paris at this time of year?"

"They're expecting me to stop at the chateau on my way back to Paris. Phébus wrote that they would all come down for three weeks so we could have a little holiday together when I passed through."

We arrived on what must have been the first sunny day of the year. Beato was playing with the children on the lawn. As soon as she saw the coach, she rushed inside to tell the others we had come, and they all came out onto the porch at the head of the double staircase to meet us, Lisette with her four-month-old baby in her arms. Mélanie, going on three, looked just like her mother at that age, and four-year-old Laurent was outgoing and full of mischief, not at all like his namesake.

Adrienne took Anatole by both hands and kissed him on both cheeks. "So at last we get to meet you," she said. "I don't know why Gérard felt he had to keep you hidden."

"I thought it was you he was hiding from me," he answered.

The children adored Anatole. He was marvelous with them. To my astonishment, he would not allow Beato to spank Laurent when he was naughty. "Make him stand in the corner," he told her, "take away his toys, don't let him have dessert, but never, never hit a child."

I waited until we were in bed to ask him about it. "I never dreamed *you* would be against spankings," I said.

"My father used to beat me."

"What for?"

"What do you think? Because I liked boys. I used to want men to hit me to convince myself he did it because he loved me."

"But not anymore. What made you change?"

"You. You loved me. Not at first, but soon enough."

"Did I? I didn't think I did."

"Maybe you didn't realize it, but I could tell."

"Did you love me?"

"I wouldn't admit it to myself, but I think I fell in love with you when you sucked my cock instead of paying me. You took charge, just like my father, but you only wanted to make me feel good. Love me now," he whispered. "Make me feel good."

"Come with me," I said. "No, put on a dressing gown, like me. Someone may see us in the corridor."

"Where are you taking me?"

"You'll see."

I held his hand and led him up to the attic storeroom, where they kept the few pieces of servants' furniture the peasants hadn't carried off during the Revolution. I took the mattress from the double bed that either Lucie and I or Julien and Phébus had shared and laid it on the floor. "My life has come full circle," I explained. "This is where I made love for the first time."

"But not the last."

"I hope not."

"With the Count's father, right? The man you really love?"

"*Really* love? I've really loved four men in my life. You're the fourth… and the last. I won't fall in love again, not at my age. We'll go home tomorrow and make love in *our* bed."

We couldn't leave the next day; half our clothing had been sent to the village for laundering. Nor would Lisette and Phébus let us go so soon. We stayed two more nights.

As we drove off in the coach, Anatole turned to me and asked, "Tell me—was my behavior satisfactory, or do I deserve a spanking?"

"No spanking. Adrienne says you're very nice, and I think so too." And I gave him a kiss.

Chapter 3

TOUSSAINT'S ribs were mending, but he was still in pain and winced as he limped around the apartment. They hadn't only broken his nose—in two places, it turned out—but his right cheekbone as well. His face would never be pretty again. Anatole looked at him gravely, shook his head, and said, "They really made a mess of you, didn't they? You have as good a chance of turning tricks as Gérard."

I pretended he had stung me to the quick. "What about Venice?"

That caught Toussaint's interest. "What about Venice?" he asked.

"That can wait. First let's hear about you."

He spoke for a long time, but we didn't learn much more than what was in his letter. All the time he was speaking, Innocent kept muttering, "The bastards! The bastards!"

I asked Toussaint if he knew who did it.

"No, but I thought I recognized Dussardier's voice. If it was him, Sénécal must have been there too."

"You didn't see their faces?"

"It was too dark. They hid in a passageway about a hundred meters from the street lamp and yanked me into it when I walked past. Before I knew it I was on the ground and they'd started kicking me."

"Kicking! What animals!" Anatole muttered.

Toussaint stopped talking to took a sip of wine; then he went on. "I covered my head with my arms to protect it, so I wouldn't have seen them once my eyes adjusted to the dark, either. Then one of them kicked me in the... well, he kicked me, and I reached for where he'd kicked me. That's when they got to my face."

His story affected all three of us, and Innocent not the least, who must have listened to it countless times. After a light supper, I sent Toussaint to his room. "But I haven't told you about the political situation!" he objected.

"Tomorrow."

We stayed up a while longer talking with Innocent, then went to bed ourselves, tired from our travels. We had undressed and were turning down the coverlet when we heard a loud "Ouf!" Even though it was only a grunt, we recognized Toussaint's voice. We had heard him grunt before.

I said, "It must be painful for him to turn over."

Then we heard another, and another.

We rushed to Toussaint's room without a stitch on. Toussaint was standing, clinging to the bedpost for dear life, his chest in a plaster (the only thing he had on), while Innocent humped him from behind. It must have hurt more on all fours or lying on his stomach.

Anatole doubled over with laughter. "A fine doctor you make!" I exclaimed.

"At least let us finish," Toussaint whined.

"Very well, but tomorrow he goes to the villa, or you'll never heal."

I sent Innocent back in my carriage the first thing in morning. He and Toussaint hugged goodbye, but not too tightly, and he said, "I'll see you as soon as you're fit to travel. But don't forget—those roads are bumpy!"

When he'd gone, Toussaint sat in my favorite armchair, stuck his tongue out at me, and grumbled, "*Now* what do I do to amuse myself!"

"You can beat off. But not here," I added, seeing him reach for his trousers, and pointed the way to his bedroom. In response he folded his arms across his chest and pouted. "Or if you prefer," I went on, "you can fill us in on the political situation.

His eyes lit up, and he launched into a diatribe attacking the King and what he had either done or tried to do while we were away. Much of what he said I already knew. Charles X had tried, repeatedly and unsuccessfully, to push through censorship laws that would have muzzled every opposition newspaper in France. In his frustration, he had dissolved both Chambers and set the next election for late spring, which meant that except for the King and his ministers we had no government. I would vote, wouldn't I? It was essential the liberals be reelected.

I did vote when the elections were finally held, and the liberals were returned to their seats in greater numbers than before. Then the King disbanded the National Guard, so the only armed forces remaining in Paris were the Royal Militia and the police.

The d'Airelles arrived in Paris just in time for the elections and stayed two months before returning to the chateau for the summer, long enough to host a ball and two dinner parties, as if the richest citizens in the capital were oblivious to the mounting tension. Phébus's liberal friends discussed the political situation in the smoking room, but most of their guests pretended things were just fine. I attended the first dinner and brought Anatole with me at Adrienne's insistence, but had moved back to the villa to start planting the garden when they had the second, on the first day of June.

At the dinner I introduced Anatole to the Marquise d'Espard. She said a few polite words and then ignored him, engaging me in conversation as if he weren't there. "We never see you anymore, *mon cher colonel*," she said. "Where have you been hiding yourself?"

"I'm seldom in Paris nowadays, *Madame la marquise*. I'm semi-retired, you know, and I've bought a villa in the country and spend much of my time there."

"Indeed? Where is it? I'm sure you have a charming little house."

"In Saint-Germain-en-Laye."

"Oh, but that isn't far at all! Not so far that you need to make yourself into a hermit."

"I'm getting old, Madame. When I make the trip, it seems very far."

"Nonsense! You look very fit."

"Appearances are deceiving. You'll see I won't stay long past dinner."

"But what do you do with yourself all day at your villa, may I ask?"

"I garden."

"You garden? How very quaint! Like Voltaire's Candide, aren't you? '*Il faut cultiver notre jardin.*' But not in winter, surely? You must live in Paris then, I'm sure."

"I spent last winter in Italy, *Madame la marquise*. I haven't been back long."

"Paris is too far away for you, and yet you go to Italy!"

"I wasn't alone, Madame. Monsieur Roubaix came with me," I said, trying to draw Anatole into the conversation.

"Well, you must stay in the city a while so we get to see more of you," she said, continuing to ignore him, and went on to speak of Italy and what a lovely place it was.

"Are salons always that dreary?" Anatole asked on our way home. "I used to have a better time at Jacques's wine bar."

Innocent was disappointed that I hadn't brought Toussaint when I came to the villa for the summer, but as Anatole had rightly pointed out, he had no one to serve him when Toussaint was in Saint-Germain. (That he might also be serving Anatole in other ways bothered me not in the least.) I told Innocent that his friend was still recovering, which was true, and not fit for hard work like gardening. He and Anatole would join us at the beginning of July.

Toussaint and Anatole arrived when I said they would, by which time we had finished the heaviest work. Toussaint was strong enough for chores like weeding and watering. The plan was for Anatole and me to stay at the villa until the last Sunday in July, then return to Paris to pack our bags before leaving on Tuesday for three weeks at the chateau.

My memory of the next few days is as vivid as my memories of the Tribunal, Saint-Lazare and the battles I fought in. In fact, I remember them as clearly as making love for the first time with Julien, or with Akmoud in a tent by the pyramids, and I don't know how many hundreds of times with Laurent. As planned, we drove the carriage to Paris on Sunday and spent the night in my apartment. We were looking forward to our trip and stayed up talking about it until past midnight, then exhausted ourselves in bed instead of resting. As a result, we slept until noon. Since we would spend the next three days sitting in the carriage, I wanted to stretch my legs, so I told Anatole I would walk him home and come in the carriage to fetch him after lunch the next day. The streets were unusually quiet, and although it wasn't a holiday, almost all the shops were closed.

I learned why when I picked up a copy of *Le Moniteur* on my way home. I seldom read that paper, but a sign in the shop window where I bought it—one of the few I found open—said it had published the text of the sovereign's latest legislative abomination, which we now know as the July Ordinances and which the liberal press had not seen fit to print. King Charles had, among other things, abolished freedom of the press, dissolved the Chamber of Deputies, taken away its right to amend laws he introduced when new deputies were elected, and deprived the working bourgeoisie of the right to vote. The shops, no doubt, were closed to protest that last act of oppression. I smelled trouble. I went home to get my carriage and drove to the bank to find out what was afoot. It, too, was closed. From there I drove to Monsieur Monceau's house in the Faubourg Saint-Denis to learn what I could from him. My inference about the closures was not only correct, but the Stock Exchange had shut down as well. He also told me that the edition of *Le Moniteur* I had bought would be the last. The conservative newspapers had ceased printing that morning and would not reopen until the government censors were ready to begin work. The liberal press had refused to abide by the laws and would continue to publish.

"Do you think we'll have another revolution?" I asked.

"Don't ask me," he replied. "I always think the worst." Then he reflected a moment and said, "The King may yet back down—he has before, after all—and the city is quiet."

"Too quiet," I thought. As a precaution, I made a long detour to get home and circled the western half of the city, crossing the Seine at the Pont des Invalides. If the people were to arm themselves and revolt, the fighting would occur in the center of Paris, and they would direct their most ferocious attacks against the Tuileries and the Hotel de Ville.

By Tuesday things had apparently returned to normal, but I was glad to be getting out of Paris before whatever was going to happen happened. Then at noon the shopkeepers bolted their doors and sent their workers home, creating a *de facto* general strike. When I left for Anatole's, the streets had begun to fill with idle men and women milling listlessly about or talking in small groups, outwardly subdued, but I could sense the slightest spark would set them on a rampage. A few blocks from his apartment, I saw what appeared to be an angry mob. They were neither acting violently nor making noise, but their animosity was palpable. In my judgment, we risked finding ourselves in the middle of a riot on our way out of the city. Instead of picking him up, I told him I would return an hour or two after dark when the streets would be empty. As assistant manager of one of the leading banks in

France, given the situation, I could count on the guards opening the gates for us after hours. Then I returned to my apartment and waited. Late in the afternoon I heard a small group of men marching outside my window. I looked out. A patrol. Another passed by about an hour later.

I heard the first shots a little after sunset. Then came more gunshots, shrieks, and people running through the streets. The concierge knocked on my door to tell me he was locking the gates of the courtyard. About half an hour later a crowd passed by my building chanting slogans. I peeked through the curtains but could see nothing. Not a single street lamp was burning. I climbed to the top floor of my building and looked out the window at the top of the staircase. The entire city lay in darkness. I didn't dare go outside anymore.

I went to bed at midnight. A hush had fallen on the city, but I did not want to chance going for Anatole. We would just have to sit it out; I couldn't guess for how long. I hoped I had made the right decision.

I had. I woke the next morning to the sound of cannons and gunfire. The noise came from all over but was loudest in the direction of the river and the Mont Sainte-Geneviève. At about eight o'clock a hundred or so men and a couple of dozen women, workers and peasants from the outlying countryside armed with muskets and pitchforks, came marching down my street toward the city center singing "La Marseillaise". The patrols had disappeared, no doubt recalled to defend the government offices and the arsenal.

At noon my cook and housekeeper, who had rooms under the eaves, let themselves into my apartment hoping to find something to eat. "We thought you had left Paris, Monsieur," the cook said.

"There's no way out now. I ought to have left Monday. There's an untouched basket of food I packed for the road we can share."

"How long will this go on?"

"It could be a day, it could be a week. No longer than that, I think. Either the soldiers will put down the rebellion or the King will abdicate.

The Chamber of Deputies must have called for him to resign already. My guess is he's left Saint-Cloud."

"What do we do in the meantime?"

"We stay inside."

The fighting continued all day, on through the night, and all day Thursday. After dark we went up to my housekeeper's room and watched the scattered fires burning in the city from her window.

Friday morning it seemed a relative calm had returned to the city. There were scattered pockets of fighting, but none of them flared up and spread. I had gone over two days without news, shut up in my apartment. By mid-afternoon I thought it safe to go to Anatole's. The streets were strewn with rubble. When I reached the rue du Bac I saw an abandoned barricade to my left at the corner of the rue de Grenelle. I turned the carriage around, left it in the courtyard, changed my clothes so people would think I was a worker, and set out again on foot. If I brought Anatole home with me, we had a good chance of finding the road open in the other direction.

The shooting came from other parts of the city. Few people ventured outside their houses, and my neighborhood seemed empty. I had to make two detours around barricades that had been left standing, and could not walk to Anatole's in a straight line. There were more people in the street on the other side of the Croix Rouge. I passed smashed storefronts and articles that looters had dropped in their haste at every turn. I saw several dead bodies and at one corner ran into a pile of corpses.

Anatole looked up anxiously when I opened the door. "Oh, it's you," he said, as if he had been expecting someone else.

"A fine welcome! Didn't you miss me? I thought you might try to come to me to see if I was all right. A building like mine draws an angry mob. Fortunately it suffered no more damage than a few cobblestones through my windows and usual pockmarks in the façade from bullets." He didn't seem to be listening. "Instead I came to you," I went on. "So you see I'm braver than you are."

"I thought you might be Toussaint."

"Toussaint?" Then I noticed the worried look on his face and asked, "What's the matter?"

"Toussaint. He showed up suddenly in the middle of the night on Tuesday, excited that the revolution had finally come. He ran through his usual litany of the King's offenses against liberty and described the new order to come in glowing terms. His eyes were ablaze. Then he grabbed the poker from the fireplace and ran to join the insurgents. Gérard, he didn't even have a firearm!"

"And he hasn't come back?"

"No, not even to sleep. I know the fighting hasn't stopped yet, but we've won, haven't we? We took the Hotel de Ville. I hear they're setting up a provisional government. You'd think he would at least have come to share his happiness with me."

"How do you know all this?"

"That's what they were saying this morning when I stepped outside to see if he was coming. So you think it's reliable?"

"Well, the fighting is pretty much over as far as I can tell, so, yes, I'd say it probably is."

I went back to my apartment to tell my cook and housekeeper that it was safe to go out and that I would be staying with a friend who lived nearby to wait for news of another friend who had taken part in the fighting. Then I returned to Anatole's.

"Not back yet?" I asked.

I plunked myself down at the table and sighed wearily. "He must have got himself killed," I said. "We can wait for him here a few days and eat dinner at my place or in a restaurant, but I'm sure he's dead. He won't come back."

My certainty that he had been killed was a premonition. The Revolution of July 1830 did not lack for victims, but I had the impression less blood had been spilled than in other Paris riots and uprisings. To me it seemed equally likely that a soldier's bullet had felled him or his fellow insurgents had turned on him because they knew he had sex with men.

I sighed. "I've had more than I can take of Paris and its revolutions, crowds screaming and throwing things, soldiers shooting people in the streets. I'm going to sell my apartment and live in Saint-Germain-en-Laye. I want to retire. It's high time I did."

"What about me?"

"I'll still pay for this apartment, but I won't come here often."

"Sell it. I'd rather live at the villa with you, if you'll have me."

"Do you mean it?" He nodded gravely. "Then we'll both move to Saint-Germain," I said.

I WAS right about Toussaint; he had disappeared forever. Innocent rushed to Paris to search for him. For two weeks he combed the back alleys, the banks of the Seine, the morgues, all to no avail. One night he came home, sat at the table, laid his face on his folded arms, and cried. I gave his shoulder a comforting squeeze. He looked up at me with puffy eyes and said, "It's my fault. I should never have let him go to Paris."

"No one could have stopped him. We all know how passionate he was about the Republic and the Rights of Man," I said. "At least we'll get to keep our Charter, which is what he wanted most. Go back to the villa. There's nothing you can do here."

We didn't go to the chateau that summer. I had too much to do, selling two apartments and the furnishings in them and training someone to take over my position at the bank. By the end of October I had taken care of everything, and we moved into the villa for the rest of our lives. I say "our lives" because I shall bequeath the villa to Anatole when I die.

We found Innocent dressed in black. He would always wear black as a sign of mourning for Toussaint.

"How lonely and despondent he looks," Anatole said. "It's awful of me to say so, but I feel sorrier for him than I do about Toussaint. We won't ask him up to our room, though… not ever. From now on it's just the two of us… forever. What shall we do to celebrate?"

"How do we always celebrate?" I replied.

WE DID not go to the chateau the summer after, either, for Phébus's stepmother died, and he brought his family to England for the funeral and stayed on to be with Julien and help him find and move into smaller lodgings, for he was alone now, his younger daughter having married and moved to the north of England.

Anatole thought Julien might come back to France now that his duty to his wife no longer stood between us, but I knew he wouldn't. "Julien wants to be English, not French," I told him.

"What if he does, though?"

"He never asks after me when he writes to Phébus, nor has he written to tell me he's free."

"I asked: what if he does?"

"Do you think I'd leave you for him? No. I'll send him back to England, or he can stay here and live with his son and grandchildren. I've cast my lot with you."

"But you still love him."

"I don't need to fall out of love in order to fall in love again. I still love all the men I've ever loved. I love Julien and Laurent and you…"

"And Akmoud?"

"If I hadn't left Egypt I would have come to love him too... in time. The culture of master and servant is stronger there than it was here under the Old Regime. They still own slaves."

"And your wife?"

"No, her I never loved, not with the depth and passion I have loved the men in my life. Do you believe that it's you I want to be with, although I love you both equally? Are you jealous of Julien?"

"Not jealous, just afraid of losing you."

"We're all afraid of losing the people we love. I was afraid of losing Julien, then Akmoud, and after him Laurent. And now I'm afraid of losing you."

"To whom?"

"To no one. Just of losing you."

I did see Julien one last time, however, and Anatole saw him, too. He passed away nine years after his wife, and Phébus brought his body back to be buried in the family crypt, the first to lie there since Phébus's great-grandparents. He felt he belonged there, where he, Lisette and his son Laurent would have their final resting place. Julien's father and mother and his sister Constance were guillotined under the Terror, Olivier was buried in Montmartre, Berthe in her convent's cemetery, and Jeanne, unless she was still alive, probably in Vienna. It was a cold winter, and two weeks after his death Julien's body showed no outward signs of decomposing, so we could have an open casket, but I did not kiss him for fear of contagion.

THERE isn't much left to tell about my life except sex with Anatole, and I've written more than enough about that already. For the first ten years we'd go to Paris for a day about once a month, once every two or three after that, and until last year we visited our friends at the chateau for a month in summer. We've grown old together, but we still swim naked in the river together (that is, Anatole swims and I wade), and Phébus and his sons join us sometimes, unless the boys are in Paris or off traveling somewhere. At twenty-four and nineteen, Laurent and Stéphane are inseparable. They've always been the best of friends.

"Grown old together"—did I really write that? *Anatole* has grown old; I've grown very old. I was about a month short of seventy-five when news of yet another revolution in Paris reached us in 1848. But this revolution spread throughout Europe. Although it was the middle of winter, Phébus moved his whole family to the Charente so the children and grandchildren would be safe (Mélanie had recently given birth to twin girls), even Laurent, who was a grown man. Adrienne told him what revolutions were like. We, of course, did not leave the villa until it was over.

It made me very happy to live in a republic again. We waited until June to drive into Paris. I thought things would be calm again after four months, but before we reached the gates we heard the gunshots and screaming inside the city. I could guess what was happening. Closing the national workshops, which had come close to draining the Treasury, had left thousands of workers unemployed. One loses one's taste for liberty when there's no bread on the table.

"Another revolution gone sour," I said, and turned the carriage around and headed back to Saint-Germain. I felt so tired after making the round trip non-stop that I had to lie in bed two days to recuperate, and I've been going steadily downhill ever since.

Epilogue

THE violence in June had resulted from the working classes' dissatisfaction with the direction the new republic was taking, and after it the government shifted even further to the right, and by the end of the year another Napoleon, the former Emperor's nephew, had been elected president with overwhelming support in the provinces. At least we are still a republic. Phébus is a member of the Assembly, and his son Laurent has said he will put his name on the list at the next elections. Everyone except Anatole urges me to seek a seat in the government. They say that as a respectable old man with a distinguished record of military service (officially, that is) and connections with the upper classes, I should have no trouble getting myself elected. If I did so, I would have for a colleague that same Monsieur Hugo who wrote the ode for the coronation of King Charles X. He has turned completely around to become one of the most outspoken liberals in the government, a leader of the opposition against the President's policies, as I should be, too, if I had the strength and wanted to serve my country. But the great events I have lived through have made me a cynic. I now believe that the vast majority of men want to be sheep, and most of those who do not act like sheep anyway without realizing it.

I go to bed early, take naps in the afternoon, and am too old to garden, too old even for a drive to Paris. By the time we get there I'm already exhausted, so exhausted that if we drove as far as the gates and turned around and went home, Anatole would have to carry me to the bedroom. We only see our friends if they come to Saint-Germain, which is not often. They lead full and busy lives, and Adrienne finds the short trip as tiring as I. In order to be with them, we spent all last summer at the chateau and will continue to do so until my strength gives out entirely.

Anatole would lie awake for hours if he went to bed when I do, so he stays up chatting with Phébus and Lisette, and the old folks, Adrienne and I, trundle off to our bedrooms. It gives us a chance to reminisce together, and sometimes I go to her room and we talk for an hour or more. Not infrequently, I doze off in the chair. Anatole knows where to look for me if I'm not in bed when comes upstairs. He shakes me awake and leads me to our bedroom. I'm quite awake by the time we get there, so we spend some time cuddling or, if we're both in the mood, we have sex. This does not only happen when I fall asleep talking with Adrienne. I haven't slept through the night in years, and I usually wake up when he comes to bed.

On our most recent visit to the chateau, as usual, Adrienne and I retired early. "You'll stay up and chat a bit?" she asked. I was sleepy and would have preferred to go straight to bed, but I could tell she had something on her mind, so I nodded and followed her to her room.

"I think you should take what we keep telling you seriously, Gérard, and present yourself at the next elections," she said.

"I do take you seriously, but honestly, what good would I do? I'd only doze off during the debates as I do half the time in this chair."

"Oh, I can't imagine that happening! From what Phébus says, the debates are very heated. The noise of everyone talking at once at the top of his voice is bound to keep you awake."

"When I'm tired no one but Anatole can rouse me. Besides, asleep or awake, I wouldn't have the strength to think clearly and follow what people were saying, much less join in. If the sessions are that chaotic, being there would only confuse me."

"Don't underestimate yourself. Your mind is as sharp as ever."

"Yes, when the people I'm with are calm and rational. The Assembly is anything but."

"Well, you ought to find some way to keep busy and occupy your mind. You can't fritter away your life eating meals and taking naps. Have you ever considered writing your memoirs?"

The very idea amused me. Laughing, I answered, "There are too many personal histories of the *Grande Armée* on the market already."

"You could focus on your travels—Egypt, Italy, Provence. Accounts of foreign lands have become quite fashionable."

"Fashionable and fictional. I'm not one to write a novel."

"No, you must tell the truth and make yourself the main character."

"How could I, Adrienne? *My Life and Loves*, by Colonel Gérard Vreilhac. No doubt it would attract readers, but what would they think when they read it? I'd scandalize everyone."

"Not me."

"You know it all already."

"Not all, but more than you think, and I'm curious to know more."

"Then ask me questions and I'll tell you here. I don't care what people think of me, but Phébus and your grandsons have their careers to think about, and they certainly won't benefit from their association with me if the details of my love life were made known."

"I admit that isn't the kind of memoir I had in mind, but I say go ahead and write it if it's what you would enjoy writing. The whole point is for you to remain active; literary fame and fortune have nothing to do with it. Of course once it's written, if you feel like a *succès de scandale*—"

"Far from it. I retired because I wanted to withdraw from the world. But it might be fun. I'll think about it. I promise."

"Good. And be brutally honest. Don't go glossing over the details to spare the public's sensibilities. They could use a little shaking up."

"And my friends? They might not like everything they read in it."

"Believe me, your friends will think no worse of you. Phébus won't mind reading bedroom secrets that concern his father, nor will I about Thibaud's."

"You know about Thibaud?"

"I took it for granted. Why should I care about what he did with Laurent in the army?—and with you, too, for all I know! He never neglected me when he was home, and it kept his friend out of trouble. I never for an instant doubted his love for me."

"Maybe you should write my memoirs."

Just then Anatole came into the room. "What's this about writing memoirs?" he asked.

"I've been telling Gérard that if he doesn't want a political career—"

"I don't want any kind of career."

"—he ought to write his memoirs."

"A splendid idea! I can't wait to read them."

"Are you sure, Anatole?"

"Absolutely, Gérard. The racier, the better."

"Yes, I'm sure you'd like that. As a replacement for my failing manhood."

"As a supplement for your undiminished virility, my dear, which will outlast mine. You're far too modest. Don't believe a word he says,

Adrienne. And he will write those memoirs. I'll keep at him until he does."

ANATOLE has indeed kept after me. He has been a relentless taskmaster, making me spend three or four hours a day at my writing desk every day all fall and winter until I finished. I read aloud what I have done before we retire for the night, and if the story has to do with one of my lovers we go to bed in a state of arousal, with predictable results. Once he entered the story, he started questioning the accuracy of what I wrote, and we have argued many times over which of us has the more reliable memory. I have seldom accepted the revisions he proposes, because my book should recount what I remember, even if I am mistaken. Besides, if I listened to him, every scene would take place in the bedroom—or on a storeroom floor, or in a tent, or on a beach by the Mediterranean—provided all the actors are men. One would think nothing else interests him. I suspect that more than once he has felt a twinge of jealousy when I read to him about Julien, Laurent and Akmoud, but he denies it. "How can one be jealous of the dead," he protests, "when one gets to do what they have right after you hear about it, and they no longer can?"

ANEL VIZ, born and raised in New York City, currently resides in the Midwest, where he has taught at the same small liberal arts college for over thirty years. He has lived about one-quarter of his life in French-speaking countries. He returned to his childhood passion of writing at age sixty, and ever since he has churned out works in a variety of M/M genres: poetry, short and novel-length fiction, humor, essays, etc. He likes to experiment. Though most of his stories are romances, few of them would be called traditional romance. His work appears regularly in *Wilde Oats* and *GayFlashFiction* online magazines.

Also by ANEL VIZ

There Are Fairies in the Bottom of the Garden

He lives alone in his little house, barricaded against the pushers, hookers and muggers who people the neighborhood, and only ventures out to go to work. Then three eccentric men move in next door, give him a new name, and fill his garden and his life with friendship, freedom, and inner harmony.

Dancing for Jonathan

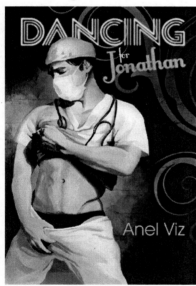

The palpable sexual attraction between Jonathan, a wealthy paraplegic, and Vince, his new live-in aide, is deepening as quickly as their friendship. But both men are trying to keep their feelings in check, keenly aware of the difference in their ages and the stresses on their relationship caused by the imbalance of power in their roles of employer/employee and patient/caregiver. Adding to the strain are the secrets Vince is keeping... secrets that might lead Jonathan to suspect he is trying to take advantage of him and destroy any hope of a future together.

The Perfect Gift for a Voyeur

I suppose I ought to feel guilty, spying on him this way, but I don't. After all, he can't help but know he's clearly visible at night in a lit apartment. Either he's a bit of an exhibitionist or he knows that another man lives across from him and assumes he has no interest in seeing him naked. If he doesn't care, why should I?

http://www.dreamspinnerpress.com

Other historical fiction from DREAMSPINNER PRESS

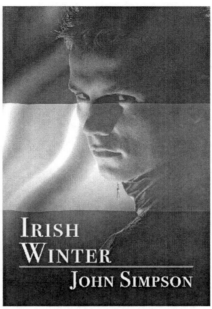

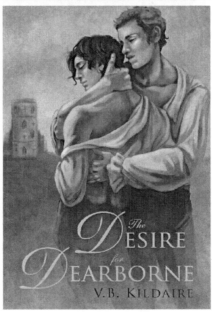

http://www.dreamspinnerpress.com

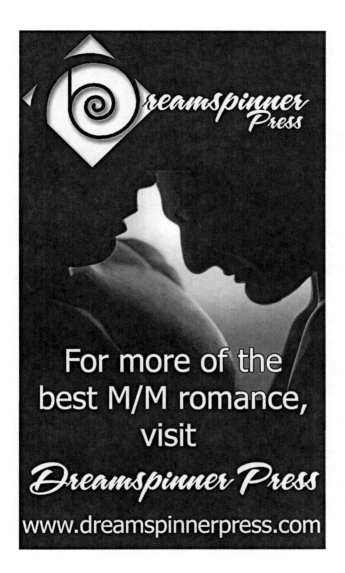

CPSIA information can be obtained at www.ICGtesting.com
Printed in the USA
LVOW010344160112

263998LV00002B/47/P